DENNIS R. DALTON

UNIT 33

A COLLECTION OF THRILLER
CRIME SHORT STORIES

**FLARE
BOOKS**

El Paso, Texas

Published by Flare Books, an imprint of Catalyst Press.
www.catalystpress.org

© 2025 Dennis R. Dalton

In North America, this book is distributed by
Consortium Book Sales & Distribution, a division of Ingram.
Phone: 612/746-2600
cbsdinfo@ingramcontent.com
www.cbsd.com

First edition, first printing
1 3 5 7 9 8 6 4 2

ISBN 978-1-963511-30-7
Library of Congress Control Number 2025936339

Cover design by Kathy McInnis of Ivy Leaf Designs

CONTENTS

UNIT 33:
DAN HOLMES' PRIVATE INTELLIGENCE UNIT

San Francisco is like any other large city when it comes to never sleeping—there is always someone, somewhere, awake, who witnesses whatever goes down. With everyone carrying their own phone, whatever is witnessed has the potential to go viral almost immediately. It's as though the whole city is continuously watching … just waiting for something, anything. Take, for example, a couple of weeks ago, just past midnight near the front of the Hyatt Hotel at Embarcadero Center.

This is a time when the only people awake are the guards in the lobbies of closed banks and commercial high-rises. Even so, the guards are just as likely to be at their posts taking their break or their heads buried in their cell phones. The cleaning staff is busily sanitizing offices dozens of stories above the street or taking their break, hard-earned or not. Out on the street, there is always that one person or a couple of out-of-town business people staggering back to the Hyatt after a night of too much to drink and too little to eat. Then again, there might be that romantic couple rushing to catch the last Bay Area Rapid Transit (BART) train.

Such was the case for Abbey and Ron, or at least that's how Ron saw it.

They were no strangers to the area. They worked at 2nd National Bank, which had just moved into the former San Francisco Federal Reserve Bank kitty-corner to the hotel on Market Street. More specifically, they worked for the company's Corporate Security department. Along with several of their co-workers, they had all but closed O'Toole's Bar and Grill a few blocks away and now it was time to catch the last train to the East Bay.

Abbey was tired and looking forward to cuddling down with her feline companion Bootsy under a warm heating blanket. She liked Ron all right, but he was more co-worker than anything else. If you asked him, though, you might get a different answer. They both lived in the East Bay. So, for Abbey, it was only natural that they would try to catch the same train. Even with all the surveillance cameras on the platforms and in each train car, at this hour it was no place for someone alone and vulnerable, which would have described Abbey had Ron not suggested catching the train together.

Strange, she thought, looking up towards 2nd National as they hurried down the street. The office lights on the sixth floor corner window were still lit. That was her boss Dan Holmes' office. She knew he kept odd hours but her gut told her something wasn't right. After all, it was well past his bedtime, as he liked to say, often referring to being in bed by 10 p.m. She had worked for him for six years and knew that he prized the weekends with his wife, Brenda.

"Ron, do you see the lights are still on in Mr. Holmes' office?"

"Probably the cleaners," Ron answered.

"You're probably right."

The usual friendly clang of the trolley car coming down California Street had long ago gone silent for the evening. The large shoeshine stand that accommodates four patrons at a time sat empty, looming near the entrance to the stairs leading to the underground train stations. Even the recessed doorways they passed were void of the usual assortment of sleeping homeless souls.

"Where are they?" she mumbled to herself.

The street seemed suddenly deserted. She instinctively picked up the pace.

Ron seemed oblivious, probably the result of two too many grapefruit martinis—his favorite libation of the evening for some godawful reason. Or his thoughts were on what he was hoping for a little later at his place.

Ron was Senior Bank Agent, a bank detective. He was Black, in his mid-thirties, and his divorce settled two months ago after a yearlong tumultuous breakup. He wanted to get on with his life in a bad way. He figured Abbey could well be his path to something better, something he had secretly longed for since he first saw her three years ago. His female co-workers teased that he was ruggedly handsome, standing more than six-foot-two-inches with the body of a workout junkie. He wondered if Abbey felt the same way.

The underground stairway to the train stations came into full view. Abbey looked up again at the sixth floor. This time the lights were out.

"Ron? Notice how it seems like all the lights above the lobby level are out in all the buildings around here?" she asked softly.

"Hadn't noticed. You're not scared, are you?"

"No, just a little anxious. I'm not used to walking around here this time of the night. Strange, how I don't even think about the area during the day when I'm working. God, I can't believe we are the only ones on the street. It's really unsettling. There's not even a taxi or police car around. Are we really the only ones?"

She slipped her arm into his.

He smiled; things were going his way. "Kind of like one of those thriller or sci-fi movies after the aliens have invaded the place and everyone is either dead or run away. Do you watch those types of movies, Ab?"

"No," she answered quietly as they briskly approached the underground stairway. "I've never been one for those types of shows." They were close enough to hear one of the underground trains pulling into the station below them. Since BART was on the level below Muni, she couldn't distinguish which train it was. Either way, trains meant the presence of people. Right now, she wanted to lose herself among the other passengers. *Safety in numbers,* she thought.

As they approached the stairs, Ron said, "Be careful not to slip, it's wet."

This was the first time she realized that it was raining—more misting than actually raining. Regardless, up to now, she had simply written the cool wetness off as the fog. After all, wet foggy nights were the norm for San Francisco, especially this time of the year.

As they approached the stairs, a black SUV accelerated towards them down Drumm Street, tires screaming. Someone ran right by them. Where had he come from, and who was he running from? He was overweight, fiftyish, breathing hard, gasping for air as he passed them, trying to maintain his balance but clearly losing the battle. Ron caught sight of his eyes as he stumbled past. He was scared—really scared.

Ron tightened his grip on Abbey's arm and literally pulled her down a couple of steps. The runner managed to cross the BART plaza and make it to Market towards the front of 2nd National. Then, exhausted, he fell. He got up but fell again. Then got up a second time; only he didn't make it more than twenty feet before he fell again. The SUV was still hurtling down the street. The driver hit the brakes and screeched through the intersection, turning hard, momentarily accelerating then slamming on the brakes, coming to rest.

The chase was over.

Ron and Abbey looked at each other in disbelief. They climbed slowly up one step to get a better view without being noticed. Abbey's heart pounded. She began to shake.

Ron tightened his grip on her arm and said in a calm voice, "Hold on, they haven't seen us."

He pulled his phone out with his free hand and hit the camera icon. He didn't know what was happening but he would have a record of it. He thought, *pretty exciting stuff, and right in front of our building. Come Monday, the ladies will eat this up. They seem to thrive on any kind of cloak-and-dagger crap.* He was smiling a little.

Ron was always full of himself, and why not? A former Navy Seal, how many guys had run several marathons and a couple of Iron Man endurance races? His outgoing personality made him popular among the office staff, especially the ladies. He was born and raised across the bay in Oakland's Hawthorne neighborhood with a crime rate over three hundred and fifty percent above the national average. He had struggled to "stay clean" and keep out of trouble. He was proud of the fact that the Navy paid his way through Cal State Hayward. He had graduated with a degree in Criminal Justice.

It was his days as a Navy Seal and growing up in a really tough neighborhood that had long ago wrung any sense of danger out of him. Oh, he knew danger when he found himself in it. He was no fool, but his training taught him how to spot it quickly and react accordingly. Yet, it was growing up in Hawthorne where he developed his jaded attitudes and sarcastic comments—something he tried to cover by always making it seem like he was joking or making light of a situation.

Suddenly, the rear door of the car opened. For Ron, everything seemed to happen in slow motion. Abbey was momentarily stunned, trying to figure out what was unfolding. The SUV was menacing, its windows blacked out. It sat there for one of those moments that felt like an eternity. Finally, a large figure emerged and grabbed the runner who was screaming. *Like a little girl,* Ron thought. Those years of growing up in a drug-riddled neighborhood, coupled with his Special Ops days in the Middle East, had deeply jaded him. This wasn't the first time he had witnessed some loser being tossed into a car, never to be seen again.

Abbey had spent six years in the Army of Defense for Israel, or IDF, as a front-line combat soldier on the Pakistani border where she lost several friends while on routine patrols. She was always on edge in situations like this. Uncomfortable surroundings, loud noises, sudden surprises—they all made her extremely apprehensive. The ominous black SUV, the large guy, the screaming—it all added to her tense alarm, but she was trained to be silent.

The big guy had a tight hold on the runner. He pushed him into the back seat, even as the runner yelled for help. His screaming went unanswered. Once he was inside the car, the street became ominously silent. Just as the SUV started to pull away, Dan Holmes stepped out of the shadows in front the bank. He stepped over to the driver's window and briefly said something then stepped back. A moment later, the car pulled away from the curb and drove off slowly and quietly, just as though nothing had happened.

Quite civilized, Ron thought cynically. "Do you think they saw us, Ab?"

"Shit, I don't know. That was Dan! I don't think so. Let's get out of here." They ran down the stairs and within a minute found themselves on the lower platform, two among a handful of others. Again, Abbey was struck by the degree of silence. Like the security people in the lobbies above, here, too, everyone's face was buried in their phones. They seemed unmindful to everything and everyone.

"Are you okay?" asked Ron.

"I think so, just a little shaken." She paused and then asked, "What was that all about? That was Dan, wasn't it?"

"It was Dan alright."

"Well, what do you think this is all about?"

"Damned if I know."

"Do you think we should call someone? You know, the police? After all, we just witnessed a kidnapping," Abbey pressed.

"Are you f'n shit'n me? With Dan involved?" Ron couldn't believe what Abbey was saying. He was flummoxed to say the least.

"Yeah, I guess you're right. What about Monday morning?" Abbey asked.

"What about it?"

"I think we should at least confront Dan and tell him what we saw." She paused for a moment and then, "Oh, I don't know. I'm not sure. But, one thing is for sure. I wouldn't advise showing anyone what you caught on your phone until we know more," Abbey suggested.

Their train was pulling into the station.

"Once we have a seat, I want to look at the whole thing," Ron answered.

"Me too."

The train blew its horn, a series of short blasts, as it came into the station. When it stopped, the doors glided open. They both hurried inside and immediately found an empty seat. As they settled in, Abbey gave a slight sigh of relief and said, "I'm glad I live only a block from the station. I can't wait to crawl into bed."

Ron had figured as much.

"Let's look at what you recorded," Abbey said. He pulled out his phone and opened the video as Abbey leaned in to get a good view.

Ron could smell her. *God, she's hot,* he thought.

The whole episode was barely a minute long. Strange how those things worked. While living through it, you would swear it was several minutes. Here was one of those real-life examples that demonstrate how your mind works—not very reliable.

"Want to see it again?" Ron asked.

"No," Abbey responded. "I'm just as confused now as I was up on the street. When I get home, I'm going to call the security console and ask if they saw anything on our cameras."

"Sounds good, but what then?"

"Perhaps I should call Dan."

"You really going to call him at this hour?"

"This is serious stuff," Abbey rebuked him.

"Personally, I would approach him first thing Monday morning," Ron countered.

"Yeah, I think you're right. I'm sorry."

Then, a few moments later, Ron leaned closer to Abbey, "I know the big guy. I can't remember his name, but he's a bounty hunter. If that's the case, then technically, this wasn't a kidnapping. Bounty hunters are allowed to make citizen arrests."

"Good to know, I'll mention that to Dan," Abbey added with a sense of relief.

"Did you see the size of that guy? When he picked the fellow up and threw him into the car, he looked like a grizzly bear I once saw. That bear snatched up a cougar and threw it at least thirty feet!"

Normally such an anecdote would give Abbey cause to smile. But not now.

Neither said anything as the train zipped through the tunnel under San Francisco Bay. Even if they wanted to talk, the acoustics sucked. *Loud and obnoxious,* Ron thought. Then he leaned close to her cheek, smelled her hair, and softly said, "Your stop is coming up. Want me to walk you home?"

Abbey smiled. "No, I'll be fine. I just want to be home with my dad and the twins."

The train crawled into the Oakland station and came to rest. By the time the door opened, Abbey was standing in front of it. As she exited, she looked over her shoulder and waved goodbye. He returned the wave with a faint smile, trying to hide his disappointment.

"Oh well," he mused aloud, "I hope there is another opportunity." The train was off again to the next stop. He looked out the window watching Oakland pass by and then out of sight, only to be replaced by another town, another stop, and then the next—and so on until he reached Hayward.

At home, Abbey called the security console. "Hi, this is Abbey. Did you see an incident out front about fifteen to twenty minutes ago?"

"Hi, Ms. Gentry. I just came on duty. I'll run the video back, but I see on the log that the other operator entered that there was an intoxicated person that was helped into a car by associates and that you and Agent Tyson were witnesses." A moment later, he added, "Yes, I see it right here on the video and it looks like you and Agent Tyson were just going down the BART station stairs. I can even see that Agent Tyson took a picture or filmed it."

Then Abbey asked, "That big black SUV, can you read the front plate?"

"Sure, give me a minute and I'll run it and tell you who owns it."

Abbey waited. Shortly, "Got it. It's registered to LA Trust."

"Interesting. Thanks, you've been a great help. I hope your evening is quiet."

Abbey decided against calling her boss. Ron was right.

By 8:15, both Abbey and Ron were in Dan's office.

"Well, it seems as though the two of you saw a little excitement outside our front door around midnight Friday."

The two looked at each other and then back at Dan.

"You surprised that I know? You know that I pick up a copy of the security log for weekends and any attendant recordings."

They had forgotten.

Dan calmly said, "Don't worry, no one is in trouble. I'll explain in a moment. First, I need your phone, Ron."

Ron hesitated, looked at Abbey, and surrendered it. Dan then stepped momentarily out. When he returned he said, "Don't worry, Ron, I was actually glad that you managed to record all or some of what you and Ab saw."

"It was just instinct, boss," he responded.

"First, can I assume neither of you have said anything about what you saw to anyone?"

They both nodded.

"You saw us then?" Abbey asked.

"You could say something like that," Dan responded coyly.

He then glanced at his watch. "I have limited time right now since my boss wants to be briefed at nine. She'll need to brief President Sands before he hears about it from some other source. The last thing we need, and by we, I mean me. Being on my case. Bosses can be such a pain at times." He missed the exchange of glances between the other two and their slight smiles. He continued, "So, let me give you the Cliff Notes version of a somewhat ingenious scheme. First, it turns out that the gentlemen in the car were the Director of Security for LA Trust, Peter Hunt, and a bounty hunter. The guy they snagged was Charles Fairfield. More about him in a minute.

"Hunt called me earlier Friday night to tell me they were busting Fairfield later at his apartment in Embarcadero 3 to hand him over to the FBI. He said he would keep me informed and called me yesterday afternoon to update me accordingly. Well, things apparently went cattywampus and Fairfield managed to bolt and was trying to outrun them.

"Whereas I wasn't involved in Hunt's plans, I did want to be close by when he collared Fairchild. That's when he ran past you and fell down. I don't think he even knew where he was going. Nonetheless, they caught him, threw him in the car. That's when Hunt saw me, so I stepped over to his car and wished him luck with the FBI. He then drove off.

"But, here's where it gets interesting. Instead of taking him to the FBI office, they went directly to Santa Clara airfield where Fairfield was shanghaied to Singapore. At the airport they were met by Singapore Global's security chief. Since Global owns LA Trust, you can imagine that they didn't appreciate him stealing millions from them. So, they drugged him, stuffed him in a crate, and listed it as a diplomatic pouch to avoid Homeland Security's searching it. And, since we are not allies with Singapore, I suspect we'll never see him again. Hunt was always supposed to take Fairchild to the FBI. I couldn't believe what he did, but I wasn't surprised. He has a reputation for being a cowboy and doing crazy shit like this."

"So, what about the FBI? After all, he was kidnapped and not arrested and we witnessed it. If we don't say anything, aren't we accessories?" Ron inquired.

"Right now, it seems this is a matter between Singapore Global, the State Department, and the Bureau. But I don't think it's going to go anywhere. With tensions high in the Far East and us wanting to keep Singapore on our side, I suspect the State Department trumps the FBI and asked that the Bureau let this one slide."

"You mean, it's as though this never happened and this guy Fairchild just goes away?" Abbey asked astounded. "Won't people miss him? What about his wife?"

"I'll get to that. For now, the short of it is that Fairchild clipped both LA Trust, as I say, owned by Singapore Global, and us for four-and-a-half million and two-and-a-half million respectively. In short, the folks at Singapore don't exactly take kindly to someone ripping them off. So, they had to do something. Especially with this guy, since he had targeted seven other banks Singapore owns. All total; he was into them for over twenty million dollars. When Global's execs found out, they decided to send their security chief over here to fetch him."

"Well, I have to ask, what did he actually do?" Abbey inquired.

"Great question, Ab. A few months ago, Sam Greene got a call from Fairchild who said he had proof that our senior private bankers were skimming their high-end customer accounts to the tune of several million over the past several years. He claimed that he had the proof on no less than six of our people. As our General Auditor, Greene wanted to see proof and Fairchild supposedly showed him their names using aliases and setting up Swiss accounts. Fairchild said it was an organized group and he suspected several others."

Dan continued, "Greene met with President Sands, briefed him, and asked him to sign a contract with Fairchild to investigate the whole matter. Sands told Greene he would go along with everything. But after Greene left, Sands called me and filled me in on what he knew. Together, we agreed to give Greene as much rope as he needed and see how things unfolded.

"About two weeks later, I got a call from Hunt at LA Trust who said that their General Auditor had been approached by Fairchild three months ago. Without telling anyone, their GA signed a contract. By the time Hunt's people got involved, LA Trust was into Fairchild for nearly four million dollars and they were going to pull the plug.

"Over here, I was doing some discreet checking and was likewise growing suspicious of Fairchild for sure and possibly Greene. Within a few days, I got another call from Hunt saying that Fairchild was somehow tipped and he was on the lam. That's when Hunt turned to his bounty hunter thug to find him. It didn't take long. You saw how it all played out over the weekend."

"So, how did Fairchild actually get his money?" Abbey asked.

"Beyond the initial retainer, for every name he could 'prove,' Fairchild got fifty thousand. By the time it all came to a head, Greene had authorized two-and-a-half million in consulting fees," Dan answered.

"Not a bad scam; quite creative, as a matter of fact. He gets an Olympic score of ten from me on creativity and having the balls to try it!" Ron laughed and Abbey shook her head with half a smile again.

"A quick question, if I may," Abbey ventured to ask. "I assume Greene wasn't actually collecting anything from Fairchild, was he?"

Dan looked at each of them, smiled, and then quietly said, "The jury is still out. That's why I want to see you both when I return from briefing President Sands. We have some work to do."

"God, it seems that Greene should have just handed the whole thing over to us. As it is, it looks like he cost the bank a few million," Abbey wondered aloud.

Ron blurted out, "Because he's been bucking for Corporate Security to report directly to him for years; so, my sources inside Audit tell me. This was his way of proving his team could investigate major crimes just as well. Besides, and please, sir, take this in the manner in which it is intended, but from what I hear, there's been some real bad blood between you two for a while."

"I wish I could disagree with you, Ron, but you're spot on."

"So," Ron asked, "does Greene know about what happened to Fairchild?"

Dan smirked. "As of this moment, I doubt it. However, after I have briefed my boss, I suspect he will call him."

"God, how I would love to be there when he gets the call from President Sands!" Ron erupted.

"If there was bad blood between the two of you before, I suspect Greene will have you in his crosshairs," Abbey added.

There was a moment of silence among the three. It was as though each of them were simply processing the matter. Ron broke the silence, "I wonder what type of fate awaits Fairchild now?"

"He'll likely end up in a Singapore prison with no chance of parole. Their system of justice is much swifter than ours. It is not unusual for people like Fairchild to sometimes have fatal accidents or commit suicide."

Abbey cut in. "Sorry, sir, but before you leave, aren't we still out two-and-a-half-million and LA Trust four-and-a-half million?"

"That's true, Ab, but our money, at least, isn't really lost. For that matter, we're out front with an extra two million. Fairchild thought he was being really cute by opening two accounts, one here and the other at LA Trust under a different name. He took the money we gave him and deposited it at Trust and vice versa with Trust's money going into his account here.

"I can't speak for Trust, but once we discovered Fairchild's lame attempt to hide our money under our noses, I had Retail IT create a back door on his account. Every time he made a deposit from LA Trust the funds were automatically transferred to another hidden account under our control. We dummied up his account to make it look like all his deposits were intact, but his actual account didn't have a penny in it. So, we have LA Trust's four-and-a-half and they have our two-and-a-half. For now, we collect the interest on the four-and-a-half and let the legal and retail folks work it out. Just a little trick I came up with a number of years ago."

Ron leaned over to Abbey and said almost inaudibly, "Remind me to never deposit money in this bank."

"You fuckhead." Dan laughed. He quickly caught himself. "Pardon the crass language, folks. For now, if there are no more questions, I suggest you get back to work before the rest of the staff starts asking questions."

Abbey hurried, knowing Dan's time was limited. "And, what about his wife?"

"Thanks for bringing that up. Hunt's people actually found out that she is in North Carolina. She left him years ago when she found out he was a thief and several police agencies wanted him. From what I understand, she'll be quite happy once she finds out—no love lost there.

"I'll see you two when I return from President Sands' office. It doesn't have to be together. As you leave, Ron, you might want to check on your phone. I'm sure it's ready. I had my Admin delete the video."

As Abbey and Ron headed for their respective offices, Abbey stopped and asked inquisitively, "So, Fairchild was actually kidnapped and we witnessed it. As I see it, aren't we actually accessories to the fact, along with Dan?"

"Maybe, maybe not," Ron responded. "Perhaps all we saw was a drunk fall down and some friends helped him up, put him in their SUV, and drove off. After all, that's what our security console operator saw and logged it accordingly."

10:30 A.M.

As soon as Dan returned to his office, he called Ron. "Are you ready to see me boss?" Ron answered.

"I can just as well tell you over the phone. I want you to have a couple of your people discreetly check with the buildings around us and see if any of their cameras picked up what happened. I think it is a fair bet that Hyatt's security people recorded it, but what about the others? See if they will give you a copy and then we can decide what we need to do, if anything."

"I'm on it."

"Not so fast, there is something else. Take a couple of your agents and hit Fairchild's place. I want everything electronic and any hardcopy materials that suggest his involvement with us or LA Trust. Then pay the building manager to empty his place. Give it all away to Goodwill or some other such organization. Or the manager can keep the stuff. I don't really care. All I want is for the place to be empty in the next twenty-four hours."

Dan called Abbey. "I'm back. Can you meet me in the lobby?"

"Sure. I'll be right there."

UNIT 33

A few minutes later, Dan and Abbey walked out of 2nd National Bank and headed up the street. On the way, Dan said, "I'm going to show you something and you are never to tell a soul." They turned at Beale, stopping at a small alley that led to the loading dock. As they walked towards it, Abbey noticed a steel door. The sign read, simply, Unit 33. To the casual passer-by, it appeared to be an entrance to something associated with the loading dock. The entrance was controlled by an overhead camera and a simple keypad.

Dan typed in a code and the door unlocked. They walked in and Abbey saw that they were in a mantrap. The outer door behind them closed automatically and locked. In front of them was another locked door with another overhead camera. Dan spoke, "Good morning, the woman next to me is cleared." With that, the door buzzed open and they stepped into a stairwell.

Abbey looked at Dan, but said nothing.

She followed him up the stairs, two flights. When they reached the landing, they encountered a third locked door, with a biometric eye and facial scan locking device. Dan stepped close to it, placing his face close to the device and opening his eyes widely. The door buzzed open and they stepped into what looked like a typical front office with a receptionist.

"Good morning, Dr. Holmes," the receptionist said, smiling.

Dan returned the greeting and asked her to give Abbey a day pass. He then directed Abbey to a small conference room.

"Sir, she called you Dr. Holmes."

"That's right. I have a PhD from Southern Cal. I received the degree more than thirty years ago. Very few people at the bank are aware of it."

"But she does, that's interesting," Abbey responded.

"Well, in a few minutes, you will likely understand," Dan answered.

"This place is only known to myself, President Sands, and now you. It's a separate entity and not part of the bank, but financed by it. I can explain all of that later. Essentially, it's a small IT operation. As I will show you, the heart of the facility is comprised of six independent workstations. Each is staffed with an operator and three monitors with a central keyboard. In a separate room, there are four processors, each dedicated to a separate function. There is an offsite facility that serves as our redundancy in case one of the usual threats befalls us. You know, water, fire, and earthquakes.

"In short, we have the talent and know-how to hack into systems anywhere in the world and within nearly any organization, public or private. Our analysts are continuously researching the internet and extracting information. They're particularly adroit with archival records, public and private.

"You got to watch these computer geeks. One of the analysts developed his own software program while attending Cal Tech. The software hid his IP address, disguising it as coming from someone else. They're continuously improving it, thus allowing them to eavesdrop on an organization or extract confidential information without their knowledge. A favorite pastime is hacking into one agency but making it appear that it was coming from another unsuspecting source. It's not uncommon for them to hack a Russian government agency, leading the Russians to believe the hack was originating from a Chinese government agency. As President Sands says, 'We have our own private CIA!'"

"Sir, can I ask a question?"

"Go ahead."

"What about malware protection software? Clearly a great number of organizations and governments have sophisticated counter measures to thwart such attacks."

"That's what I thought, but as one of our analysts pointed out, they may think they're protected, and for a brief period of time, they may be, but it doesn't take long for us to be ahead of their game. To them, it's only a job. For us, it is what we live for. We're really good at this."

Dan went on to explain the unit's history. "When Unit 33 was originally set up, 2nd National was not only expanding its footprint in several countries, but also financing other organizations doing business in the same or nearby areas. Our Board of Directors were concerned that we might end up inadvertently financing regimes that posed a threat to our interests, or underwriting corporations that served as a conduit for drug lords, terrorists, etc.

"It didn't take long to discover that local foreign office managers, by virtue of their position, already served as a conduit for ascertaining sensitive information and passing it along to U.S. intelligence agencies—or others. The Board's directive to President Sands, and therefore me, was to make sure our 'skirts' are clean and if not, give us enough time get out. The Board didn't want to know the details, so Sands directed me to do what I do best. And we never looked back."

"So, why me, why now, sir?" Abbey asked.

"Because we want to pass the baton to you to run this operation. I've watched how you manage our department's Background Investigations Unit and Executive Drivers Unit. You've got the people skills and know how to keep your mouth shut. You don't piss people off. Besides, I'm in my sixties now and I need someone like you to take over this operation sometime, so why not now? As I see it, you'll have three to five years to grow into the position under my guidance. Sands agrees. He has also approved a very nice pop in pay and corporate title."

Abbey smiled; the money would definitely come in handy.

Abbey was a widow, having lost her husband several years earlier when he was deployed to Iraq, leaving her with twin boys, now in their mid-teens. Her tough-mindedness had earned her a reputation as someone who could hold her own in the heavily male-dominated Corporate Security department. She had, as the saying goes, "thick skin," and could "dish it out" with the best of anyone, including the sexist comments that still pervaded the department. Those were some of the qualities that convinced Dan she was the right person.

Moreover, as he told President Sands, "She's smart, graduating from UC Berkley in International Relations, magna cum laude. You would not readily know this since she rarely talks about her personal life. She always dresses professionally and carries herself with a definite air of confidence. She's got executive potential, especially within the bank's International Division."

What Dan failed to mention to Sands, seeing no added value, was that she was born in Israel. Her father was an American doctor from Boston and her mother a native Israeli, born in Jerusalem. Abbey always felt very close to her natural homeland and on a number of occasions she was approached by Mossad, Israeli's Intelligence Service, to become an agent. She always declined, but that didn't mean she was opposed to espionage. And, on occasion, she would draw on her resources to help others out when asked. Over time, she developed a close relationship with one young woman, only to discover later she had been recruited by Mossad. Ellen Fischer was now Abbey's closest friend.

Dan rationalized that combining management of Unit 33 with overseeing the executive drivers could prove to be exceptionally strong under Abbey's direction. Unit 33 was all about gathering intelligence, not unlike what the executive drivers did. The drivers did more than ferry executives around. Unbeknownst to anyone getting in an executive vehicle, everything was recorded.

Experience had taught Dan years ago that executives are perhaps among the biggest gossips in their own organization, not to mention how they liked to brag among themselves or at dinner parties, and so on. They freely talked in front of their drivers as though somehow the drivers were deaf or indifferent. So, demonstrating special appreciation at Christmas, on birthdays, and on their employment anniversaries, Dan was typically ahead of the curve regarding most bank matters at the executive levels. Coupled with Unit 33's technology, he was—as they say—in the proverbial catbird seat. And, when necessary, such strategies proved invaluable when applied to lower-level managers or bank officers, such as General Auditor Sam Greene or any of his cronies. Who better to run the combined intel units?

"What about Ron? How is he going to take my promotion?" Abbey asked, sincerely concerned.

"Well, that should not be a problem. I want to transfer the BIU to him and with that comes a pop in pay and title as well. You have the Background Investigations Unit humming with our usual due diligence on loan applicants, credit checks, employee background checks, and ad hoc special requests. So, the transfer should be seamless. For him, all he needs to know is that you are working on a special project for me. Hence, the transfer.

"And, oh by the way," Dan continued. "When I told you and

Ron that it was Hunt's people that broke the Fairchild case and found his ex-wife, that was only partially true. It was Unit 33 that not only discovered the fraud, but also tracked down his ex. But Ron doesn't need to know this. Okay?"

"I hear you, sir."

Dan had long ago given up having Abbey call him Dan. As she explained, her father was a surgeon and he taught her that people with advanced degrees worked hard for them and it should be acknowledged, even in casual conservations. Similarly, people in authority, like one's boss, should always be shown respect by referring to them as either Mr., Mrs., Ms., or sir or ma'am. She had apologized, explaining that because she was raised that way, she felt more comfortable calling him sir. He told her he understood. The subject never came up again.

When Dan called Ron in and told him that the BIU was now reporting to him, he was more than delighted. For him, this was the kind of recognition he wanted. A new corporate title, increase in pay, and being able to actively integrate himself into so many new business units was more than fantastic. It was a dream come true for a guy who battled "a slum upbringing," as he called it.

Dan teased, but cautioned, "Ron, don't let this go to your head. I can see it growing as we talk."

A few weeks had passed since the Fairchild matter. Even so, Corporate Security was still actively investigating Greene to see if he had some sort of sidebar deal with Fairchild. Unit 33 was working extended hours to track Greene's assets.

Dan was at his desk when he received a text from Abbey. It simply read, "Our sources have confirmed that Fairchild is dead in a Singapore jail while awaiting trial. It was reported by prison officials that he committed suicide."

In turn, Dan called President Sands' office. He talked to his Executive Assistant and asked that she relay the message. He then called Ron. "I want everything that your folks pulled out of Fairchild's place put in my SUV today. Have somebody stop by my office for the key fob. Okay?"

"No problem," Ron answered. "I'll personally retrieve the fob. Can I ask what you intend to do with it?"

"You can ask, but in this case, the less you know, the better off you are if ever asked about it."

THE FOLLOWING SATURDAY EVENING

It was approaching 9 p.m. when Dan's phone rang. "What's up, Ab?" he asked, half looking at one of his favorite TV shows.

"I think we've neutralized one of your more worrisome threats, sir. And if we play this right, Greene is going down."

Dan stepped away, leaving his wife Brenda alone.

When Abbey finished talking, he smiled. She was right, Sam Greene was no longer someone to worry about. Whereas taking someone off the street in the middle of the night may be messy business, misappropriation of bank assets for personal gain and blackmail was another matter. She briefly explained that Unit 33 had traced payments from Fairchild's LA Trust account to an account Greene had with an investment house in Boston.

But that wasn't the worst of it. Greene had another arrangement with the bank's armored carrier service, Rossi Armored Services. So, he was actually receiving kickbacks from two vendors at the same time. Dan thanked her for her unit's excellent work and said he would meet with her Monday morning.

"Sir, is this what you mean when you say that an unsuspecting person does not know it, but they've just been mentally terminated?"

"Maybe not tonight, but as soon as President Sands hears of this, it most certainly will be the case. I suspect he will want to give Greene a little more rope to make sure it's nice and tight when the time is right."

Dan hung up and went back to Brenda. "Everything okay, Dan?"

"You bet. Do you think it's too late for a little ice cream with chocolate sauce? I feel like celebrating."

START OF A NEW WEEK

On Monday, Dan and Abbey met and he received all of the reports on both cases. They agreed that, for now, they would set the Fair-child matter aside and focus on Rossi Armored Services and their business relationship with the General Auditor. He would pass the Rossi case on to Ron as information coming from a whistleblower within Rossi's company, thus protecting Unit 33's involvement.

It didn't take long for Ron's agents to start putting the case together. The investigation was steadily progressing and Ron felt it was only a matter of a few more days, a week at most, and they would be able to hand over their investigation to the San Francisco Police Department. That's about the time when Sam Greene received a phone call from one of his auditors.

"Hello Mr. Greene, I have some information. I'm not sure it's legitimate, but your involvement was implied and I thought you should know."

Alarm bells began ringing in Greene's head. "I understand. When the weather is nice, I always enjoy having lunch in the Embarcadero plaza. Why don't you meet me there at noon and we'll grab a sandwich from one of the food trucks and have a chat?"

At noon, the two of them met, ordered their lunches, and sat down on one of the nearby benches. After a few pleasantries, Greene asked his auditor what he had. "I was having a drink last night at O'Toole's with one of Corporate Security's agents. We're friends from way back. Anyway, my friend was getting a little more than drunk when he let it slip that they were investigating a bank executive. No names were mentioned but he did say it involved a kickback to one of our executives."

"Interesting, but how does that translate to implicating me?" Greene asked, trying to keep a straight face.

"Well, a few weeks ago, again at O'Toole's, he said that you were pissed as to how the Fairchild matter unfolded and then he said something like, 'Hey, maybe Greene is pissed because his under-the-table money has dried up.' Then he laughed and added, 'That's my theory anyway. Too bad Ron and the others don't want to take me seriously.'"

"And that's it?" Greene asked.

"No. At first, I thought he was talking about Fairchild again, then he said he wasn't allowed to use names but based on Corporate Security's investigation so far, it involved one of the bank's money carriers and then added, 'Audit knows something but they're not telling.' That was it, that's all he said. I just thought you should know."

"Thanks. Let's keep this between us for now. I'll do some poking around myself. Maybe we can use our resources and not only remove any suspicions about me, but also pull their investigation out from under them and score our own victory," Greene offered, smiling and then added, "Say nothing to anyone and I'll get back to you. If your agent friend has anything to add, let me know right away."

A FEW DAYS LATER

Dan was planning lunch with Ron, but Ron called and begged off due to a family matter. This was not problematic for Dan, since it was his custom to take a staff member to lunch each month, as a show of appreciation. He decided to ask Abbey's Executive Drivers' supervisor. They met in the lobby and leisurely strolled up to 33 Beale Street, exchanging small talk. Along the way, Dan explained they were going to meet Abbey and her friend, Ellen Fischer, in the front lobby. From there, the four of them would walk to one of Dan's favorite restaurants nearby.

As they walked down the street, neither noticed the two men behind them. It was a little past one o'clock and the street was jammed with the usual assortment of taxis, buses, Muni trains, and messengers darting between all of them on their bikes. The sidewalks were equally full as office workers hurried back to their office after lunch—most with their heads down, buried in their phones. No one was casually strolling along, that was something reserved for afterhours in the financial district. For now, it was all about getting from one place to another with the least amount of hassle.

It was a great day weather-wise. As Abbey and Ellen waited just inside the revolving door, Dan and her Executive Drivers' supervisor walked towards them. At the same time, she saw two guys running up behind them. A single shot rang out. The supervisor dropped immediately, fragments of his brain flying through the air.

One second all was normal; a second later, chaos reigned. Pedestrians screamed, some running—nowhere in particular, just trying to get out of the way. Vehicles screeched to a halt. Several drivers abandoned cars where they stopped. Instinctively, Dan began to crouch down. A second shot rang out just as Dan was going down. He fell face-first onto the pavement. His body jerked when the second bullet entered him at near point-blank range. The shooter turned, ran across Beale Street, and started running towards Market.

Horrified, Abbey pushed through one of the doors to see the other taking aim at her. A third shot rang out. She went limp, blocking the revolving door. As she lay there motionless, the assassin fired off another shot into her lifeless body. She was bleeding from the front of her neck where the first bullet struck her. A second shot quickly followed into her side near her ribcage.

Then the second assassin turned and started running up his side of the street just opposite his fellow assassin. By this time, Ellen had cleared the adjacent front door with her weapon drawn. She dropped to a kneeling position and took aim at the assassin fleeing ahead of her. She squeezed off a shot and he dropped. The woman that he had just pushed aside stood there screaming hysterically.

From behind him, the first shooter heard a voice identifying himself as the police and yelling for him to stop. The assailant kept running as he felt two bullets whiz by his head from the detective's weapon. As the shooter approached Market Street another shot rang out. He dropped dead on the spot. Ellen had pivoted on her knee and deliberately squeezed off another shot, hitting her target in the back of the head. A marked SFPD unit screamed to a stop. The officers jumped out as the detective ran up to them waving his gold shield. The three officers approached the assailant. He was bleeding from his leg and right side. Two of the detective's bullets had hit his target. Part of the back of his head was missing.

Abbey was still breathing, albeit shallowly. Ellen leaned in to comfort her. There was nothing more she could do. She knelt in a growing pool of Abbey's blood as she tried to cradle her friend in her arms. Tears began to flow. Blood was everywhere, the sirens were not far away and getting closer, horns were blaring as buses and cars tried to get around or out of the way. As the three lay there, people tried to step or jump over them.

And then, it was over.

It was quiet, eerily so. No traffic on the street, no wailing sirens, no one on the sidewalks except for police officers and paramedics.

It was purely coincidental that the detective just happened to be walking on the sidewalk opposite where Dan, the supervisor, and Abbey had fallen. He saw the first assailant cut in front of him with the gun still in hand. That's when he first called out, identifying himself as a police officer, and began his pursuit.

At first count, it appeared that two others were injured, each hit from presumably the detective's weapon as he fired at the fleeing assailant. One lay face down on the sidewalk where she had been hit; the other was sitting up and being attended to, the extent of her injury unknown but she was talking.

Ellen stood against the front wall of the building, covered with Abbey's blood. She silently watched the paramedics lift Abbey onto a gurney and race off to a waiting unit. As for the supervisor, his body lay where he had fallen, but the paramedics and two police officers were carefully examining him. Dan was unconscious as he was lifted onto a gurney and put into another waiting paramedic unit. Once in, he was sped away.

A police officer stepped in front of Ellen.

"A witness told me that it was you that shot and killed the two perps. Is that so?" she asked.

"Yes."

"Where is your weapon?"

Ellen pulled back the front of her coat, exposing the holstered Glock. "I have a permit to carry," she calmly said.

"I take it that you are law enforcement then?"

"No. I'm actually Special Ops, Israeli Consulate."

"We're going to need a detailed statement, ma'am. You in a position to come with me?"

"I guess so," Ellen said.

On the eighth floor of 2nd National Bank, Sam Greene was at his office corner window straining to see what, if anything, he could take in on the street below. His phone rang. He answered it. The voice on the other end said, "It didn't go exactly as planned, but the three targets are down. It appears there was some collateral damage. My two guys apparently didn't make it, but that's probably best." The caller hung up.

Greene went back to his desk and sat down. He smiled broadly.

Toni Rossi saw what was happening on the television in his office. As he watched, his phone rang. When he answered, the same voice that had just spoken to Greene calmly said, "It's over. What do you want me to do with Mr. Greene?"

"Take care of him, sooner rather than later," Rossi responded and then hung up.

A moment later, on the executive floor, President Sands' Chief of Staff interrupted a teleconference. "I'm sorry, but there's been a shooting. It's several of our people. They've been shot on the street in front of 33 Beale."

"Who?" Sands asked, stunned.

"People in Corporate Security, sir. Dan Holmes and two of his managers."

President Sands hung up on the teleconference with a group of analysts. No explanation, nothing about calling the parties back. He simply hung the phone up and said, "My God." Then dropped his face into his hands.

LATE THAT NIGHT

It was close to ten o'clock before Abbey left the operating room and was wheeled to ICU. The doctor met her twin boys, her dad, and the boys' coach in the waiting area. The doctor told them that they should prepare themselves, he was not hopeful she would make it through the night. One of the twins slumped to the floor and the other knelt next to him. Granddad let the tears freely roll down his cheeks and the soccer coach leaned down to talk softly to the boys.

Brenda was in a daze. In all of the close calls he had experienced before, Dan was never seriously hurt.

It was then that President Sands walked into the waiting room. He sat down next to Brenda. She leaned into him and he embraced her. Her hands shook. The two had gone through tough times before, but nothing like this.

Another doctor walked into the room and asked if Brenda Holmes was there. Everyone looked at him as Brenda stood up.

"He's alive, but in critical condition," the doctor said. "The bullet went through the back, nicking his spine, and shattered into fragments. It was one of those bullets designed to cause as much damage as possible. One of his ribs was severed and is lodged up against the back of the heart. There's a bullet fragment there as well. It's a miracle he's still with us but we cannot operate any further tonight. He needs to stabilize. Hopefully, we can remove the remaining fragments late tomorrow but it will take a long time. We've already removed them from the lungs, the stomach, and liver. They seem to be everywhere, but we know where they are and we'll get all of them."

"Once everything is out, will he be," Brenda paused momentarily, "okay?"

"I wish I could give you the answer I know you want to hear. But I can't. It's simply too early. In the long run, I think he has a chance, but that all depends on his health, will to live, and getting the remaining fragments successfully removed. Right now, he's in critical condition and the slightest movement of that fragment near the heart could be fatal. Trust me, we're doing everything we can. Right now, he's one of the two lucky ones that are still alive."

Sands looked at the men just a few feet away. "Are they here for Abbey Gentry?" he asked the surgeon.

"I believe so," the doctor said.

"Is there anything you can tell me about her condition? She works for me."

"I wish I could discuss her status, but I can't," the doctor replied. "You'll have to discuss that with the family's doctor."

Regardless, President Sands could read from the surgeon's tone and eyes that it was dire. He heard the other surgeon say to Abbey's family, "Let's pray. It's all we can do right now."

Sands went to his office. There he extracted a file from his middle drawer entitled *Corporate Security Line of Succession*. He had a similar file for every major department in the bank, something he required to be annually updated. He located a sealed envelope at the rear of the file, entitled Unit 33. He scrolled down to the unit's supervisor, the person who oversees the daily operation of six people, and dialed the number listed. When the person said hello, Sands identified himself. "I want the work your unit is doing to continue. You folks may not fully understand your importance, but I do," he said almost matter-of-factly. "Until further notice, you report to me, and me alone. Is that clear?" And then, "What do you have so far?"

"Mr. President, we know the shooters belonged to one of the city's most dangerous Hispanic gangs, the 5th Streeters. Their leader sometime back swore to avenge his father's death. He believes that Dr. Holmes was responsible for his father's death because it was his testimony that led the father to San Quentin where he was killed. What we haven't firmly established is whether or not this was a simple revenge shooting or whether someone hired them out."

"And if it was a hit job, who else wanted Dan out of the way?" Sands asked.

"Right now, that question might be better answered by Ron Tyson's group. They're working on a sensitive case involving one of your executives."

"I'll call Ron, but you're talking about Sam Greene, right? Dan's been keeping me in the loop on that one. I was just wondering if we had someone else."

"Not to our knowledge, sir. Just Mr. Greene."

"Thanks. Keep up the good work, I'm calling Ron now." With that, President Sands ended their call and dialed Ron right away. "Hi Ron, Sands here."

"Yes, sir," Ron answered.

"Where are you now?" the president asked.

"I'm at the hospital with Mrs. Holmes."

"We must have just missed each other."

"That's what she told me," Ron answered. "Is there anything I can do to help you, sir?"

"Yes. Until further notice, you will serve as Acting CSO and report directly to me."

"Yes sir."

"What do we have on Greene? Is he behind this?"

"My money says yes, but we have a few more loose ends before we can turn this over to the Feds."

"Alright. But before you do, set up a time with me. I want a full briefing before this leaves the bank. I'll need time to prep the Board and have Corporate Communications ready with a statement and press release."

"I've got it, Mr. President," Ron answered.

THE NEXT MORNING

Sam Greene kissed his wife goodbye and asked her to say the same to his son, who was still in bed. Yesterday was a good day for him, his team having won their championship soccer match. It was a quiet Saturday morning and Greene's usual golf buddies were going to meet him at the Presidio Golf Course. It looked like a perfect day for a round of golf, no wind, with a beautiful California blue sky. Sam backed his Mercedes onto the street and drove off. Approximately one block later, there was a loud explosion. The car was history, as was the driver.

At the hospital, Ellen Fischer found Brenda sitting in the hall-way alone. Abbey's family had gone home, advising Brenda they would be back in a couple of hours.

"Hi, I'm Ellen. I don't think we've ever met, but Abbey is my best friend. I've been calling all night checking on her and Dan's status. I would have been here sooner, but I was making certain arrangements. Do you know anything?"

"No, other than they are both still with us, but remain in critical condition in the ICU," Brenda answered.

"Do you have someone to stay with you?"

"I've called our daughter and she's trying to get here as quick as she can, but she's coming in from North Carolina."

"I didn't know you and Mr. Holmes had a daughter."

"Well, Dan keeps his private life pretty private. He doesn't even carry pictures of us in his wallet."

"Trust me, I understand and it's a good thing he doesn't."

"I get it. You're from The Company. No wait, Dan has told me a little about you. You've worked with him before, in the Middle East. I think he once told me you're not only friends with Abbey but also work for some other country's CIA. Israel, right?"

"Sounds like Dan has been doing a little talking out of school. But I'll forgive him, he's a great guy," Ellen teased slightly.

Brenda smiled. Then, "Does Abbey know?"

"Oh yes. We met when we were both in the Israeli army. Eventually she went her way, I went mine, but we've stayed in touch all these years. When Dan was looking to hire someone for a special assignment at the bank, I recommended Abbey. That was some time ago."

"Do you know who did this?"

"I'm not sure about who's behind it, but I know who pulled the trigger."

"I hope the bastards rot in hell!" Brenda said, crying audibly.

"Mrs. Holmes, we're working on that as you and I speak. And, can I trust that all of this stays between us?"

"Your secrets are my secrets. Just nail the fucking swine," Brenda swore aloud.

"Well, if you want, I can stay until Abbey's family comes back."

"Thanks, but that isn't necessary. Besides, it seems as though you have some work ahead of you."

Ellen smiled. "That I do."

Just before noon, Ellen Fischer and Peter Rosenberg, her spotter for the past fifteen years, slowly drove down the alley behind Carlos Chaval's home in Hunter's Point. As leader of the 5th Streeters, Chaval allegedly spent most of his time away from his home. In reality, he spent nearly every night there. Ellen had tapped her sources in the local San Francisco office of Mossad. She discovered that they had a lengthy dossier on Chaval, since the 5th Streeters were highly antisemitic.

Previous surveillance by Mossad revealed that Chaval was a creature of habit, arriving at home within minutes of the same time each evening and leaving at the same time each morning. He came and went in an SUV driven by one of his gang members and another riding up front serving literally as the shotgun person. Chaval always entered and exited the rear of the vehicle just behind the shotgun.

His home was four doors down from the rectory of Our Lady of Lourdes Parish in the Hunters Point District. There was no mistaking the target. There were no street lights in the alley so the only illumination came from a pair of flood lights on each end of a long community garage that ran the length of the alley directly across each house. Upon inspection, they discovered the flood light fixtures at each end had no bulbs. It looked like this had been so for some time. The roof was flat the entire length and a three-foot-high parapet extended along the entire roof line. It was perfect for someone to crouch down behind it and go unnoticed.

As they drove off, Ellen continued their conversation just as they entered the alley. "We can take him out when he's going from the car to the house or vice versa. If anyone steps outside the house, I'll drop them. The same goes for the driver and the other."

"I'll park the truck behind the garage and we can access the roof with my ladder. Should be easy on, easy off," Peter said.

Ellen nodded approval. "I'll set up on the far end, across from the rectory, and you can take up a position midway down. You should have a clear vantage point to spot me and keep an eye on the street and the rear of the church property. What do you think?"

"I like it," Peter said. "Tonight, when we return, I can mount the cameras on the street lamps out front. That will give me a clear view of when his car is arriving via my iPad. I'll then activate the self-destruct mechanism on each camera."

"I'm thinking that a morning hit might be best," Peter offered.

"Great. Tomorrow morning we'll do a dry run to get our timing down. The Mossad report says that his morning ride always arrives between 7 and 7:10. If so, we'll be set to go," Ellen directed.

By 6:45 the next morning, they were in position to observe Chaval's departure. Crouching behind the parapet about halfway down the garage roof, they watched as Chaval's driver pulled up just before 7 and a bodyguard on the passenger's side exited the vehicle. He opened the rear door and positioned himself by it. He looked up and down the alley, and waved his hand facing the house. The target exited almost immediately. As he walked down the steps quickly, his wife came out and stood on the landing, waving goodbye. Chaval hurried down the sidewalk and entered the rear seat. The bodyguard closed the door and then slipped into the front passenger seat. The SUV drove away, gaining speed as it went down the alley.

Once the vehicle exited the alley, Ellen and Peter made their way back to the truck. "I'll be using my usual weapon. I won't need my tripod since the top of the parapet will serve nicely."

Ellen had over twenty years as a professional sniper. Early on, she was seen as one of Israel's best and brightest youths and was recruited directly into Israel's navy and shortly thereafter into the elite commando unit, Sayeret Matkal, as a specialist in foreign counterterrorism. Ellen had demonstrated a remarkable ability as a sniper under any condition her trainers put her through.

Peter, on the other hand, had a basic working knowledge of military style rifles, having trained and carried one in Afghanistan serving in Dan's special forces unit as a "consultant on loan" from one of Israeli's commando units. His real forte was doing advanced reconnaissance for these types of assignments and serving as a spotter for the shooter. It was here he met Ellen, who was also on loan. They soon realized they worked well as a team.

The plan was simple.

They would park Peter's truck on the street to the rear of the garage. Accessing the roof under the cover of darkness, Peter would take up a position midway along the parapet, allowing him the maximum vantage point for serving as Ellen's spotter up and down the alley. He would track the arriving SUV on his iPad and signal Ellen as it approached the alley.

Ellen would position herself behind the parapet aligned near the rear of the rectory entrance. That would allow her to take the target out as he made his way to the awaiting vehicle. Her second shot would take the wife out and the third would take down the bodyguard. This would then allow her to take the driver out as he sped by her below. All in all, four shots, less than ten seconds with spare rounds if needed.

Once they were off the roof, Peter would quickly pull the ladder down and put it in the rear of the truck and then jump in. All in total, it would take less than sixty seconds to get into position and then wait to execute, and less than a minute to get off and pull away. They had the drill down pat.

By 6:45 a.m. the next morning, they were in position. It was close to 7:11 when Peter saw the vehicle on his iPad. He signaled Ellen, who indicated she was ready. A moment later, Chaval's vehicle entered the alley. As the SUV pulled to a stop, the bodyguard exited, looking around just like he had the morning before, never bothering to look up. The bodyguard gave Chaval the signal that it was safe to come on out.

As the bodyguard opened the rear door to the SUV, Chaval exited and began to hurry along. A second later, there was the sound of a rifle shot and Chaval was down. His wife, having stepped out onto the porch, looked on in horror as he fell. A second later, she, too, was down.

The bodyguard was running to Chaval when a third sound occurred and he, like the other two, fell. There was a momentary delay as the driver processed what was happening. Then he gunned the motor and started to speed down the alley. He had not traveled twenty yards when he drove by Ellen, who stood up and shot him in the head as he passed by. The SUV swerved to the left and crashed into the garage.

Four shots, all in the head, all in under ten seconds.

Ellen turned and began running towards the ladder right behind Peter.

In less than a minute, Peter and Ellen were off the roof, the ladder was stowed and the truck slowly pulled away. As they passed by the alley, Peter looked down and said there were two people leaning over one of the victims. As they pulled up to the main street, they could hear distant sirens. Peter slowly turned left and drove away at the speed limit.

In less than an hour, an all-white Gulfstream G450 left Santa Clara airfield with no tail or other markings. On board were two pilots, one flight attendant, and two passengers. It headed east; no flight plan filed. The waiting plane was courtesy of Mossad.

As the plane jetted across the country, Ellen wrote a letter to Abbey. She explained that taking Chaval out was the least she could do for their friendship. She explained that she would be gone for some time, but they could communicate through Mossad just as they had done before. Ellen wished her a full recovery and signed off saying, "I once told you that I would kill if it meant saving you. I guess in a way that came true today. You're my best friend. I love you like a sister. Please hurry and get well." She sealed it and gave it to the flight attendant, asking her to make sure Abbey got the letter.

A MONTH LATER

With the help of Ron's investigators and Unit 33 intelligence gathering abilities, Rossi, along with several managers of Bay Area casinos, were indicted for money laundering, racketeering and illegal gambling under the federal RICO (Racketeer Influenced and Corrupt Organizations Act). They had used these casinos as money-laundering fronts and had an arrangement with Sam Greene to deposit funds into their commercial account.

As General Auditor, Sam had been able to control Rossi's roll-over service agreement as the bank's sole money courier, thus enabling Rossi to move deposits in and otherwise legitimate funds out at will. They are currently awaiting trial and being held in the San Francisco County Jail. Sam Greene's family was denied any bank severance or death benefits.

For Dan and Abbey, their mutual recoveries were long and painful. Dan returned to the bank three months later. As for Abbey, she returned six weeks later. She still goes to physical therapy twice a week.

BANK ROBBERS JACKIE MCGREGOR AND CARLOS VALDEZ

THE BANK ROBBERY

"Come on, babe. It's getting late. We need to be there in less than an hour," Winston said.

"I'll be ready in five minutes and it's only a twenty-minute drive, Winston, even in traffic. We'll be okay."

Jackie McGregor actually beat Winston to the older model Ford F150 they had stolen the previous night. She was wearing latex gloves as Winson instructed and sat behind the steering wheel. Winston carried his backpack, also wearing latex gloves. The gloves meant no fingerprints left behind when they ditched the truck later.

"I'm ready," Winston said. "Let's get going. Just drive the speed limit and don't do anything that'll draw attention."

Fifteen minutes later, they pulled up across the street from the 2nd National Bank branch and parked against the curb. From this vantage point, they could see both the front entrance and the reserved loading zone parking spot on the side street. Winston had pulled out the red western style bandana from his backpack and tied it around his neck. The hood on his blue rain jacket was down.

Within a minute, a Brinks armored truck pulled into the empty loading zone spot and a guard exited, weapon drawn, and went to the rear of the truck. She briefly looked around and then gave three short quick raps on the door.

Another armed guard exited, carrying two large canvas bags. The first guard closed the door. Together, they walked to the rear of the building and disappeared.

This was the moment Winston was waiting for. He exited his truck and quickly crossed the street, entering through the front door, the hood of his rain jacket obscuring most of his face.

The guards had entered through a rear entrance and put the bags on a cart that was next to the open vault door. One of the tellers was logging them in. Along the teller line, each employee waited on customers at their respective windows. No one was paying attention to what was transpiring behind them.

Winston lingered at one of the kiosks, posing as a customer, watching the transaction between the guards and the vault teller. Shortly, the guards left the way they came in, leaving the vault teller alone to complete the logging-in procedure. Winston approached the end teller window, having pulled the red bandana over his mouth and nose. He held a Colt .45 in his left hand.

Stopping at the corner of the teller line, he looked at Teller 1 and said, "Don't say anything. Don't scream. Just calmly turn around and take the unopened money bag off the cart and hand it to me."

The teller was shocked but managed to do what he directed her to do. She walked over to the cart and picked up the bag, all the while looking at the vault teller who, in turn, was trying to comprehend what was unfolding.

Outside, Jackie had swung the pickup around and parked immediately in front of the bank, waiting for Winston to come running out.

Teller 1 handed Winston the bag. He took it and turned to leave. And then he stopped, turned back to the teller, raised the Colt, and squeezed the trigger. The teller's expression was one of horror as she fell to the floor, lifeless.

Winston ran out to the awaiting vehicle. He jumped in and the Ford F150 roared away. Neither he nor Jackie spoke. Three blocks later, Jackie turned into a parking lot, pulled alongside a white Toyota SUV, and stopped. The two of them jumped out, climbed into the Toyota, and left, but not before Winston ripped his gloves off and threw them on the ground next to the stolen truck. The police would discover the vehicle later that afternoon. They began by checking for the vehicle's registration and running the license plates and discovered, not surprisingly, it had been reported stolen. A crime scene was set up and the Crime Scene Investigative Unit, or CSI unit, began processing it for fingerprints and DNA. It didn't take long to discover the gloves, which they bagged, marked, and inventoried.

As Jackie sped away, she said, "I heard a shot. What happened?"

"Don't worry about that now, just drive and keep to the speed limit. The last thing we need now is to be stopped," Winston answered.

Fifteen minutes later, they were back in their apartment.

Winston emptied the large money bag on the bed and the two of them just stared at it. Jackie let out a scream of excitement. "Just look at it!" she shouted and laughed hysterically. "I've never seen so much money in one place. How much do you think there is?"

"I don't know, but it's a lot. There must be tens of thousands of dollars."

For the next several seconds they both just stood there staring at the bed. "Well, let's count it. It's not like it's going to bite us," Jackie giggled.

It was almost sixty thousand, they discovered.

THAT AFTERNOON

Ron Tyson, manager of Corporate Security's Bank Investigations Unit, BIU, answered his phone. It was the security console. "Sir, there's been a robbery at one of our San Leandro branches. It was the Red Bandana Robber. One of the tellers was killed."

"Anyone else hurt?"

"No sir. I've dispatched an agent to the branch."

Ron thanked the operator and asked to be transferred to Dan Holmes, his boss and Chief Security Officer for 2nd National Bank. On the second ring, Dan answered. "What's up, Ron?"

"We've been hit again by the Red Bandana Robber. One of our agents is enroute so we should have the details shortly."

"If it's anything like the other two, it will likely be the end teller."

6 P.M.

While driving home, Dan noticed a car following him from the parking structure. It stayed close behind him, all the way across the Golden Gate. When he crossed the bridge, he pulled into the parking lot of the observation point looking back on the city. The car slowed as it passed the parking area and then did a U-turn and headed back to the highway, proceeding southbound. Dan couldn't get a look at the driver because of the darkness and the vehicle was too far away to get the license plate number. But it was an older Oldsmobile, red bottom, white top. He thought it was a convertible. It looked like it was in excellent condition.

Dan waited another ten minutes and then departed for home, calling his long-standing friend, Commander Hines of the San Francisco Police Department. He explained to the police executive what had just happened and added that, even though he wasn't certain, he believed that this was the third time he had noticed the car following him. It didn't have a front plate and always turned off sooner than expected so Dan was unable to get the rear plate number. Hines took the vehicle description and told Dan he would have one of his detectives call him in the morning.

Dan continued his drive home, thinking about the events of the day. As he approached his turn into Tiburon, his phone rang. It was Unit 33, Dan's highly confidential analysis unit. "What's up?" He was accustomed to receiving phone calls on his commute home. Typically, it was one of his direct reports or, on occasion, President Sands wanting him to handle some matter sooner rather than later.

This time, the caller's voice suggested a sense of urgency. "Dr.

Holmes, the heavy rain that is due to roll in this evening is setting up to be more of a severe storm. Some of the meteorologists are reporting that we should expect sixty- to seventy-mile-an-hour wind gusts with up to four inches of rain overnight, which translates to flash flooding in your area. Also, it's possible that cliff homes might be washed away. Ms. Gentry is talking to Retail Banking now so they can inform their branches. She asked me to call and inform you." The caller continued, "If it's like past storms, a number of our branches will lose power."

"As long as they have no power, we don't need to worry about any of our vaults automatically unlocking as they are timed to do. Just advise Abbey that she ought not worry about overtime costs for the uniformed security officers. We need to get them to where they are needed, for as long as we need them. I'll keep President Sands informed; Abbey can direct all her efforts to assisting Retail Banking," Dan directed.

Then he added, "Thanks for the heads-up. Have someone in your shop keep me informed. I'm sure Abbey has already started the conversion of our security console into a command center."

7 P.M.

It was shortly after seven o'clock when the bank agent finished up her initial investigation. She could have been finished earlier, but she wanted to stay clear of the police since it was an active crime scene until they said otherwise.

At Jackie and Winston's apartment, they were getting drunk and snorting coke. "So, from the gunshot, I assume you killed this teller just like the other three? I just don't get it. Do you get some sort of kick out of shooting innocent bank tellers?"

"I don't know. I guess I do kind of get a kick out of watching their expression as I raise the gun and then the look on their face just before they fall."

"I get it," Jackie responded. "No, I really do. They have all that money. It's just not fair. I bust my fuck'n ass off all day and what do I have at the end of the day? Nothing!" she screamed. "It's just not fair!" she said, looking at all the money that they had moved to a small table and stacked high.

"Don't lose your cool, girl," Winston shot back. "It's not like the money is theirs. They just work for the bank. They can't keep any of it."

Jackie went silent and sat there staring blankly, lost in her drug-addled world.

9 A.M. THE FOLLOWING MORNING

By nine, Dan had provided President Sands an overview of the robbery and the status of the storm's impact on the retail branches. The rain was still coming down hard. Nonetheless, Dan felt confident he could make it into the city, and therefore to the bank. "Listen, Brenda, I think I'm better off there as opposed to here. If I go in, will you be okay? If not, let's grab the dog and we can get one of the corporate suites at the Hyatt across from the bank."

"Go, Dan. I'm sure the dog and I will be fine. We've got the whole-house generator if the power goes off. We have plenty of food and water. Go, but keep me informed. We have faced scarier times than this. Roscoe and I will be okay." Then, looking at the dog, Brenda added, "Isn't that right, Roscoe?" The dog barked as though he understood what she was saying. "See?"

Dan smiled, put on his rain parka, and left. An hour later, the rain began to intensify along with the wind. Brenda went about her usual routine getting ready for the day. Roscoe was lying on the floor in front of the shower, one of his favorite spots for some inexplicable reason. Suddenly his head shot up, his ears perked, all of his one hundred and ten pounds on full alert. He growled as he walked cautiously to the sliding glass door in the master bedroom. The curtains were drawn back, providing an excellent view of Brenda's wooded backyard. Alarmed by Roscoe's behavior, she knew something—or worse, someone—was out there.

But who would be out in a rainstorm? The Holmes' house was bordered by a small woodlot to the rear of the property, which led to a steep hillside. There was a six-foot wooden fence around the entire backyard, affording privacy and containing Roscoe. The only way to access the rear yard was through the side gate or by jumping the fence.

They had neighbors to both sides and were situated at the end of the cul-de-sac, providing a spectacular view of the San Francisco Bay beneath them. The street was always quiet, and the neighbors knew each other, nearly everyone being long-time residents.

Brenda slowly advanced to the sliding glass door. Roscoe crouched, growling loudly. Peering out into the heavy rain, Brenda saw somebody approaching the door. She screamed and turned to her bedside table, pulling out a .38 Special revolver. Roscoe was jumping wildly against the door, trying to get out, barking loudly and ferociously.

The individual stepped up onto the deck. He wore a long heavy black coat that extended past his knees, the hood pulled up and over his head. A surgical mask covered his mouth. He was carrying what appeared to be a shotgun at his side.

Brenda yelled, raised the gun, and took aim.

He backed away and ran towards the side of the house and presumably the side gate. Brenda unlocked the door, and started to slide it open. Roscoe bolted through, barking wildly. As the dog raced to the side of the house, Brenda heard a loud gunshot then the gate door slammed shut. A few seconds later, Roscoe came back up on the deck, limping and whimpering.

Brenda raced for her phone and dialed 911.

Three marked police cars responded within a matter of minutes. They found Brenda in the bedroom, shaking and crying. Roscoe lay on the wooden floor, licking his leg.

Brenda handed one of the officers her phone and asked her to call Dr. Williams, a neighbor and a veterinarian. Brenda was hoping he might still be home. A few moments later, the officer returned and advised Brenda that the vet would be over shortly.

As the police were responding, Brenda had called Dan and briefed him. Despite wind gusts of fifty-five miles an hour, Dan headed home. By the time he arrived, Dr. Williams had examined

Roscoe and was treating him for a gunshot to his left front leg. The police had canvased the back and side yards and determined the intruder had gained access through the side gate. They found muddy prints indicating both his entry and exit, along with one shotgun casing. Dan was also advised that a neighbor, returning from the nightshift at St. Luke's Hospital, was nearly hit by an older model red and white car racing away.

Brenda had calmed down enough to repeat to Dan what she had told the police. Together they decided it would be better for her to spend the next week at her sister's place in Healdsburg, an hour north. Roscoe would need to wear a cone to keep him from chewing on his leg dressing for the next week. He would go with Brenda. Dan would stay over at the Hyatt Hotel for the next several days.

The police were treating this as an armed assault by an unknown suspect. Dan called Abbey and asked her to have Unit 33 work every possible lead. They would search archived records for anyone who might fit Brenda's description and felons who used a shotgun since the police were able to determine that was the type of weapon used to shoot Roscoe. He also asked for a progress report on the red and white Oldsmobile. So far, the search had yielded nothing.

THREE DAYS LATER

Jackie enjoyed being "economically flush." It didn't take her long to enhance her wardrobe, restock her makeup drawer, buy that new iPhone she had been nagging Winston to get for her, and start looking for a new car. Winston was completely the opposite. Having been raised in a poor family, he had been taught to conserve, especially when it came to money matters. The arrangement with Jackie was straightforward—a fifty-fifty split. For the past eighteen months, it had worked just fine.

Regardless of his view towards money and saving, he was always financially broke.

Winston was a hopeless addict and his habit was expensive. Long ago, he had graduated to heroin and lately found that fentanyl as an additive kept him continuously high. The recent robbery was by far their largest score. For him, this meant no need for another robbery anytime soon, or so he thought. It didn't hold true.

Seeing his latest victim die the way she did had given him an incredible thrill. He wanted it again. Jackie said she got why he did it, but she didn't have a clue. Shooting his victims had nothing to do with money, nothing at all. It was all about the thrill. For that one moment, he was God. He controlled everything. He decided who lived, and who didn't.

Jackie woke up early the following morning not feeling well. She felt bloated and her right shoulder hurt. She couldn't remember bumping her shoulder or getting hit there recently. "Oh well, how can I remember much of anything? I've been drunk for the past week," she mumbled aloud.

Winston came into the bedroom and asked if she wanted to get some breakfast.

"No, I don't have much of an appetite right now," she said. "For that matter, I haven't felt like eating much lately. I guess that's why I'm losing weight. God knows I could afford to lose a few pounds."

THE LARKIN STREET LIBRARY

Meanwhile, Brenda and Dan had decided that it was safe to return home, and the Tiburon police assured them that added drive-by patrols would be increased. After a few days, it appeared that life was back to normal. Brenda had decided she was going to the San Francisco library after lunch to do research associated with her genealogy. Dan had a meeting with Commander Hines later that afternoon, so he, too, would be in the city. On his way in, Abbey called.

"Unit 33 has narrowed the likely Oldsmobile down to a couple of owners. One is a 1973 Olds Cutlass. It has a red bottom but a white vinyl Landau roof. That style of roof was popular for GM cars and could easily be mistaken as a convertible. It belongs to a woman who is overseas in the Army and the vehicle is being stored in a warehouse in Richmond.

"The other is a 1974 Cutlass similar in appearance to the first.

47

It belongs to a Carlos Valdez who lives in South San Francisco. He works out at the airport and parks in Lot D. That's the employee parking lot. I've already notified the police and they're sending a unit out to check the lot."

"Great work, Ab, this could be the break we've been looking for," Dan said with a note of excitement. "I'm on my way to a meeting with Commander Hines. I'll let him know the good news. Where exactly does this Valdez guy work at the airport, and do we have a home address?"

"He's a baggage handler and should be working now. He lives right there in South San Francisco. We've passed his address on to the South San Francisco Police as well and they've got another unit on their way, sir," Abbey answered.

Dan's meeting with the commander began at three o'clock. As his meeting was about to begin, Abbey called again, informing him that Valdez had not shown up for work and he was not home. So, the police had put out a BOLO (be on the lookout) for him. Dan said he would inform Hines and stepped into their meeting. They had barely begun when Dan received a text from Brenda. He glanced down. It read, HE'S HERE.

Dan showed the text to Hines and then called Brenda.

"Dan, I just walked out of the main library and that guy is here. I recognized his coat. I know it's him. He was inside when I was there. I just knew he was following me. I'm really scared, what should I do?"

"Honey, I have you on speaker. Commander Hines is here."

Hines calmly asked, "Brenda, are you okay physically?"

"Yes. I'm just scared," she repeated.

"Where exactly are you?"

"I just got in my car. I've locked it, but, what good will that do if he shows up? He'll just break the window out or something."

Dan turned to Hines. "She's at the library on Larkin."

Commander Hines yelled to his Admin, "Get dispatch to roll a couple of units to the Larkin Street Library. Code 3."

"Honey, stay where you are. SFPD is on the way."

"Oh God! He just ran by. Hurry, please hurry," she pleaded. A moment later, "He's getting into a red and white car!" she screamed. "He's headed for Larkin. He's getting away," she cried.

Dan jumped in. "It's a red 1974 Olds Cutlass with a white Landau top. No plate number, most likely no plate at all."

Hines relayed the description. Both men looked pensive when Brenda spoke up. "I hear the police arriving now. Should I blow my horn or something? Listen, I think he was carrying a gun."

By this time, Hines was on the line to dispatch, "Advise responding units, the perp is believed to be armed. Consider him dangerous." Then to Brenda, "If you think it is safe, exit your vehicle and wave to the police officers so they can see you."

Dan jumped in a second time. "Brenda, you're safe now. Do whatever the police say, and I'll be there as fast as I can."

Over the commander's phone, Dan heard dispatch. "Shots fired, one of ours is down!"

"Shit!" Hines exclaimed. "Come on, Dan, we're going now!"

"Brenda, I'll see you soon. I love you."

Abbey was in the security console room and heard the police dispatch exchanges. She heard that an officer caught the perp but was shot and the gunman got away just as other units were arriving. They had sealed off the area.

WINSTON'S GOT BUSINESS

Oblivious to the events unfolding at the Larkin Street Library, Winston checked in on Jackie. She said she was feeling better, but felt listless. "Listen, I'm going out, so I'll be back in a while. You don't need the car, do you?" Winston asked.

"I don't think so. I feel tired and want to roll over. I'll see you later."

Winston left, intending to get something to eat, but knew he needed to make a quick stop. He called his drug dealer. "I need to see you. I've got the cash. How much can you give me?"

"You have the money; I have the stuff. Usual place. I'll be there in thirty minutes, don't be late."

"I'll be waiting for you," Winston responded.

Thirty minutes later, Winston was standing next to Terminal #3 at the Port of Oakland. This time of day, foot traffic was light, and it was remarkable how little security there was. It was a perfect place for a drop. As his peddler approached, Winston was thinking, *I wonder if there is as much excitement in shooting a male? My previous victims have all been female and helpless. This guy is actually a real scumbag.*

As his drug dealer drove up, Winston walked over to the driver's side and slipped his left hand into his jacket pocket. He wrapped his hand around the grip of the Colt. When his pusher lowered his window, Winston quickly pulled the .45 out of his pocket and pulled the trigger twice. The look on the peddler's face was one of shock and horror as he realized what was happening. And then it was over. His head fell back, and Winston grabbed the door handle, quickly opening the door and pulling him out. When he hit the pavement, the plastic bag was visible on the center console. Winston reached in, grabbed it, and shoved it into the right pocket of his jacket. He walked away, smiling.

"God, was that great!" he said loudly to himself. "The look on his face was fantastic! I feel so alive." Winston drove to the Best Eats Diner a few blocks away. He left the Colt .45 locked in the glove compartment, the drugs in his jacket pocket.

About an hour later, he arrived back at their apartment. Jackie was up getting ready but moving slowly. Winston opted not to tell her anything about his encounter with the drug pusher. For him, the challenge was to find a new source. He didn't think it would be that difficult.

"Listen, Jackie, I have an uneasy feeling about staying here. I feel it in my gut. I have a cousin who owns a place just south of Fremont in the Milpitas hills. It's off the main road and is quiet. Great views of the Bay, I think you'll like it."

"When do you want to leave?" Jackie answered.

"Right away. If you can be ready in thirty minutes, we'll be settled in there before the sun goes down. Okay?"

"I've always trusted your gut. I wish I could trust mine," Jackie responded. Her joke fell flat.

Each of them packed what money they had left in their respective backpacks, what few clothes they had, their toiletries, Jackie's pillow—she never traveled or moved into a new place without it. It didn't take long and just as Winston said, they were soon settling into his cousin's home overlooking the south end of San Francisco Bay.

"You're right about the view. What's your cousin's business so that he can afford this place? The view itself is worth millions!" Jackie asked in amazement.

"He's some high-tech guru. Right now, he's in Ireland negotiating some deal. He owns a place there and told me he'd be there through the summer. He said I could use this place and the one in Ireland anytime. Maybe we should take a vacation and pay him a visit."

"If you don't mind, I'd like to hang here for a while. Like I told you earlier, I haven't been feeling that great lately." Trying to make light of how she felt, she joked, "I think I need to change my brand of rum."

A FALLEN OFFICER

As the assailant fled down Larkin, a responding police unit pulled up directly behind the Olds and signaled him to pull over. The Olds slowly pulled around the corner onto Folsom and parked. The officer told the suspect to turn off his vehicle and place his hands above the steering wheel and on the dashboard so the officer could see them. The driver did as he was instructed but then immediately opened his door, hurried out, and started running up the street, revolver in hand.

The officer notified dispatch of the perp's actions, exited his patrol vehicle, and chased him. The weight and length of the perp's coat slowed him down enough to allow the officer to catch him. They both began fighting for control of the assailant's gun when it discharged and the police officer fell. The perp tore the jacket off and began walking briskly up the street.

A Muni bus passed by and stopped at 8th and Folsom. The driver was unaware of what had just occurred. Several police vehicles were descending on the area, marked and unmarked. The bus pulled to a stop, and no one got off, but the gunman got on from the rear door. Slowly, the bus pulled away from the curb as he made his way to the front, all the while digging in his pocket for bus fare. It proceeded up Folsom to Moscone Center, less than three blocks up. When it pulled into the bus stop, the gunman jumped out without paying and ran towards the Convention Center.

Hundreds of people were attending a conference of some sort. Many of them were simply milling around the plaza out front, waiting for the next round of presentations to start. Some of them had walked to the street and were looking down Folsom, trying to see what the police action was all about. Above them, the SFPD helicopter flew by. The onlookers could also hear other aircraft nearby when suddenly a drone flew over the area, hovered for several seconds, and then continued to fly by.

The gunman entered the Center in a hurry, looking for the men's room. Finding it, he entered one of the stalls. He checked his revolver. One bullet was spent, he could smell that it had just been fired. Along the way, he had dropped his phone, but wasn't overly concerned since it was a standard burner phone that he had purchased at Walmart several days earlier. He knew his prints were on the phone; however, never having been arrested before, he was sure it couldn't be traced back to him. He had heard once that the police can lift DNA from the phone's speaker, but again, he knew he wasn't in their system, so he wasn't that concerned. That would prove to be a big mistake.

After several minutes, he exited the men's room and saw a vendor selling jackets, t-shirts, and hats sporting the words "22nd Annual Meeting" and then some sort of logo. He purchased one of each. He then returned to the men's room, took off his shirt, and shoved it into the trash bin. He quickly pulled the shirt and jacket on and put the cap on his head. When he exited the building, he looked like many of the other conventioneers. He was safe for now. He walked briskly towards the Transbay Terminal.

Back at the library parking lot, Dan and Brenda decided it would be best if she stayed in one of the corporate suites at the Embarcadero Hyatt for now. He would join her after work, and they would stay there until things settled down and the police had a better idea of the identity of her stalker, now a police killer.

While the fatally injured officer was transported to the hospital, other officers began a search of the abandoned Olds. It didn't take long for them to discover who the registered owner was. When they opened the trunk, they discovered a 12-gauge shotgun, several shells, an M16 with a loaded magazine, and a loaded Glock 19. They also found a burner phone on the pavement near the front driver's side door, presumably dropped by the gunman as he exited the Olds and ran away.

THAT EVENING

By seven o'clock, the Oakland Crime Scene Investigation Unit had finished their work at the Oakland Port and sent their evidence to the crime lab. The drug dealer's body was in the morgue. His autopsy was scheduled for the next day, given the volume of business. The lab had also determined that he had been killed by the same gun used in the 2nd National robberies.

Unbeknownst to them, Dan had already received a phone call from Abbey, advising him that their Unit 33 had intercepted communication between the city morgue and OPD about the weapon. The Colt .45 belonged to his brother, killed about four years ago.

"Do we have any DNA or witness statements that can actually connect him directly to one of the robberies directly, Abbey?" Dan asked.

"Unit 33 is still working on that. How do you want us to communicate our findings to Ron and his bank agents?" Abbey asked.

"I'll advise Ron and President Sands. Just let me know as soon as your people can confirm he is our man. Until then, I'll just let President Sands know we have a person of interest. It isn't much, but it ought to hold Sands for now if he knows we're making progress. Great work, Ab. Please let your team know how they continuously impress me. They make me proud."

A moment later, Dan was on the phone to President Sands.

TWO DAYS PASS

Two days passed and the rains had moved out of the Bay Area. The bank was trying to get back to business as normal. Although the police and Unit 33 had identified Vernon Winston as the Red Bandana Robber, he was still at large. President Sands was pressuring Dan and his people to locate him before another robbery occurred.

It was then Winston approached Jackie with the idea of pulling off another bank heist. He said he was running low on money, which surprised her. "Seriously? You've blown through nearly thirty grand? I can't believe it."

"Well, I have, and don't you judge me. I'm going to slip out and check on a couple of places to see which one will make for the next target. It might be several days before we find the one that matches our criteria. While I'm out, I need to meet with a guy." That was Winston's code for locating a new pusher. Jackie noticed he had left his .45 behind and the rest of his cash, so she wasn't too worried about his return.

About three hours passed when Winston returned, smiling broadly. "I think we have our next target. It meets our conditions. All that's left is to figure out their armored carrier schedule, which should not take long." It wasn't surprising that Winston found his target so quickly, considering 2nd National Bank used a standard floor plan for nearly all of its retail branches and located them on the corner of busy streets with a loading zone on a side street. The retail managers preferred such a layout. This made their armored deliveries low-key and therefore less susceptible to being robbed.

4 P.M. THE FOLLOWING DAY

The Oakland Police SWAT Team took up a position approximately half a block from 239 Delancey Street, out of sight from apartment

351, which overlooked the street. This was the known address for Vernon Winston and his girlfriend. On signal, the team proceeded quickly down the street and entered the building, rapidly ascending the stairway and down the hall to Apartment 351. They stopped, lining up against the wall, and the team leader loudly announced their arrival. A moment later, one of the officers smashed a battering ram through the door and the rest of the team flooded in, only to discover it was empty. As the SWAT team exited, members of the CSI unit came in and began their meticulous search for any DNA, fingerprints … anything to confirm the identity of the occupants and possible evidence suggesting where they may have gone.

ONE WEEK LATER, NOON

Winston and Jackie were sitting on the patio at the local deli, The Best Sandwiches. Neither noticed the man approach their table. "Pardon me, but aren't you Vernon Winston?" he asked, smiling. Both were taken aback, wondering who this man was. "Don't be alarmed, I was friends with your brother. We were in Afghanistan together."

"Okay," Winston said cautiously.

Jackie stared at the man.

"We also had a friend that I think you know. He supplied you things, if you catch my drift."

Suddenly Winston understood clearly who this person was. There was no doubt in his mind. This guy was a hitman for the drug cartel that supplied Winston's pusher. He jumped up. As he did, the paid assassin pulled out a Glock 19 and discharged two rounds into Winston's chest. Winston fell forward, dead. Jackie screamed. The man ran around the side of the deli, disappearing.

ANOTHER WEEK LATER

Once the coroner confirmed that Winston had died of two shots from a Glock 19 at close range, his body was cremated and buried at the county cemetery. No one showed. Jackie read about it online. She wanted to go to his funeral but thought the police would be watching. She assumed that by now the police knew Winston had a girlfriend but had yet to identify her.

After the shooting, she had raced back to his cousin's home. She was safe there for now. She pooled what was left of Winston's share of money from their last robbery with hers. He had less than five thousand dollars left. Her share was approximately eighteen thousand dollars. Jackie knew it wouldn't last more than a couple of months. That's when she decided that she could follow Winston's plan and execute his latest robbery. They had been going over the details when he was assassinated. With the added robbery money, she would drive to Mexico and disappear. But first, she needed a safe place for the money she had. What better place than a safety deposit box at the very bank she was going to rob? she concluded, chuckling at how smart she was.

That afternoon she drove to the branch bank to check the layout for herself. An armored truck pulled into the side street loading zone. She watched and, just like other times, observed one of the guards exit the truck, weapon drawn, and walk to the rear of the truck. He knocked three times and the door opened. A second guard emerged, turned around, and pulled out two large canvas money bags, then closed the door. The two then proceeded around the corner to the back of the branch.

Posing as a customer wanting to open a safety deposit box, Jackie entered the bank and observed the same transaction Winston had described several times before. *This looks fairly straight-forward,* she thought. She had to figure out a way to escape since there would not be a waiting getaway car. *But first things first,* she thought. She opened an account and, in the privacy of the safe deposit vault, she put the balance of the earlier robbery money in Box 515. She then returned to the cousin's home. She was still sick and not eating very much. She was getting worse but wanted to pull off this one last robbery before going to see her doctor.

Over the next few days, she returned to the branch, double-checking everything and then rechecking it again. She felt that she could do it. To her good fortune, she discovered that there was a small parking lot kitty-corner across the street. It was a private lot, reserved parking only. There were not only several empty spaces, but it had a rear entrance and exit. Her plan was to park as close as possible to the rear of the lot and then take up a position directly across from the branch to observe the coming and going of the armored truck. Once it departed from the bank, she would walk briskly across the street and enter, posing as a customer. She would pull Winston's red bandana up over her mouth and nose and go to the end teller, just as Winston had done.

The next day Jackie was ready to execute her plan. However, she knew that to do so required a boost of encouragement. In other words, a couple of good snorts of coke with a vodka chaser. The armored truck came right on time and left within a matter of minutes. She raced into the bank, pulling her mask up and pulling Winston's Colt from her waistband. Since she was about the same size as he was, she wore his blue hooded jacket with the hood up.

She quickly approached the end of the teller line and demanded that the teller grab one of the bags off the cart right behind her. Like the other robberies, the vault teller was caught totally by surprise. Jackie grabbed the bag and turned to run. Then she stopped, turned around, and raised the Colt. She fired off two shots in the direction of the teller and then ran quickly out of the branch and across the street.

She ran to the rear of the lot, unlocked the car, and jumped in. She quickly raced out of the lot, and then turned up the side street. At Main Street, she turned right and ran into the back of a city bus. Since the Toyota was an older model, there was no airbag to soften the impact. She fell unconscious.

ON THE RUN

Carlos Valdez was, as the saying goes, on the lam. He knew he had lost his car. He couldn't go to work, nor could he go home. He also assumed that public transportation was not safe, which meant no flying, no riding a train or bus, and, lacking a phone, no calling a friend. The one thing he did know, however, was how to steal a car.

As evident by his owning a classic Olds, he knew cars, especially older models.

He headed to the Transbay Terminal. There he could find any number of commuter cars in the adjacent lots. He remembered his cousin, who worked for one of the lots, telling him how the lot attendants were very casual and how easy it would be to steal a car. It didn't take long before Valdez was driving off in a blue Dodge Challenger.

He crossed the Oakland Bay Bridge into Oakland. He knew he had only a few hours before the owner would discover his or her car had been stolen. His plan was to find the nearest BART customer parking lot and swap the Dodge out for something else. Since these lots were generally not staffed and police patrols infrequent, he would be in luck. He headed east towards Sacramento. Fifteen minutes later, he saw the Walnut Creek BART sign. He exited the highway and drove into one of the lots. He noticed the cameras but didn't much care since he knew that even if he was observed, it would take some time for a patrol unit to arrive.

He began slowly driving up and down the rows of cars and pickup trucks. On the third row, he spotted what he was looking for—an older Kia Sportage. He knew their reputation for being one of the easier cars to steal. He found an empty spot a few spaces down and pulled in. He then quickly ran back to the Sportage and within a minute was driving out of the lot.

For the next several days, it was as though Carlos Valdez had disappeared. No one knew where he had gone—not his family, not his fellow employees, and more importantly, not the police.

In the meantime, Dan had found out from one of the detectives where Valdez lived. He called Ron and asked him to send a staff member over to his house and try to ascertain why Valdez was targeting him and his wife. Later that evening, Dan got his answer.

According to Valdez's mother, he blamed Dan for the death of his father and uncle while the three of them were in Iraq. Dan had headed a Special Ops mission and the Valdez brothers were members of his unit. While out on an assignment, the unit came under attack. Heavy gunfire was exchanged. When it was over, five of Dan's men were dead, two of whom were the Valdez men. Carlos was only a young teenager at the time. Regardless, for years he kept saying, "One day, I'll make him pay." But he never did anything about it so she always thought it was just Carlos' way of venting his frustration for not having a father in his life.

That evening, Dan pulled into a gas station. After filling his tank, he went inside the convenience store to purchase a soda. Unbeknownst to him, Valdez followed him in. As Valdez drew a gun, the clerk thought the store was going to be robbed. The clerk pulled out his gun from under the counter and yelled, "No, you don't!" Surprised, Valdez turned towards the clerk, who shot him three times. He was pronounced dead on arrival at the hospital.

That evening, as Dan and Brenda sat down for a glass of wine, Valdez's death was the first thing they talked about. For Brenda, Valdez's death was a godsend. There would be no more sleepless nights; no more being on edge in her home; no more wondering if she were being followed. For Dan, he, too, was relieved that the whole episode was over. He was happy for Brenda. As for himself, he felt strangely at peace, but knew something like this could easily repeat itself. His life was a history of assassinations, needless murders, and dying army buddies. He kept a lot of this to himself, not even sharing most of it with Brenda ... well, at least for now. There would come a time, just not yet.

JACKIE'S HOSPITAL STAY

Jackie woke up in the hospital to find a man sitting in the chair next to her bed. "Who are you?" she asked groggily.

"Well, first, I assume you know you are in a hospital, right?" the man answered.

"Yeah, I guess so."

"Do you remember driving into the back of a bus?"

Jackie nodded her head slowly but affirmatively.

"I'm a police detective and I was just finishing an addendum to my report. Welcome back to reality."

Jackie stared at him blankly. "Do you remember robbing the bank just prior to your accident?"

"Yes."

"Well then, I am required to advise you of your rights before we can go further. Okay?"

"I have a headache; can I get something?"

"Sure. I'll just push this button for you, and someone will come." The detective hit the call button and about a minute later, the attending nurse came in smiling.

"Hi, I see you have joined the land of the living. How are you feeling?"

"I have a screaming headache," Jackie responded, grimacing.

"That's not surprising. I'll get something for you. In the meantime, Detective, I'm not sure this is the best time."

"You're probably right. When can I come back? There are several people who would like to see her statement since she's a suspect in several robberies, four of them involving homicides and the killing of a local drug pin."

"My, my, hasn't she been busy of late," the nurse said. "I would suggest you stop by tomorrow. She'll still be here and in a much better position to answer your questions."

The detective smiled. "You're no doubt right. Thanks." Then he stood up to leave. As he did so, he asked, "Just one quick question. Where do you live? I'd like to let your family know where you are."

Jackie responded, "I don't know exactly. Just up in the hills near the airport."

The nurse said quietly, but firmly, "You better go." The detective turned to walk out of the room. Then he turned back. "I'm not sure you are aware of this, Ms. McGregor, but we have a police officer stationed just outside your door. You know, just in case you feel like taking a walk or something."

By the end of the week, Jackie was transferred to the Santa Clara County Jail to await her arraignment and eventually her trial. She never mentioned Winston. Likewise, she never told anyone about the safety deposit box. Since the prosecutor could only prove Jackie committed the last robbery, Jackie was charged with only the one robbery. She pled guilty and was remanded to the Central California Women's Facility in Chowchilla, California.

ONE YEAR LATER

Dan had just returned from a luncheon meeting with the security director of LA Trust. As he sat down behind his desk, his Admin, Erin, walked in, asking, "Did you have a productive lunch?"

"Actually, I did. Thanks for asking. What's up?"

"I'll give it to you straight. Remember Jackie McGregor?"

"Sure. What about her?"

"In a couple of days, she's going to be released from Chowchilla."

"What?" Dan fired back, not believing what Erin just told him to be true. "How? She's a lifer without parole! God! She killed four of our bank tellers and seriously wounded one of our customers, all in cold blood. This has got to be a mistake."

"Sorry, Dan, but it's true. Here's a copy of her release order signed by none other than Judge Nelson."

"Nelson? He wanted her to hang! How can this be?"

"Well, read it and you'll see she'll be under house arrest and required to wear an ankle bracelet. Apparently, she's going into hospice. She's got late-stage liver cancer."

"Okay. That's sad enough, but why the release? Chowchilla has an infirmary. Why can't she stay? I've got to get to the bottom of this. I wonder if SFPD is aware?"

"I don't know, Dan. Do you want me to put a call into their office?"

"No, I'll call right away. Thanks anyway."

He picked up his phone and dialed Abbey. "Sir?" she asked, answering his call.

"I need Unit 33 to pull everything on the Jackie McGregor robberies, including the videos. She's being released to her home in a couple of days under hospice care. I need your people to find out who's behind her release and why."

"We're on it, sir."

Dan then called the lead detective of SFPD's Bank Robbery Division. "Hi Dan," she answered. "Let me guess, Jackie McGregor. Right?"

"Who's behind this?"

"The ACLU," the detective responded.

"Hell, I should have guessed so."

"Yeah, they're pleading it out as the humanitarian thing to do."

"Fuck," Dan said quietly.

"Ditto. But there's nothing we can do at this time. Besides, we all know she was involved in the robberies where your people got killed; however, she was only convicted on the last robbery, and no one was killed."

"Yeah, only paralyzed for life," Dan shot back satirically.

"Well, I've never been satisfied with the whole damn thing. I've asked my people to pull everything we have on her. Dan, if you're going to let her pass away and close out your case altogether, I want a last look since there are a number of unsolved homicides and one murdered drug kingpin still on our books."

"I agree. I've asked my people to investigate them as well. I'll let you know if we come up with anything," Dan offered.

THREE DAYS LATER

Dan and Abbey were stood at an analyst's workstation. "What have you got, Brian?"

"I'm pretty sure that Jackie McGregor didn't commit any of the robberies, save for the last. For that matter, we can't actually prove she was there at all. Whereas we have video of the getaway car, we don't have a clear view of the driver. So, she may or may not have been the driver. And, as you'll see, she wasn't the robber in the others."

"That's interesting," Dan said.

"Let me bring up the last four robberies just before the last one." As he did, he continued. "All are nearly identical. The robber in each case goes to Teller #1. He pulls a .45 from his jacket forcefully and damn near sticks it in the face of the teller. You can clearly hear him demand she pull one of the bags on the table just beside the vault door behind her. He had to know that our courier had just delivered them, and the bank vault teller was in the process of making the deposit. You can see her working on them."

"Okay, I think we all know that was the robber's MO," Abbey said, growing a little impatient.

"Wait, this is only the beginning. You'll see in a minute. After the robber grabs the bag and turns to leave, he stops. He then turns back at the teller and shoots her at point-blank range. He turns sharply to his left and exits in a hurry. All these actions are his MO. He never varies.

"Then you have the last robbery. Here, we know we're dealing with the McGregor woman. She's got to be about the same size as the first robber or else everyone would have noticed the difference in size and know they were two different people involved. Anyway, at first glance, you think she's the same person.

"She pulls out the .45, but notice, she really doesn't have total control of it. That's because it would seem a little heavy to someone not used to carrying it. She even slightly fumbles with it as she extracts it from her jacket. In this video, you don't clearly see her face because it's covered with the same red bandana used in the others. Since we assume it's the same person, our mind's eye fools us. We hear what we want to hear but in reality, it's different. The teller does as she's instructed, just the same as the others. There are the two bags on the cart, but these are lighter since we were trying out different courier services and they were picking up smaller amounts."

"And this is relevant, how?" Abbey asked again.

This time Dan answered. "She didn't know how heavy the bags were. So, when she grabs the vault bag, we assume it must be the first robber since she does not carry it lower. The bag is lighter, so she can easily carry it. And we assume that the robber must be a male because that is what we expect to see."

"You got it, Mr. Holmes," the analyst said, smiling. "But here comes the real giveaway. She's not used to how loud the sound is discharging a .45 indoors, in a confined area. I'll bet she hasn't fired that weapon more than a dozen times, and all outdoors. That's why she flinches from the recoil and in this robbery, there are two shots. The first bullet misses the teller altogether even though she is but a few feet away and the second ricochets off the side of the counter and hits the customer in the groin."

"This is a bit of great analysis. I've got to say well done. Well done indeed. What do you think, Abbey?"

"Why didn't anybody ever see this before?" she asked, somewhat astounded.

"Because there had been these previous robberies, all with a near identical MO. Again, everyone wanted this over. She had been caught, confessed, and the gun was the same. Her MO was close, but her execution severely flawed; yet no one cared. The nightmare was over. I think it was as simple as that." The analyst seemed pleased that the other two were both astonished and proud of him.

"You know, this begs the question," Abbey interjected. "Are we sure the robber in all of the others was Winston?"

"With all due respect, Ms. Gentry, I think she clearly knew who her 'partner in crime' was. He must've been someone very close to her. There are details of the other robberies that were never released, but she tried to mimic them. My guess is that knowing she didn't have much time on this earth, she stepped up and committed the last one because she either needed the money or in her own sick way—mentally sick, that is—was somehow honoring his memory."

"I see where you are going," Dan noted. "And, you may have something about her motive. But what remains a mystery to me is the motive for deliberately turning to walk away and then swinging around and shooting the teller in cold blood. McGregor may well know why but isn't talking. It's hard to believe her motive was driven only by money. Unless they were heavier into drugs than what we might have thought and/or living a very extravagant lifestyle, they spent nearly two hundred thousand of our dollars from all their robberies."

"And then you could postulate that she actually had a good

chunk of it hidden away and wanted one last score before running off to Costa Rica or some other such place," Abbey added.

"What about love?" Dan added to the speculation. "Maybe she saw herself as a sort of Bonnie and Clyde character. While some would call her stupid, others might see her as a sort of romantic heroine. Unless she opens up, we'll never know one way or another."

JACKIE MCGREGOR'S SECRET

Despite knowing she was in hospice, Jackie never understood how seriously ill she was. Without a family, she left no will or instructions about the disposition of her assets. She never told anyone about the safety deposit box and was declared a pauper by the court at the time of her death. Like Winston before her, she was cremated and her remains buried in the county cemetery.

A day later Ron received a call from SFPD's Crime Lab. They advised that initially the red bandana was not tested for DNA, a simple evidentiary oversight. The analysis found DNA belonging to both Winston and McGregor. Such a link would have been enough, especially when bundled with the other circumstantial evidence, to have charged her with all of the previous robberies and homicides.

Dan didn't stop with her death. Knowing the depth of Unit 33's abilities, especially their archival prowess, he asked them to do a deep dive into McGregor's past and interests. He wanted to determine if there was a way of discovering where she may have hidden the monies from the previous robberies. It took them two days to get back to him and advise that she rented Safety Deposit Box number 515 at the bank she robbed. She rented it under the name of Vernon Winston.

GANG WARS AND
FOREIGN FILE EXTRACTIONS

WAH CHING AND THE 5TH STREETERS

Just off Sacramento and Grant in San Francisco's Chinatown, behind the Canton Building, there are a number of nondescript residential buildings. They're home to several families of one of Chinatown's more active street gangs, Wah Ching—a criminal organization notorious for drug trafficking, racketeering, and murder. The San Francisco Police Department's Gang Taskforce ranked them among their top five most dangerous gangs. Their activities are not restricted to Chinese gang activities, especially when supplying illegal drugs. They will do business with almost anyone, provided the buyer adheres to their ground rules and does not compete. Yet, over the past few years, the 5th Streeters, another one of the top five San Francisco gangs, had been actively encroaching on Wah Ching's business interests.

The 5th Streeters had become convinced that Wah Ching was responsible for the death of their leader Carlos Chaval, his wife, and two of their members. Despite the fact that SFPD had ruled out the idea that Chaval's assassination was gang-related, the 5th Streeters held fast to the belief that it was Wah Ching. To say otherwise, they held, was to play down the seriousness of their turf war.

Or, it was just another example of how the police were being paid off by Wah Ching. Regardless, they needed to send an emphatic retaliatory message. In short, they were tired of the recent street skirmishes. Passions on both sides were escalating and the Gang Task Force knew blood would soon be flowing. They wouldn't have long to wait.

CHINATOWN ROCKED

It was approaching 3 a.m. when three explosions rocked Chinatown. One of the residential units behind the Canton Building was totally demolished and the resulting fire spread to the two adjacent units. Windows were shattered throughout the immediate area and within a matter of minutes, fires broke out over a three-square block area. The San Francisco Fire Department sent out a mutual aide call and within the hour, eleven neighboring departments were staged in the area, either directly engaging the fires or standing by; SFPD had effectively sealed off Chinatown.

As the morning hours crept by, onlookers and rescue workers could hear trapped victims, some screaming for help, others whimpering as death overtook them. The air was thick with black smoke and, given the age of the buildings, both lead and asbestos exposure were clearly on the minds of public health officials, the media, and environmentalists. The social networks were jammed with conjectures and the blame game was full-on. Hundreds of families had lost everything, while sixty people were known to be missing and presumed lost. Most of the victims were mothers, children, and the elderly. It would be days before official numbers were adjusted upwards as bodies or body parts were recovered. The final total was one hundred seventy-five lost. Of these, forty-seven were believed to be affiliated with Wah Ching.

10 A.M. THE FOLLOWING MORNING

Dan Holmes, EVP and Corporate Security Director for 2nd National Bank, arrived early for work. Throughout the night, he had been kept informed of the situation since two of the bank's branches were severely damaged and a number of bank employees were either killed or injured. He called his Deputy Director, Abbey Gentry. "Anything Unit 33 can tell us besides what's in the news regarding Chinatown?"

"I have a preliminary. Wah Ching is convinced that it was the work of the 5th Streeters. The city officials are likely to blame faulty gas lines and blame the building owners. If they can get away with it, it'll be a perfect cover story to avoid any mention of an escalation of the war between the two gangs. There's a lot of finger-pointing going on between the city and the landlords, and then of course there are our properties."

"Anything going on within either gang?" Dan asked.

Abbey responded, "Clearly Wah Ching is planning something, but nothing concrete right now. As for the 5th Streeters, as the saying goes, all's quiet on the western front."

LATER THAT DAY, DAN RECEIVES TWO SURPRISE VISITORS

As though having his attention primarily on the Chinatown events wasn't enough, Dan's cell phone buzzed and he looked at the text. It read, "Two men in lobby unannounced. They want to see you. From their IDs, I think you should see them." He looked at his CCTV monitor and switched it over to the lobby view. He recognized them and responded, "Send them up." He wondered what the CIA wanted.

A few moments later, Dan was standing in his office doorway when the gentlemen stepped off the elevator and joined him. They all shook hands.

"Good morning, gentlemen," Dan said. "What a nice surprise. It's not every day I get a visit from the CIA, especially when one is the chief honcho himself. Please come in and have a seat." Dan pointed to a seating area—a sofa, two side chairs, and a coffee table at the far end of his office. "Do you want something to drink?"

"No thanks," the SAC declined firmly, but politely. "Let me get right to the point, Dan."

"Sure. How can I help?" Despite the apparent formality, Dan and the SAC were actually long-time golf buddies.

"We need a favor. There's a certain gentleman who has been in the news of late, suggesting he might make a run for the presidency next year. He's backed by some powerful people, but we're not sure most of them know much about his background."

"Okay," Dan answered hesitantly trying to assess where this was going.

The younger agent began, "Our person of interest started a non-profit a few years back, supposedly to aid the less fortunate. Like other organizations, this one receives donations from around the world. Our sources tell us his non-profit received a recent donation. His organization has an account at your bank and the donation was deposited there. Two days later, money equaling that donation was wire-transferred into his personal account, also here at 2nd National. And then, almost immediately, it was wire-transferred to a numbered account in the Caymans."

"Other than the questionable transactions, why exactly is all of this of interest to the CIA? Unless, of course, his donor is either on your watch list or is believed to be an enemy of the state. And of course, if you folks had a copy of those transactions, that might prove helpful for some reason farther down the road," Dan responded.

The younger agent nodded while the SAC gave a slight shrug of his shoulder, and then added, "This stays between us. A sort of pay it forward, if you will. You help us now and when the time comes, we help you." The SAC gave a slight sigh. "The originating financial institution is the Central Bank of the Democratic People's Republic of Korea. In this case, the North Korean government didn't even go through their normal foreign exchange bank, Joson Trade Bank. But it doesn't really matter since everything is either owned or controlled by the government."

"Which means Kim Jong Un," Dan concluded for the SAC. "Who's the target and how much was transferred?"

"By asking those questions, can we assume you'll be assisting?"

"Your words, not mine," Dan responded, cautious.

"Senator Hillside and the amount is three million."

"Let me take a look." Dan went over to his desk and pulled the senator's account up on his desktop, which sat adjacent to his printer. It was but a moment and Dan said, "It's all right here should ever anyone need a warrant. In the meantime, if you'll excuse me, I need to step out to use the restroom."

After Dan left, the younger agent went over to Dan's desk. A few minutes later, Dan met them outside his office. "I'm sorry for taking up your valuable time, Dan, and I apologize for coming unannounced. But as always, you were very gracious."

As the elevator doors opened, Ron stepped out. The two agents smiled and walked into the elevators. Suddenly the younger agent recognized Ron and, smiling, yelled loudly as the doors were closing, "Ron! It's been a while. Hope all is well."

"Couldn't be better," Ron yelled back just as the doors closed. Ron turned to Dan, "I know that guy. Was that his boss?"

"Yes."

"What did they want, if you don't mind my asking?"

"They just stopped by to ask a favor."

HAVING A GREAT DAY

Over the next few weeks, the tensions in Chinatown remained high, but Unit 33 reported that there was no chatter about an imminent retaliatory strike. They would keep Dan and Abbey informed daily, especially Dan since he was leaving in the next few days for Texas.

Despite the unsettled atmosphere within the street gangs, Dan felt it was still alright to leave for a couple of days. He had returned to his office, having just met with his boss, Fred Sands, the bank's president. It was approaching four o'clock and Dan was alone in his office, reminiscing over the twenty-five years of service as the Chief Security Officer for 2nd National Bank in San Francisco. Earlier, there had been an Open House his Deputy Director, Abbey Gentry, hosted for both his department staff and anyone else who wished to stop by and congratulate him. Quite a number of bank employees had made their appearance as well as local and federal law enforcement friends. There was one special person who came, his brother John. The brothers were very close.

Abbey knocked on his door, seeing that it was partially open. John was with her. They had only started dating a few weeks ago and until now were keeping it low-key.

"We thought we'd just pop in and see how you're doing," Abbey said, smiling.

"I feel great. I didn't know there were so many people that liked me," Dan answered, laughing aloud. "It's a shame Brenda couldn't be here; she would have enjoyed it. But, being in Texas by our niece's side to help with the birth of her sister's first grandchild trumps today's festivities for sure."

"What a day, huh, Dan?" John remarked, smiling broadly. "Just think, a twenty-fifth anniversary, a birthday, and a new family member, all on the same day. It doesn't get much better than that, bro! When is Brenda coming back?"

"We're not quite sure; I suspect it will be in a couple of weeks. But I'm planning on slipping over there for a couple of days, so we'll all be seeing each other soon. But first, I need to discuss a few business assignments that our beloved president just laid on me— or should I say, you and Ron."

"Ah, I know what that means," John told Abbey. "I'll make my exit. Maybe I'll see you on BART. I'm planning to catch the 5:18."

"Okay, honey. I have some cleanup from the Open House, but I should make it."

"That shouldn't be a problem as far as I'm concerned," and with that John made his exit, stopping momentarily in the office doorway and turning to look at Dan. "Send my love to everyone when you see them."

MERGERS AND EXTRACTIONS

"Well," Dan said, "Unit 33 has their work cut out for them. On the QT, our friends at Singapore Global are back in our lives. It seems that they are interested in buying us out. They call it a merger of equals, but you saw what happened when they bought out our friends down south. It wasn't a year before LA Trust's entire executive staff had been let go and a new board elected. Other than retaining the name LA Trust, they are for all intents and purposes Singapore Global."

"Wow, when's it going to be announced, sir?" Abbey asked.

"Not for a month. That should give your Unit 33 analysts time to do a deep dive. They may be publicly traded, but I've never trusted them, especially after some of their recent acquisitions. And, since our governments are not officially allies, they can do a lot of damage and we can't extradite any of the top brass."

"Okay, anything else?" Abbey asked, anticipating more.

"Yes. It seems as though the time has come for us, and by us, I mean our top brass, to extract some rather sensitive documents from Syria. I'll fill you in tomorrow before I leave. For now, I need to meet with our EVP of International. I'm thinking it might be wise to have Ron accompany me since this is going to be one of those 'boots on the ground' operations."

"Are these documents new to you?"

"No, Ab, I first heard about them shortly after I arrived. For us here in the States, there's no criminality involved. However, our friends in Syria have a much different perspective. Should these files fall into their hands, several CIA operatives and their families will be at risk, not to mention they'll issue arrest warrants for several of our past and current execs. This is just the thing that could quash any merger talks, not to mention potential congressional inquiries."

"How many files are we talking about, sir?"

"I can't say for sure but President Sands wants everything in our Damascus office back here or some other safe place—London, Paris, Geneva, those type of places. Once they're secured, we'll have them shipped here and stored or destroyed, but not before 33 has had a crack at them."

"Well, so much for a low-key day of celebrating," Abbey mused.

"Oh, I don't know. As for the merger, I'm not surprised and with that, it logically follows that the new owners would be rather skittish if they knew of the existence of these files. So, for you and me, it's business as usual. For now, I have a wife, a niece, and a precious one to go see," Dan concluded smiling.

LATER THAT AFTERNOON

Abbey knocked on Dan's door. "You wanted to see me, sir?" He waved her in and pointed to the chair in front of his desk. When she sat down, Dan turned his Montblanc pen and pencil desk set around. "Take a look. Do you see anything that might appear to be out of the ordinary?"

"No, sir," Abbey said as she closely examined the set without touching it.

"Well, look closely at the tip of the pencil. It's the one on the right."

"Sorry, sir, not seeing it, whatever it is."

"Keep your eyes on the tip as I say something," Dan continued. "Now do you see anything?"

"Oh my God!" Abbey exclaimed. "What's with the little red light?"

"That tells me that the conversation is being taped," Dan answered calmly. "That's for my benefit. And, if you were wearing a wire, the tip of the pen would light up blue. While you might think you were recording our conversation, in reality all you would be getting is a bunch of garbled sounds. Inside my pen is a device that scrambles any conversation. You think you leave having a recording of our conversation, but you don't. And if anyone is listening in on your side, all they hear is squelching and are unable to communicate with you."

"This is unbelievable, sir. So, every time I come in, or someone else, you're recording our conversation?"

"No, only when I lift the pencil a little and then let it fall back into its holder. As for the pen, it's on all the time."

"In all due respect, sir, you have a much darker side than I imagined," Abbey said with astonishment.

"Well, hold on then because it's going to get a little darker," Dan responded.

"I'm almost afraid to hear or see. And why are you showing me this now, after all these years?"

"If the Singapore Global merger becomes a reality, there will be times when people you least expect will pay you a visit. Their purpose will be to get information from you, information that could prove—oh, how do I want to say—deleterious to our interests. This is particularly true for the security people at LA Trust. I can't get into the details now, but I will when the time is right. For now, I've ordered two sets, one for you and one for Ron."

"Does he know about this?"

"Not yet, but he will shortly. In the meantime, I need you to send me your best analyst for erasing a few things from my laptop and printer."

"Okay, but do you want my person to eliminate what's on the cloud and our main server?"

"That won't be necessary. This computer and printer are stand-alone; they are not on our servers and not on the cloud. Right after they were issued to me, I had a friend of mine come in and take both offline. I have my own backup and would just all the same, leave it at that."

"No problem. I'm fairly certain I don't want to go there anyway. When would you like to see her?"

"ASAP."

"She'll be here within the next fifteen minutes. I'll call her and ask her to come right away."

It was not even ten minutes later when there was a knock at Dan's door.

"Hi, come on in. I think we've met before. Right?" Dan asked.

"Yes sir, we met at your Christmas party last year."

"Great. Here's what I need. Earlier today I accessed a certain customer's account and made a copy of a certain set of transactions. Sit here in my chair and you'll see what I'm talking about. A printed copy of those transactions was made on my printer. I need all of this to go away and I mean go away. Okay?"

The analyst began clicking away on the keyboard and within

a matter of minutes, she looked at Dan, smiled, and said, "You're good to go. No one will ever trace what you saw or what you did regarding the senator's account."

"Except you. I don't want you to share any of this with anyone, not even Abbey. Understood?"

"Sir, I don't mean to be disrespectful, but I've seen a lot worse since joining Unit 33. I don't suppose you can tell me anything about what this is all about?"

"Not really. In short, you cannot testify to something you know nothing about. Thanks for your help, and send my regards to the rest of the team. And keep up your amazing work," Dan said.

With that, the analyst pulled away from Dan's desk, stood up, and walked out of his office.

SINGAPORE GLOBAL

Two days later, as Dan was preparing to leave Texas, he received an initial report of Singapore Global. According to Unit 33, thus far, SG appeared to be clean of anything that might prove later to be compromising. The institution had its business warts, so to speak, but nothing that would cause alarm or be embarrassing for 2nd National Bank. The report contained personal information on some of the executives, both at the corporate level and among their field offices and subsidiaries, including LA Trust. Dan had this information extracted since the report was to be forwarded to President Sands' desk. He asked that Unit 33 continue with their deep dive to determine if there was anything else.

UNIT 33

Before he left, Dan felt he needed to address an open business item with Ron. He began to feel that the time was now to fill Ron in on Unit 33. He called Abbey and discussed the matter. She agreed. For that matter, she wondered why it had taken Dan so long. He asked her to set up a meeting later that afternoon.

When Ron and Abbey arrived, Dan asked them to sit down. "Before we begin," Dan started, "Ron, I have an early Christmas present for you. A few days ago, I gave Abbey one and she's really excited about it." He smirked as he gave Ron the pen and pencil set and explained how they worked and why he was giving the two of them the pen sets now.

"This is all rather cloak and dagger. Thanks, I suspect they'll get a lot of use. I only wish I had an early Christmas gift for you that was as intriguing, boss."

Dan gave a slight chuckle. He filled Ron and Abbey in on the pending merger announcement with the admonition that nothing about it was to leave Dan's office. The two of them nodded in agreement.

Shifting gears, Dan asked, "Ron, what do you know about an organization called Unit 33?"

"Is that the consulting firm located in our IT center on Beale Street?" he asked.

"Right," Abbey answered.

"Well, to be candid, I only know that they do some sort of classified work. I assume it's some government thing. They're very close-mouthed and you can't get into their offices without some sort of clearance. They seem nice, but you really don't see much of them. They come and go through an entrance off the loading dock. I think they operate around the clock so I assume their work is global."

Dan asked, "Do you know if there is anyone in IT there or over here that knows anything about them?"

"If there is, I don't know. I've told my staff to stay clear and not talk about it. They know that if they start asking questions, I'll fire them. The last thing I need is to have some federal agency poking their nose into our business. So, it's kind of like a China wall. They stay on their side, we stay on our side, and neither knows what the other does. It works out okay."

"Well, you understand the basics, but Ab and I need to fill you in on a few details," Dan started.

Ron looked curious.

Dan continued, "First, Unit 33 is a private non-profit organization designed to gather intelligence. Their network is global, so yes, they operate 24/7/365. Secondly, I'm the president and Abbey manages them and their operation on a pro bono basis. Thirdly, as of now, there are only four people in the bank that knows anything about them, the three of us and President Sands. Got it? Any questions?"

"Can I ask what kind of intelligence they gather and why?" Ron asked as he sat back in his chair.

"They handle highly discreet information. For example, currently Unit 33 is doing a deep dive into Singapore Global and their subsidiaries. President Sands and the Board of Directors want to know if there are any business relationships, sponsorships, or connections that could blow up in our faces."

Abbey added, "You will be surprised how widespread and cavernous their network and abilities are. Since our bank has offices across the globe, our international operations are continuously financing ventures and underwriting various government enterprises. All the while, we're monitoring that activity here. If we see a red flag, Dan advises President Sands. You'd be surprised how many business ventures we've nixed before they were given the go-ahead."

Ron sensed that another shoe was about to drop and he wasn't sure it would be something he would like. "And so, why are you telling me all of this now?" he asked suspiciously.

OPERATION EXTRACTION

"Don't get worried," Dan assured. "We have an assignment for you, one which may require you to draw upon 33's resources. Some time back, we closed our office in Damascus. Our employees had to bug out quickly given the escalation in their civil war. When the U.S. officially intervened in support of the Syrian rebels, parts of the regime obviously fought back and it was unsafe for Americans, let alone for 2nd National, to continue our banking relations.

"When we bugged out, dozens of highly sensitive documents were left behind. Our offices were in the World Bank building.

They too have left. Several other foreign banks were officed there as well. When all was said and done, the abandoned building was left standing there as a stoic reminder of more peaceful times.

"President Sands wants those files out of Damascus, ideally here. This is where you come in." Dan went on to explain the Damascus project. He then explained that Ron's first meeting would be with International Banking's EVP to get the details necessary for the file extractions. These details involved the number of files, how they were marked, where they were located in the offices, and anything that might possibly hinder the operation. For example, were they in a vault with a time lock? That would drive the extraction team's arrival and departure.

Following this meeting, Dan and Ron would meet with an international import/export business run by two brothers, the Segals. For anyone casually walking by their office, their unassuming signage would suggest a firm specializing in textiles. For those in the know, it was the west coast office for the Mossad, Israel's Central Institute for Intelligence and Special Operations. They were there to discuss the necessary resources required to accomplish the mission, most importantly, the selection of the extraction team.

Despite Damascus being a city of two million plus, the presence of Westerners, especially Americans, would be seen as suspicious. And even though Ron was Black, the way he dressed, carried himself, and the food he ate would all be telltale indicators of his being an American. They would point out that the same kind of caution would prohibit them from using any Israeli operatives. Success would require employing Syrians, which would prove doable if the price was right.

Ron asked exactly when all of this was to unfold. Abbey was the one to cut to the chase.

"You start today."

Ron asked, "If things are going to move fast, what happens when I'm gone? Who steps in here for me?"

Dan was quick to answer. "You'll still be able to do a lot of things. It's just that you'll be doing them remotely, likely somewhere in

Europe or Tel Aviv. Abbey will fill in for you on anything that requires in-person handling here. I suspect that by the end, you two will know each other better than you do now."

"Well, you know that just being engaged I'll need to talk to my fiancée about my being out of the country. What can I tell her?" Ron asked.

"Just tell her you're on a bank security project, and leave it at that," Dan suggested.

Abbey burst out laughing. "As though she'll just say, 'Okay dear,' and leave it at that. You have to be joking, sir. With all due respect, I think your wife has spoiled you."

They all laughed together and then Dan suggested, "Ron, I'll let you and Abbey figure that one out."

"And, the nature of these files that need extracting?" Ron asked.

Dan responded, "Essentially, they are loan documents and letters that outline, shall I say, terms of certain business ventures. Nearly all of the documents are at least ten years old; however, the people and nature of these businesses are still operating today. If these files fall into the wrong hands, it could prove to be embarrassing for a number of our executives and current congressional members. And then there is the matter of certain individuals getting killed.

"In several cases, the Syrian government might find the businesses to be illegal even though they are legal here. President Sands and others in International Banking also advise that members of the World Bank have cause to worry. In short, the documents could be used for either blackmail, extortion, or in some cases— execution. Regardless, in the wrong hands, they would make for some great propaganda to discredit the U.S. and our bank, not to mention others around the world," Dan reiterated.

Ron nodded. If he wanted to say anything or ask questions, he elected to keep quiet for now.

"Good. Your goal is simple. Get the files out of Syria without anyone suspecting otherwise. And, hopefully, no one gets killed or arrested," Abbey reinforced, smiling pleasantly and showing her devilish dimples.

"One thing I don't understand. Why are they in hard copy and not electronic?" Ron asked in a puzzled tone.

Abbey smiled. "Back then, there was no cloud and even if there were, we couldn't trust it and in several of our overseas locations there are countries where it is illegal to transfer certain electronic files without going through their networks. If we don't trust them now, think about what it was like back then."

Ron shook his head. "I had no idea. I thought the internet seamlessly crossed borders."

"A lot does, but there are certain requirements and restrictions. If you get caught, things can get ugly really quick. That's why we use microchips, bundle them, and have them sent out under diplomatic pouches. It's actually a foolish way to do business, but everyone does it. That's why we don't do direct business in a country where we do not have a consulate."

Ron just sat there dumbfounded for a moment, and then muttered out loud, "Fuck, who would have thought?"

Dan and Abbey smiled.

TWO DAYS LATER

Dan had arranged a second meeting with the Segals to bring Ron further up to speed. He went in somewhat jaded, thinking they might be better off using the CIA or even Military Intelligence. It didn't take long for Ron to see why Dan had chosen the Segal brothers. Their demeanor was low-key and at times it was hard to understand them since both talked low and with thick accents. Nevertheless, they struck Ron as being very competent. It didn't take the four of them long to get to the point of talking about how to get the files out of the country.

Dan was speaking, "I've used the folks at Control Risks for years. They can be trusted. If you can get the files to the Port of Beirut, I'm certain they can find the ship that will transport them to Liverpool. I'll take care of getting in touch with them and we'll arrange a place where all of us can iron out the details."

"So, let me get this straight," Ron tried to summarize. "Mossad lines up the team, executes the extraction, transports the files across the Syrian border into Lebanon to the Port of Beirut, and hands over the operation to a British group. They, in turn, arrange cargo passage to Liverpool. Right?"

"Yes," said Dan as the Segals were trying to figure out what Ron's point was.

"And why can't your team get them out of Beirut?"

Jacob Segal gave a brief smile. "We don't have the resources to effectively negotiate with either the port authorities or the shipping companies that operate out of there. Sadly, even we have our limits."

"Well, gentlemen, with all due respect, doesn't it take two to three weeks for a cargo ship to make its way up to England from Beirut? It stops along the way several times, loading and unloading containers at several ports. My father was in the Navy and spent a great deal of time in the Mediterranean Sea. He often told me of his seafaring ways and how long it took the big ships to go from the Middle East through the Strait of Gibraltar and then up the Iberian Peninsula to England. I actually worked on one of those ships one summer." And then he added, "Isn't having all those files in the hands of strangers for that long a tad worrisome?"

"You have a point. Let me discuss this with Control Risks; they're in the area a great deal," Jacob Segal said, essentially confirming Ron's input.

"Okay. But allow me one more question. Why can't we simply load them on the next flight out of the country to our destination of choice?" Ron asked.

"Oh, if it were that simple, Ron," Dan cut in. "We're told it could be as many as nine to ten four-drawer filing cabinets. And, if I know our EVP, you can double that number. Besides, they're mixed in with other files, which makes it very difficult to determine what could stay and what needs to be removed."

"Then maybe we load the whole damn bunch, furniture and all, then sort everything out later when they are safely on our home turf?" Ron offered.

"Because time is of the essence. Think of it this way. Draw to your days as a Navy Seal. We need you to put a team together, get in there, take possession of the materials, exit rapidly and without notice, and secure them, preferably here or in London. And perhaps you're right, Ron, maybe our plan should assume everything goes, but that means more trucks, more men. With that comes a higher risk. I don't think any of us can afford that," Dan answered matter-of-factly.

Even as he answered Ron, Dan thought, *This reminds me of my days as unit commander in Iraq.*

A "USELESS" EVP

While Dan was off to Texas for a few days with his family, Ron had managed to get a half hour meeting with the International EVP, but he wasn't all that helpful. When Ron informed him that he would likely be working out of Paris, the EVP was quick to offer the names of several restaurants that were exceptional. *You've got to love it,* Ron thought to himself, *we're trying to keep this guy's butt out of a sling and all he can talk about is great places to eat.*

Ron had gone into the meeting hoping to learn roughly how many files there were and where exactly they were located. "You know, in someone's office, a storage closet, etc." But no such luck. Then it dawned on him, *I'm talking to the wrong guy. I need to find out who the branch manager was at the time the decision was made to skip out. And, was he or she still around?*

Ron asked pleasantly, "I'm sorry, sir, but who was the branch manager and where can I find him or her?"

The EVP thought for a long moment and then answered, "Damned if I know. Ask our London manager. She's been around a long time. She'll probably know." With that kiss-off, Ron got up and left.

6 P.M.

On the drive home, Ron decided that the plan to remove the sensitive documents needed a code name. Hence, it was he who actually choose Operation Extraction. Perhaps this was a throwback to his earlier Navy Seal days when every operation had a code name. He had met with the Segal brothers and International Banking, now it was time to work through the logistics and get this operation underway.

At the Segal brothers meeting, it was decided that Jacob Segal and Ron would begin by meeting face-to-face with Control Risks in their London home office. From there, they would go to Tel Aviv. The decision to have Control Risks involved proved to be a great decision when he met since the EVP was from London. He had voiced a high level of confidence when he was told about Control Risks employing former MI6 operatives. In this case, "familiarity breeds comfort." He was unaware, however, that Jacob and Ron would be largely relying on the services of Mossad. "You just got to love spy work," Ron confided in Jacob since even the initial planning involved its own secrets.

Nevertheless, both meetings allowed Ron the opportunity to meet key assets and understand how operations such as these in the past were carried out. His own military background allowed him to pick up on the nuances of using operatives in foreign countries. He did not feel out of his element, but came quickly to see that this type of mission required experienced assets.

The plan was simple: secure the services of hired Syrian operatives and have them enter the building under the guise of being a local moving company. On-the-ground Mossad agents were reporting that given the ongoing skirmishes, companies were continuously relocating. This meant that the presence of a moving company would seem routine.

For now, the decision was to have them transported across Syria into Lebanon at the Masnaa crossing to the Beirut Port, and have them secretly shipped to Liverpool, England. Even though this route was longer, it was not only safer, but also less likely to be checked. The crossing border at Masnaa was selected since it was used every day by local truckers, thereby lessening the odds of being stopped and searched. Moreover, the Beirut Port would be easier since the authorities were much more open to receiving "certain considerations" for their cooperation. The same was true for the ship captains.

In what would serve as an initial dry run, the Mossad team leader would surreptitiously visit the former bank posing as a utility inspector, access the office area, and photograph everything. This would give Jacob and Ron an understanding of the magnitude of the inventory. Ron would be in Tel Aviv and the leader would wear a helmet camera, allowing Ron to stream everything the leader encountered. He would be close by if needed but the team leader would have the flexibility to do his job without someone second-guessing him. Ron would do all of this from a private office within the Tel Aviv Museum of Art, compliments of Mossad.

Operation Extraction would take place during the day. This would draw the least amount of suspicion since it was common to see moving companies working throughout the city during these times. To further reduce attention, they would disguise their vehicles and mover uniforms to look like Ahmad International since it was one of the larger commercial moving companies and an accredited member of the International Association of Movers. In all, the team leader determined that extraction would require three trucks and eight movers besides himself. This would enable them to be onsite less than an hour. Along with the filing cabinets, they would include some furniture to make it appear like a legitimate move.

Two days before Ron left, Jacob called and advised Ron that they had made an arrangement with Control Risks to take over the operation once the trucks arrived at the port. CR would use their business contacts to work out an arrangement with one of the local merchant ships operating out of the Port of Beirut. Besides meeting the agreed upon transport fee, as part of the "arrangement" with the ship's captain, he would also receive a large solid mahogany desk, complete with matching chair, and a large leather sofa that was the bank office manager's "pride and joy." Everything would be loaded onto the ship at night just prior to the ship weighing anchor.

Dan was back from his short family visit and he and Abbey were discussing how things would operate with Ron in the Middle East. Dan's phone rang; it was Commander Hines from the San Francisco Police, a long-time friend. He was hoping to see Dan sooner rather than later. They set up a luncheon meeting.

"I guess your theory about Chaval's death somehow being linked to your attempted assassination went up in the smoke in Chinatown. Excuse the pun; it was unintended. Our resources clearly show that this is all about one gang infringing on the other and a revenge hit trying to send a message."

"Hmm," Holmes quietly responded. Then after a moment, "I guess I was wrong." It was as simple as that. The two men were talking about an attempt on Dan's life. He, Abbey, and one of her supervisors had been shot outside 33 Beale Street about two years prior. The supervisor died and he and Abbey were seriously wounded. It was Dan's theory that the hit was actually put out by the bank's General Auditor out of fear of being caught in a racketeering scheme.

Dan believed the GA hired the 5th Streeters as assassins and some other unknown assassin actually killed the gang leader, Chaval, and his wife. As for Abbey, she knew Chaval was taken out by her best friend, Ellen Fischer, a Mossad trained sniper, in retaliation for attempting to take Abbey's life.

While fleeing back to Israel to avoid arrest, Ellen had written a note for Abbey, explaining everything. After reading the note, Abbey burned it. As far as she was concerned, the truth would be buried with her. And that included Dan, who did not need to know. Even so, Dan always suspected that the Chaval assailant was Ellen, but never brought it up directly with Abbey. As the saying goes, "It's better to let sleeping dogs lie." The good news was that with the Chinatown bombing, Ellen, for now, was no longer a person of interest.

"How bad do you think the street war is going to be?" Dan asked.

"Bad. Beyond hearing what's in the media and politicians butting in, our Gang Task Force is putting plans together as we speak. Intelligence tells us that it will be fought out. We just don't know exactly where at this time. One thing is for sure, Wah Ching will not settle for a simple retaliatory bombing. Dan, I'm really concerned. I fear there's going to be a lot of blood shed before this is all over. It's one thing for a rival gang to encroach on another's territory, but this was sabotage on their home turf. Now it's personal."

City Hall and the SFPD were speculating that a large-scale gang war could break out anytime. The governor's office was prepared to announce that the National Guard was on notice. And the media was stepping up its coverage, reporting that city and county officials were developing plans for a city-wide curfew should gang-related violence begin to spike.

"So, how can I help? I don't think you wanted to have lunch just to discuss the current state of affairs," Dan surmised.

"Yes. I need all the information I can get, especially anything that would indicate a breakout before it actually happens. Our intelligence is good, but always limited. And then there's the politics involved. That means more road blocks, which means time, and I can't afford to lose time. If this thing goes as some project, we're talking about a lot of lost lives. I don't know how your bank agents do it, but they do a fantastic job digging up shit and passing it along well ahead of everyone else. I need them to keep ahead of the situation."

"Of course we'll do what we can," Dan said, leaving the police commander believe such intelligence work was part of a bank agent's job as opposed to his confidential Unit 33. "Let's finish up here and then we can go back and meet with Abbey. We have a couple of rather sensitive analyses underway, but I'm sure she'll somehow juggle things around to make this a priority. In the meantime, as a quick diversion, do you want to see someone who's awfully cute?"

"Well, okay, I guess," Commander Hines responded, somewhat puzzled.

"Here, it's a couple of snaps of my family's new addition. He's going to kill the girls," Dan said, smiling just like all new grandfathers, had he actually been one.

"He's a handsome lad, Gramps."

After the commander left, Abbey voiced her concerns. "It's going to be tight, Dan. We've got the Singapore Global merger and we're working with Ron with his Operation Extraction."

"Do what you can and let me know if I need to run interference."

THE EXTRACTION

The Damascus bank office was located on the fourth floor. The building itself had suffered considerable damage several times from artillery shells. Nonetheless, the team leader was able to gain access to the floor without difficulty. Unfortunately, he found the bank's office doors locked. He wondered who had the keys. He called his contact in Mossad, who in turn called Jacob Segal, who in turn called Ron. When Ron got the call, he lost it.

"What!" he exploded. "He's looking for a key to the goddamn door of an abandoned office? Tell him to bust the fucking door down, or bust through the wall! This is unbelievable. We're going to hold up the entire operation while someone goes looking for a fucking key? You've got to be shitting me!"

Why didn't he call me directly? Ron wondered. Was he messing with Ron's head because Ron was a Westerner or simply following orders? The more he thought about it, the more pissed-off he became.

Jacob listened calmly. When Ron stopped shouting, Jacob responded, "It's a cultural thing that you will probably not understand. Busting through doors and walls is just not done, even if the roof has been blown away. We have to find the key. Who can you call?"

"I can't believe this. What would happen if I went there and accidently put my foot through the door?"

"That would be most unfortunate," Jacob said.

"Hold tight. I'll call our EVP and explain the situation. Maybe he knows where the fucking key is. I'll be right back," Ron continued to yell.

He waited for a minute to allow his blood pressure to lower and then put a call into the EVP. When he came on the line, Ron explained the key fiasco. When he finished, the EVP calmly said, "Oh yes, it's a cultural thing there. Let me make a few calls. I'll get back to you right away."

Ron couldn't believe it. If this were part of a movie script, no one would believe it. To his Western mind, this was simply unbelievable, but he was there and living through it. He called Jacob back and told him they were trying to track the former manager down. As luck would have it, Ron got a call back a couple of hours later. The manager said he had the key with him. He was in Paris. Ron asked him to standby and called Jacob. "We've located the key. It's in Paris. The former manager stopped long enough to lock the door as he fled," Ron explained.

"That's understandable," Jacob said, his voice remaining pleasant, almost serene.

He and Ron worked out how to get the key to Damasus as quickly as possible. It would be flown in on the next Pegasus Airlines flight. The Mossad liaison, a paid Syrian operative, would receive the package and get it to the team leader, who would have it the next morning.

Late that night, Ron got a call from Jacob saying that the plan was back on track. The next day, as Ron watched, he could see that there would be sixteen four-drawer filing cabinets photographed, inventoried, and extracted. And yes, the team leader asked Ron if he knew how to get into the vault.

Ron lost it.

Later that afternoon, the Paris manager texted Ron the following: "It's on a time lock. It opens every morning at 9 a.m. local time and locks at 5 p.m."

He couldn't believe it. The more he thought about it, he began to muse: *Was someone expected to believe that this vault had been unlocking and locking every day for over ten years? No way, it was impossible.* But sure enough, the next day he received another text, this time from Jacob. It read, "Vault opened, four additional filing cabinets."

Given the recent volatile history of street fighting and shelling, it was strange that businesses carried on as usual. Movers were continuously seen crisscrossing streets and alleyways as they relocated businesses and organizations from one locale to another. Ron had seen his share of wartime environments, but nothing was quite like this.

On Monday, Ron heard from Jacob that the extraction team had tried three times to drive to the bank over the weekend, but were unable to do so as a result of localized heavy fighting. For now, Operation Extraction was on hold. Throughout the ordeal, Ron kept Dan informed almost daily. He accepted the updates as calmly as if Ron were reporting on soccer matches. "Be patient, Jacob will not let this go south," Dan reassured him.

Two weeks would pass before the Syrian operatives made it to the bank and set about photographing, recording, and loading file cabinets and furniture. After five hours of loading everything, the caravan was ready to roll out.

At six o'clock the next morning, Ron's phone rang. He answered it, expecting it to be Jacob or the team leader. The caller identified herself as a lieutenant at the U.S. base Al-Tanf on the border between Syria and Iraq. She needed to know what he wanted them to do with twenty-four drawer filing cabinets delivered earlier from Damascus.

Ron was dumbfounded but quickly gained his composure. He asked for her callback number and immediately called Jacob Segal. Jacob suggested he call their contact at CR for instructions, which he promptly did. The contact wasn't surprised at all. He told Ron to instruct the lieutenant to set the cabinets aside and she would receive her instructions from Major Vogel within the next thirty minutes. Ron did as he was instructed and then called Jacob back.

"Can you explain? What happened at the ship and how did the files get to some military base out in the desert?"

"Well, contrary to what you may have been led to believe, we were never going to use the ship. No matter how much you pay those mariners, you can't trust them. So, between CR and ourselves at Mossad, we always knew the materials were going to be driven out of Damascus to Al-Tanf since it's only a three-hour drive.

"But why wasn't I in on the loop?"

"Well, whereas I have come to trust you, the Brits are another matter altogether. Remember, you are still somewhat of an unknown to them. They know and trust Dan, but you have to earn their trust and one mission alone does not make it. Consider it this way, the mission was your bar mitzvah," Jacob answered.

"I'm not going to even ask how you got the military to do all of this."

"It's probably best that you don't."

"What happens now? We got a shitload of filing cabinets belonging to an American bank sitting somewhere on a miliary base in the middle of the fucking desert."

"Whoa, Ron, slow down. Later today or tomorrow, they will be put on a C-5M cargo carrier and flown to Ramstein Air Base in Germany and then on to Travis outside Sacramento. Once there, you name the day and time and we'll make arrangements to move them wherever you like. In a matter of a few days, they'll be secured in an airforce hangar. Security doesn't get any better than that. Besides, that lame EVP of International Banking that you told me about will think that you not only work miracles, but you have the U.S. military at your beck and call."

Ron laughed aloud. "Yeah. That SOB needs to understand that he isn't God's only gift to humanity." Perhaps Ron's feelings were still smarting, but he was beginning to see the upside of what Jacob and Control Risks could add to assignments like this.

TWO DAYS LATER

Ron was in his office when Abbey popped her head in and asked if he would like to join her and Dan for a cup of coffee at a local bakery. Once the three of them had settled into their chairs, Abbey asked Dan and Ron if they had had a good weekend. It was then that Ron gave them the final status of Operation Extract.

"And where are the files now?" Dan inquired without any sign of amazement.

"The last I heard was that they were still in some hangar at Travis. I put in a call to our EVP but he has yet to return my call. When he does, I'll advise him accordingly. He'll no doubt want to know the final location."

Dan responded, "His soul will be rotting in hell before you ever get a call from him. And I dare say President Sands feels the same way. For now, don't worry, I'll make arrangements to have them moved."

Abbey and Ron laughed out loud and then she asked, "What about the desk?"

"Well, the ship's captain knows where it is at. And don't worry, they left the door unlocked."

THE GANG WAR ESCALATES

Just as Unit 33 had reported, city and county officials and landlords actively engaged in finger-pointing; everyone knew blame would ultimately be affixed to the owners. In time, the investigation showed that the cause was due to a ruptured gas line. However, the actual cause was inconclusive as to whether it was failure with the line or sabotage.

For now, however, Wah Ching was certain that the explosion was the work of the 5th Streeters. If so, this would most certainly end in more deaths. Unofficially, the SFPD Gang Task Force unit agreed with Wah Ching and believed that sabotage was the most likely cause based on intelligence being provided by their Gang Unit. Moreover, two independent Vice Unit confidential informants had as much said it was a retaliation hit by the 5th Streeters. They were rarely wrong. Unit 33 agreed.

NOVEMBER

From Unit 33's initial involvement, Dan had asked Abbey to monitor any form of communication between the Wah Ching gangs in San Francisco and Los Angeles. Dan had this nagging feeling that the LA operation was not going to let SF handle this on their own. She instructed Unit 33 accordingly. It wasn't long before Unit 33 was reporting that a great deal of activity in the form of texts and emails between the leaders was beginning to materialize. Dan decided he would stop by Unit 33 and see first-hand and notify Commander Hines as promised.

Unit 33's day-shift supervisor briefed Dan and Abbey. "There seems to be a plan underway to develop a three-tiered approach to their retaliation on the 5th Streeters. There are no definite dates as to how this will unfold, however, we know that the first plan of attack will involve sending about two hundred LA members here to Chinatown. The second plan will involve using another gang from here to do their dirty work if Tier One fails. Again, we have no details about who that will be, nor the timing. Finally, there is a great deal of consideration being given to some form of retaliatory bombing.

"I think they're flushing out the details, priorities, and timing because there seems to be a lot of back and forth as to the likelihood of making the greatest impact. The LA leaders want the 5th Streeters eradicated. There is no doubt of this," she finished.

Abbey then asked, "Is there a pushback from the Wah Ching people here in San Francisco? Why would they do that? It seems they, above all, would want them gone."

Dan answered, "Balance. These street gangs know and respect each other's territory. When one is eliminated, others will battle to fill the void. For Wah Ching here, it's a matter of knowing one's enemy and dealing with him versus allowing an unknown to get a toehold and becoming a new and, perhaps, bigger threat down the road. Or, as the great ancient military strategist Sun Tzu said, 'If you know your enemy and you know yourself, your victory will not stand in doubt.' For those in LA, it's all about sending a message to the other gangs and establishing themselves as the pre-eminent force in town. It'll be interesting to see who wins this internal battle."

Abbey looked at her manager and smiled. "That's why he gets the big bucks." They all laughed.

"In any event, stay on top of this and let me know the minute you pick up on anything to do with timing and which approach they'll be employing," Abbey instructed Dan.

On their way back to their offices, Abbey asked, "Are you going to update anyone?"

"I'm rolling that one around in my mind. I will, I'm just not sure who and when," Dan answered.

THE NEXT AFTERNOON

The next afternoon, Dan received two texts from Abbey. The first one simply read, "The Singapore Global deep dive is complete. They're clean and good to go." Dan quickly called President Sands and informed him. He was very pleased and said he would pass the word through to the Board of Directors. For Dan and Abbey, this meant the assignment was closed.

About an hour later, Dan received the second text. "There's been a big break in the gang war intelligence."

Dan asked her to hurry over. Within a matter of minutes, she was in his office.

"If you are okay with it, I'd like to get Commander Hines on the phone."

"No problem," she agreed. Hines came directly on his private line.

"This thing is going to go down sooner than anyone here anticipated. We've intercepted a detailed email from LA. Here's a copy." She handed it to him. It was in Chinese, with the English translation below. As Dan read it, he smiled. "Actually, this is quite ingenious. Please explain what I'm holding to the commander."

In essence, the email detailed a plan to send two hundred gang members out of the LA area in groups of three or four over several days. Each group would arrive by bus and walk from the bus depot to Chinatown. This meant having them pass through 5th Streeter territory, allowing them to familiarize themselves with the area. Using several departure points and taking different bus lines would enable them to assemble the entire group in San Francisco over a matter of three or four days.

The out-of-towners would stay with Wah Ching members so as to blend into Chinatown without being noticed. Once everyone arrived, a general meeting would be held in the basement of the Ma Su Temple. This location was chosen because of the secret tunnel that could allow a fast escape to another area three blocks away, should they get raided.

The commander knew from long ago not to bother asking Dan about his sources. He did, however, want two of his lead gang force detectives to join them. While they waited, Hines asked if Abbey had fully recovered since she had been shot and if Ellen Fischer, her sniper friend, had returned from Tel Aviv. Dan picked up that Hines was playing some sort of cat and mouse game with her regarding Ellen. Clearly, the commander was still convinced that somehow Ellen was involved in the Chaval shooting. Dan played along, and, putting on his poker face, told him that Abbey was nearly one hundred percent recovered and to his knowledge, Ellen was still out of the country.

Shortly, the two detectives arrived.

Dan proceeded to lay out what Unit 33 had recovered without mentioning them. When he finished, Detective Riley asked, "So, who exactly is this source of yours?"

Commander Hines responded, "You're wasting your time. I've learned over the years that if Dan wanted you to know his source, you would already know. Just accept it as being highly reliable and leave it at that."

Riley frowned out of frustration. Johnson then spoke up. "Riley, it doesn't matter. We can check this out pretty quickly. What I'd like to know is why we haven't heard anything from our own sources."

"That's simple," Dan responded. "This news is just breaking. My guess is that within twenty-four hours, your folks in Chinatown will know something since we believe that this whole thing is about to go down."

Hines directed, "Let's not sit on this. Get your team together and make sure you cover the Transbay Terminal. Starting tonight,

I want photos of everyone that gets off any bus. And I mean any-one of Asian descent, male and female, and I don't care how old they are or how healthy or unhealthy they look. Follow anyone that walks from there to Chinatown, especially if they linger along the way. I don't want any contact, just surveillance."

After a brief moment, he added, "Riley, you're the lead on this. Why don't you and Dan exchange numbers and Dan can text you with the latest developments on his end as they unfold?" And then to Dan, "Want to project when this whole thing will actually go down?"

"Haven't a clue."

"I do," Johnson said. "Thanksgiving. We'll have a holiday force on duty so that means our patrols will be radically reduced and they could move two to three hundred people into the temple and we would never be the wiser. They could move that many people in a matter of minutes. If their intent is to hit the 5th Streeters that night, they'll let the word drop that about fifty or sixty will be gathering in an empty lot sometime after midnight on 5th Streeter turf. This is how they always do it. They'll sucker those idiots right into their trap. Once they arrive, Wah Ching will have them surrounded. All that will be left is to have us mop up the carnage."

Hines responded, "It makes sense and will likely play out some-thing like that. So, we let them drop the word and let it play out like that. Or, at least that's what Wah Ching believes will happen. Say it is Thanksgiving; we'll have our own gang of two hundred. Once we know everyone is inside the temple, we can seal it off and snag the whole lot of them."

Hines, you're such a smug SOB at times, Dan thought.

"You know there may be a good reason Wah Ching has chosen Ma-Tsu Temple," Dan said. "It's likely it has an entrance into a tun-nel that will dump them out three or four blocks away. It seems that anywhere you go in Chinatown, you can enter one place and come out someplace else. Once everyone is in the basement, they'll barricade themselves in and by the time we bust through, the place will be empty."

"Do we know for a fact that there is such a tunnel?" Hines asked.

"I can't say for sure, but if I were a betting man, you know where my money would be," Johnson answered.

"Gentlemen," Dan interrupted. "If I may, I think I can be of some help here. We have a couple of retail branches in Chinatown. With the proper incentive, I think any one of our employees might be able to do a little surveillance work. I think I know just the person. I'm sure she can gain access to any tunnel that might be below the temple. She'll be able to map the route from inside the temple to where it emerges. If you would like, we might even be able to assist with discreet video equipment along the way."

"That's interesting," Riley pondered aloud. "But these cameras. If you place them in the tunnel, they'll be spotted by the first person to enter."

"I doubt they'll see ours, at least not right away. And if the tunnel is as long as we believe it is, what if there was a power outage once everyone enters? They're not likely to turn around since they know who will be waiting for them. Once the lights go out, we can set up emergency lighting on the other end so they can work their way through slowly. As they come out, they'll be greeted by another group of your finest. And as for the cameras, don't worry, they work in total darkness."

"Sounds a little like the type of video equipment we found after the Chaval shooting," Hines verbally jabbed.

"But what I want to know is, what follows?" Riley asked. "Let's assume our Thanksgiving plan works. What then? You said Wah Ching's Plan B is to use some other resource. I take that to mean another gang. And if so, who?"

Dan smirked and then teased, "Come on, Detective, do I have to do all of the work here?"

The others didn't think that was particularly funny.

"Hey, I'm sorry," Dan said. "That was unnecessary. I don't have an answer to your questions, and let me hasten to add, they're very good questions. All I can say is that I expect more intelligence and as soon as I have it, as we've already agreed, you'll have it. Please accept my apology again."

Unit 33 had sent over their latest to Dan. He called Detective Riley. "Your partner nailed it. Our resources tell us that the day is Thanksgiving and that if for any reason the plan fails, they will have contracted with another group to basically do the same thing."

"Great," Riley said enthusiastically, "your sources must be really good. Late last night, two of our confidential informants said that something big was about to go down involving Wah Ching and the 5th Streeters. They thought it was going to go down in the next week or so. That means Thanksgiving is certainly in play. Anything else?"

"Their Plan B is to have the Hells Angels 'carry out the mission.'"

"You're shitting me?" Riley said laughing loudly. "Really?"

"Well, how does the old saying go? 'The enemy of my enemy is my friend,'" Dan replied.

"I'll let the commander know. He's going to love it. And, if I know him, since they'll no doubt be coming across the Bay Bridge, he'll have the highway patrol meet them at Treasure Island, have a few words with them, and turn them right around."

"I thought you might like that," Dan said, smiling on his end.

"Anything about Plan C? That's the one that really has me concerned."

"No word yet, but I'll keep you posted." Dan hung up and dialed Abbey.

"Sir," she answered.

"Say, I just want you to know Hines and the Gang Squad is loving our intel. I'm hoping to hear that they're going to take me up on my offer to check out the possible tunnel under the temple in the next day or so."

MID-DAY, THE NEXT DAY

The call from Riley came in shortly before noon. They wanted to take Dan up on his offer to have one of his branch employees check out the temple for any sign of a tunnel.

"No problem, we should have it done within twenty-four hours. What about the cameras?"

"If you think we can pull it off, Commander Hines says he'd love to have them."

"Okay," Dan answered and then asked, "Anything else? If not, I got a few calls to make."

"Nope. That's it for now," Riley answered and ended the call.

Dan could smell a rat. *Sure, the commander would love to have my cameras especially if they just happened to match the ones left at the Chaval shooting.*

He called Unit 33.

When the console operator answered, Dan asked, "Is Brian in?"

"Sure, I'll get him." When Brian picked up, Dan asked, "The cameras we'll be using in the temple tunnel, whose are they?"

Brian hesitated momentarily. "I was going to use Sony's new night-vision unit, the one they developed for the military but you can get it through the Janes catalogue. Why? Do you want me to use something else?"

"No. They have the Sony logo and are serialized?"

"Yes, but we grind the manufacture run number and the serial number off."

"Perfect. Thanks." Dan rung off, knowing Ellen's cameras were specially made by Mossad. Unit 33 was safe.

THANKSGIVING

One couldn't ask for a better day weather-wise. The evening temperatures called for the mid-fifties, light winds, and no rain. Mother Nature was cooperating, something she sometimes failed to do this time of the year. Four buses were parked behind the 3rd Street San Francisco Police Station. Two hundred riot police offices were boarding. Two of the buses would soon be deployed to the front of Ma-Tsu Temple while the other two would be sent to the rear of Sheng Hing Market.

Following the map drawn by the Chinatown branch teller, two nights prior, Brian Hatfield and another Unit 33 member, Sue Wong had not only discovered the tunnel leading between the two locations, but also had traveled the length, installing their night-vision cameras.

Beginning at two o'clock, members of the Wah Ching gang from both the LA area and San Francisco began drifting into the basement of the Ma-Tsu Temple. There was a mix of men and women and the atmosphere was festive, complete with dining, singing, and dancing. To an outsider, it appeared to be the Chinese version of an American Thanksgiving feast. By 10 p.m., the festivities were over and anyone not a member of Wah Ching was escorted out.

At 10:30, the leaders were just completing their briefing when one of them received a call alerting the meeting that two buses were less than a block away and filled with police officers. Immediately, the entrance to the tunnel was opened and the attendees began hurrying through. Just as the last two gang members passed through, they closed the tunnel door. A moment later, the tunnel went dark. Panic started to set in. For a few moments, it was pandemonium as the men yelled and shoved each other.

Then ahead, a light shone. It was above their heads and appeared to be coming from a source at the top of the stairs at the end of the tunnel. They rushed forward. Several men stumbled and fell, only to be trampled by the crowd coming behind them. Over a loudspeaker, they heard the police commands. "Do not panic. This is the police. Walk slowly forward with your hands empty and above your heads. Ascend the steps in a single file." The commands were repeated as the lights came back on.

As the Wah Ching members came out of the tunnel to the rear of the market, they found two city buses waiting to load them, along with two police buses. Other empty buses began arriving to accommodate everyone. They were searched for weapons as they entered their bus. Several knives were confiscated along with an assortment of firearms.

Once the last person reached the top of the tunnel, the police SWAT team entered and made their way back to the other end under the temple. Along the way, they discovered three gang members on the tunnel floor. Each were seriously hurt, but they were alive. In addition, they seized dozens of additional weapons.

It was after eleven when Dan got the call advising of the mission's success. He texted Abbey in turn and asked her to send his appreciation along to Unit 33 and Brian and Sue in particular. The following Monday morning, Commander Hines called Dan to personally thank him and advised that the three cameras would be retained as part of the evidence. He said that he was amazed at the clarity of video given the near dark environment. He then passed along the mayor's personal thanks and noted, "As our beloved mayor told the reporters Friday morning, it was a good day for San Francisco. Lives were saved and known criminals from outside the area were taken off our streets. It was an especially good Thanksgiving for the city and the men and women in blue."

Then, almost as though it were an afterthought, he asked, "Dan, do you always use Sony cameras?"

"Always," Dan answered, smiling on his end.

DECEMBER 1ST

Unit 33 had picked up the latest communication within Wah Ching and had advised Dan that it appeared they were going to initiate their second plan to seek out the 5th Streeters and settle the score. The exact details would soon be following; for now, this was simply a heads-up. Dan, in turn, had alerted the commander, who alerted the Gang Unit Taskforce and the California Highway Patrol, or the CHP as the locals call them.

The next afternoon, Unit 33 was providing the necessary details. In essence, Wah Ching was asking the Hells Angels for assistance. The logistics called for the Hells Angels to come into the city on Friday, December 7th at 5 p.m. Members of Wah Ching would rendezvous with them at the rear of the Transbay Terminal, under the elevated highway and out of sight. The two gangs would wait until 7 p.m. to allow for darkness to settle in and the evening commute to end.

Prior to that, Wah Ching would call out the 5th Streeters to defend their turf at a designated location and time. When the two gangs encountered one another, a signal would be given and the Hells Angels would ride in and, in essence, corral them and assist Wah Ching in overwhelming the 5th Streeters. Unit 33 forwarded one final text from the Wah Ching leader. It read, "We take no prisoners, we leave no witnesses."

SFPD developed a coordinated plan with the CHP to intercept the bikers on the bridge and escort them into the city. The police would then direct them into a fenced-in area—their version of a corral. The bikers would be given two choices. First, be escorted as a group back across the bridge into Oakland, or go through a search of their person and bike. Any contraband or weapon found would result in an immediate felony arrest.

At 5 p.m., the local news agencies began reporting on a breaking news story occurring on the Bay Bridge. It was the peak commute hour for a Tuesday evening. The California Highway Patrol had set up a roadblock at Treasure Island and were directing a group of fifty Hells Angels to the right lane. From there, they were escorting them across the rest of the bridge to a parking lot at the Bay Area Metro Center on Beale Street.

Despite the traffic congestion, the traffic helicopters took it in their stride. For them, this was just another type of activity that routinely occurred on one or another of the bridges. They advised their listeners to be patient if they were in the area and assured them traffic would return to normal shortly. That was that—no follow-up on the 10 p.m. news and no mention on social media, just another nuisance to frustrate the evening commuter.

The police held the bikers until 7 p.m. to ensure Wah Ching would not show. They didn't and, as expected, the Hells Angels were escorted back to Oakland.

In the meantime, Unit 33 kept their daily monitoring for any sign of a Plan C. It never came.

5ᵀᴴ STREETERS END

Just as Commander Hines feared, since the gang wars erupted, the evening news continuously ran one story after another. Yet, with multiple arrests and extended curfews, the street wars were slowing down. Tourism was down, but not as bad as city and county officials direly predicted. For that matter, the Tourism Bureau was reporting that, despite the gang violence, most visitors saw it as largely confined to the lower-income neighborhoods and not something to be overly concerned about. Despite the callousness of this attitude, SFPD found it difficult to refute. Their official posture was that the gang activity needed to remain a high priority. They continued to dedicate considerable resources to the situation.

It was late in spring when the San Francisco gang war essentially came to an end but at a heartbreaking cost. A fire of suspicious origin broke out in a four-building cluster of low-cost housing. It was home to more than thirty families of the 5th Streeters. All of the buildings were destroyed within a matter of minutes. There were actually four separate infernos, each in exactly the same spot in each unit. All were of a suspicious nature and SFPD didn't take long in their investigation to label it arson. Some city officials wanted to call it a case of domestic terrorism. Regardless of how one labeled the loss, forty-five women and children were dead, along with sixteen males and several pets. Those severely burned or injured trying to escape the flames accounted for another thirteen victims.

RON HEADS TO SOUTH AMERICA WHILE ABBEY GOES SAILING

ABBEY AND JOHN

Most out-of-state or out-of-country visitors commonly assume that summer weather in San Francisco is mild and sunny, with a warm ocean breeze. That is, they assume this before they visit. That's a big mistake. The fog, with its cold and sometimes biting chill, arrives with more punctuality than Japan's express train, Hokuriku Shinkansen. The morning may start off sunny, but one can rest assured that by mid-afternoon, something heavier than a light sweater or jacket is a must. The locals take it in their stride and embrace it as one of those quirks that makes San Francisco unique.

Fog aside, summer time has always been Abbey's favorite season. The scents from plants, flowers, and trees wafting through Japantown or along the avenues, and in so many other tucked-away parks, always lifted her spirits. This summer, it was particularly noticeable to her. For the first time in a long time, she had allowed herself to be vulnerable and commit to the feelings she had for someone—Father John.

Not long ago, Abbey had worked for 2nd National Bank of San Francisco, or simply 2nd National, as Deputy Director for Corporate

Security, reporting to Dan Holmes. As part of her responsibilities, she managed several business units, not the least of which was a secret intelligence gathering organization known as Unit 33. Unlike its big sister, the CIA, they only collected information. However, now it was a standalone non-profit entity, owned by Dan as a side venture and managed by Abbey. This arrangement, as unusual as it might seem, occurred when Abbey fell in love with Dan's brother, John. As their relationship strengthened and talk of marriage started, Dan wanted to avoid any hint of a conflict of interest since corporate policy prohibited family members reporting directly to other family members.

As a separate operation, Dan was able to establish his own organizational policies, thereby allowing Abbey to continue managing Unit 33. As a non-profit, they were funded by grants from the bank, thus ensuring 2nd National Bank's needs were a priority. Equally important, the bank had a strong influence over who contracted Unit 33's resources and capabilities. This was the result of a previous vendor taking advantage of Unit 33's unique abilities.

John and Abbey met at Dan's annual Christmas party. At that time, no one knew that Father John had petitioned his bishop to be released from his duties as a local Assistant Pastor for St. Leo's Catholic Church. From the outset, John confided in Abbey about his plans to leave the priesthood in a matter of weeks.

Abbey was Jewish and a widow, having lost her husband in the U.S.-Afghanistan conflict. Dating a priest was an entirely new experience. Even though John had assured her several times about his decision to leave the priesthood prior to meeting her, she still wasn't convinced that God wouldn't somehow blame her for luring John away from his sacred calling. Moreover, she wasn't sure how her twin teenage boys and her father would feel about having a Catholic, let alone a former priest, in the family. Still, she felt as though she had found her second soulmate and everything would eventually work itself out.

The bank's president, Fred Sands, needed to see Dan right away. Dan rarely received texts from his boss, let alone with such a sense of urgency.

As he entered the president's office, he found Fred Sands literally pacing back and forth in front of his window. Dan wanted to joke, "Thinking of jumping?" But this was clearly no time to joke. "What's up, Mr. President?"

"Dan, our Vice Chairman is in the hospital in Sao Paulo. He's in critical condition with his throat slashed."

"First, we're talking about Sao Paulo, Brazil. Right?"

"Correct. It seems he was sitting at a table in some bar when a fight broke out. As I understand it, he was getting up, trying to get clear of it, when one of the assailants apparently swung at the other assailant with a broken beer bottle. He missed the guy, but struck our Vice Chairman, slicing his throat."

"Son-of-a-bitch," Dan responded. "Who was he with?"

"Our EVP for International Banking, Alan Font. He's the one who called me and told me all about it."

"Just don't tell me he was at Paulo Churrascaria's."

"Font said they went to some barbeque joint that was a short walk from their hotel," President Sands answered.

"It's a nice restaurant but it has more than their share of bar fights. We specifically pointed this out on his Foreign Travel itinerary and advised staying away."

President Sands shouted, "Well, then this is just fucking crazy. Why did he—that is, why did they go?"

"You called it. They were being stupid and thought nothing would happen. Unfortunately, a lot of our foreign travelers think they're above things like travel advisories."

"Well, then why do you give them those things?" Sands shot back, getting angry.

"Because we want to cover your ass, sir. In all due respect, they allow us the ability to say that we, the bank, told the traveler to stay away. If they choose to ignore us, then it's on them," Dan answered.

"So, what do we do now? We've got to get him out of there and back here so our doctors can begin caring for him. Should we send one of your people there?"

"Not right now. We'll call MediVac. They're the outfit out of Miami. We have them on retainer to fly wherever we need anywhere in the world on short notice. We used them last year when one of our junior auditors was killed trying to stop a mugging in Rio. In the meantime, I'll send one of my people to investigate the matter first-hand."

"That sounds great. Thanks, I'll let the Board know what we're doing," President Sands said, clearly feeling much better about the situation.

For Dan, the choice was obvious—Ron Tyson. He had the investigative experience and Dan wanted to give him the necessary South American experience. As he thought about it, he decided he would send Ron out for a two-week swing through a few of the other South American countries where 2nd National had offices. This would give Ron an opportunity to meet the other branch office managers as well as introduce himself to American Consulate staff. If the timing was right, Dan hoped that Ron would meet some of the on-ground operatives that worked for private companies and were former intelligence officers. Over the years, their knowledge and contacts had bailed Dan out of many tough assignments.

TWO DAYS LATER

MediVac reported that the Vice Chairman was still in intensive care and the hospital was balking at the idea of transporting him back to San Francisco. MediVac's recommendation was that 2nd National maintain the status quo for now. When the okay was given for him to be transported, they would be ready. The flight would be over eight hours so the medical team on board would fly in, spend the night near the airport, and then return the following day. This time it would be a ten-hour day due to the paperwork involved.

In the meantime, Ron called Abbey, requesting her team to do a deep dive into each of the three countries he would be visiting. He wanted intelligence reports on political stability and drug cartels operating in each country. He would need the names and contact info of key U.S. operatives. Dan advised Ron that he would get the latter since he had an in with the CIA's Special Agent in Charge of the San Francisco office. This individual would be able to make the necessary arrangements. Within forty-eight hours, Ron was finalizing his own units and booked on a red-eye to Miami. From there, he would accompany the MediVac team directly to Sao Paulo.

THE FOLLOWING SUNDAY

John's pastor, a Franciscan Friar, had seen several men opting out of the priesthood and leaving his order. He didn't want John to step away, but he understood that times were changing faster than their church. It was a shame, but it was also a reality. John's diocesan bishop had given permission for him to step away from being an active priest, as he told John in a rather melancholy way, "for the good of everyone's souls." John didn't quite understand what the bishop meant, but he wasn't going to push the point. He graciously thanked him and said that the bishop would be in his prayers. That seemed to placate him.

That Sunday, at all of the masses, John's pastor read a brief announcement informing the congregants that John had decided to step away from being an active priest. His reason was simple: he no longer felt that he should wear the mantle of the priesthood while he was struggling with issues of his faith. He needed time away for counseling and contemplative prayer.

Having read the formal statement, his pastor looked at those present and publicly thanked John for his assistance. He pledged his support and ended by asking everyone to keep John in their prayers. His new contact information would be available upon request in the parish office. He did add, however, that John had asked if he could stay associated with the parish as a member of the laity and participate as a volunteer where and as needed. The bishop gave his approval. Candidly, it was good news for the pastor since he wasn't completely losing John and finding his replacement would take some time.

Later that Sunday, over dinner, John, Abbey, Brenda, and Dan were discussing what John would be doing going forward. John surprised everyone by telling them he had been accepted as a doctoral candidate in history at UC Berkeley. And then he paused. "I have some other news. Dan, I know that you probably don't want to talk business here, but I received an interesting phone call on my way over here from one of my parishioners. She told me that two FBI agents came to her house on Friday and questioned her about what she saw the day Chaval and his wife were killed."

"Interesting. I didn't know there was a witness," Dan said. "It's strange that Commander Hines has never said anything to me about it. That killing was over two years ago. I thought the assassination was either a professional hit by one of the drug cartels or a rival gang. I figured that both SFPD and the FBI considered it a cold case and put it on the back burner, so to speak."

"I figured as much myself. We were both in the parish rectory when we heard the gunshots. We raced outside and saw a vehicle crash into the garage right in front of us. I ran over, looked inside, and saw that the driver was hit. She yelled that there were people lying on the ground a few houses up and ran to them. I never saw the shooter and assumed she didn't see anything either."

Dan then asked, "Do you know what she told them? The FBI, that is."

"Well, I'll tell you what she told me. When she ran out, she looked up at the roof of the garage. She saw two people—one about halfway down the garage and the other almost directly above us. She didn't see that the first person had a gun, but the second one— the one above us—had a rifle and was doing the shooting. Both were wearing ski masks and the actual shooter was a woman."

"That's interesting," Abbey said. "How did this woman know the shooter was female?"

"She told me the shooter had long dark hair sticking out from under the ski mask and a much smaller frame. And, when she ran off, she ran like a girl."

"What did the FBI say to all of this?" Dan asked.

"I don't know. I asked that as well, but she said that they told her it would be better if she didn't say anything to anyone. But she felt she couldn't not tell me since we were both there."

"Did she say anything else?" Abbey asked.

"Yes. She asked me if I saw the white roofing truck. In all of the initial confusion, she forgot about it until she remembered a couple of days later," John answered. He continued, "I told her that I vaguely remember seeing a vehicle slowly drive by as it passed the alley, but I couldn't recall anything in particular. In any event, she told the FBI agents that it was one of those panel trucks with the word roofing across the side in big letters and some smaller words beneath it, but she couldn't read them."

Dan and Abbey looked at each other briefly. They both knew.

Dan turned to John. "I'll bet that truck no longer has the word roofing on the side. It's a pretty old trick bad guys employ. They'll use a fake sign that can be easily destroyed to throw witnesses and law enforcement off. You can rest assured there was another sign under the one she saw. I'll bet that once they were out of sight, they stopped and pulled the roofing signs off. By now, the truck is another color and says something completely different on the sides and probably the back. And don't worry, the FBI knows this as well."

"That it, John?" Abbey asked.

"Yeah, I think that's it. But let me give it some additional thought, Dan, and I'll call you if I think of something else."

"Fair enough," Dan said, concluding the discussion.

"Wait," Abbey cut in. "John, she said she knew the shooter was a female by the way she ran. Just exactly how *does* a girl run?"

John was quick to see Abbey's trap. "You'll have to ask her. I'm just the messenger here."

Nice, John, Dan thought, *nice answer indeed.* He smiled. So did Brenda. And with that, the four of them finished their meal with much lighter things to talk about.

As John was finishing up paying the bill, Brenda excused herself and went to the ladies' room. Now that they were alone, Dan turned to Abbey. "Is Ellen still in Tel Aviv?"

"As far as I know. We chat via Zoom regularly. Why do you ask?"

"Knowing how close you two are and given her background, I've often felt that she could have easily been the Chaval shooter. I also suspect that our friend, Commander Hines, would love to have a chat with her."

Brenda had returned to the table. "I'm glad that she was stateside when the whole thing went down," Dan said. Brenda clearly heard what Dan was saying, but said nothing. When she sat down, she gently put her hand on Dan's leg and smiled.

EARLY THE NEXT DAY

MediVac had called to say that they would be leaving for Brazil in two days. Ron advised them that he would be taking the bank's plane to Miami so he would meet them at their hangar. Dan wanted Ron to leave immediately so he could visit with the Ackerman Group before rendezvousing with MediVac. Having been in business since 1977, one of their specialties was providing intelligence on terrorists and criminals in South America. Similar to Control Risks out of London, the Ackerman organization was a resource Dan relied upon for executive protection, and, should the need arise, hostage negotiations throughout Latin America. It was their report on Paulo Churrascaria's that alerted Dan to the safety issues, which he had incorporated into his Travel Advisory for the Vice Chairman.

While Dan and Ron's administrative assistants finished collaborating on Ron's itinerary, Dan brought Ron up to speed on a number of current issues throughout South America. They decided that Ron would meet face-to-face with the bank's office managers in Sao Paulo, Buenos Aires, and Santiago. And then Argentina and Santiago, Chile. As the travel arrangements were being ironed out, Dan reached out to his network in each city, introducing Ron and making arrangements for them to meet with him personally.

It would be a whirlwind two-week trip, longer if necessary. Ron could see that it was going to be exhausting, but he was up for it. His training as a former Navy Seal and daily workouts kept him in excellent strength and health.

SAO PAULO, BRAZIL

The first order of business was to see that the Vice Chairman made it safely onto the MediVac plane and was enroute to Miami and then San Francisco. Everyone knew that it would be a long and difficult journey home, but his family felt the risk was worth having him home, in a hospital nearby. They were told that his physical therapy would be several days and that he most likely would need a tracheotomy for quite some time, perhaps even permanently.

Meanwhile, Ron met with the Sao Paulo police and was allowed to view the video from behind the bar at Paulo Churrascaria's the night of the incident. Initially, the degree of violence and the suddenness caught Ron by surprise, but he was able to maintain his composure. The video showed that when the Vice Chairman was trying to stand up and move out of the way, he was directly facing the camera. Any viewer could clearly see that the angry customer was intending to strike his combatant by swinging a broken bottle at him, but the VC stood up at that moment and took the full brunt of the swing across his throat. He grabbed his throat, choked, and fell forward.

Ron had seen enough.

At first the police captain was cold towards Ron, believing that this was just another incident of an American tourist being in the wrong place. And now some corporate company man was there to prove that the bar owner was at fault and the police were not guilty of malfeasance. But when Ron explained how his department had given their Vice Chairman a travel advisory and warned him of the danger he might encounter at places like Paulo Churrascaria's, the captain began to drop his guard.

Ron explained how he and Dan were upset that the Vice Chairman deliberately went against their advice and, "speaking off the record," felt the executive should be fired for not following Corporate Security's travel advisory. He then quickly added if he were ever quoted, he would deny saying anything. The captain smiled and knew they were like-minded. He invited Ron to lunch and offered to provide him a copy of the video, which Ron quickly and graciously accepted. By the end of lunch, Ron knew there was nothing more needed for his investigation. The police knew the assailant and had the case covered. The only thing left for Ron was the paperwork; or so he thought.

The next day, Ron met with the security chief at the American Consulate and a member of the Ackerman executive protection team. Over a late dinner, according to Ron's stomach, the three discussed a number of security issues, the professionalism of the local police and their capabilities, and the escalating crime rate in the city. Ron was told that a robbery occurs every five minutes and that there was a widespread feeling of insecurity. Ron shared how one of their junior auditors was recently stabbed to death in Rio when he was trying to stop a mugging. Though Rio wasn't Sao Paulo, it underscored why the general public felt insecure. The other two nodded, indicating they understood Ron's point. The security chief reinforced the fact that overall, the two cities were still considered safe, but there were areas and places that the novice traveler needs to avoid; evidence Ron's Vice Chairman.

As dinner came to a conclusion, each man exchanged business cards and Ron made a point of paying for the drinks and meals. Both Brazilians expressed their gratitude and told Ron if he ever needed anything, he shouldn't hesitate to call. When he returned to his hotel room, he sent an email to Dan, updating him on the Vice Chairman's trip home and detailing his meetings with his dinner companions. He felt as though his trip was starting out strong. Tomorrow, he would be headed to his next city.

CRIME WHEN AND WHERE YOU LEAST EXPECT IT

The next morning, the hotel manager was standing with Ron outside the main entrance, waiting for Ron's car to arrive and take him to the airport. The front of the hotel stood several yards off one of the busier streets. It was already getting crowded with pedestrians hurrying to work. Taxis and buses streamed by like fish in a rushing river. For the hotel manager, it was just another morning of business people and tourists bustling about, minding their affairs.

As they were waiting, the manager pointed ahead and said, "Here comes my wife. We said we were going to meet at the hotel restaurant for a late breakfast, but it looks like she is early." He had no sooner said this when a motor scooter approached from the opposite side and jumped the curb in front of them. Two men were riding it. The driver sped up and as he passed the manager's wife, the man sitting behind the driver reached out and yanked the necklace from around her neck as they sped away.

Surprised, she screamed and fell down from the force of being pulled forward. Ron and the manager were approximately thirty feet away when Ron bolted ahead to see what aid he could render. The manager ran up as well, arriving a few seconds later. A small crowd had gathered, more out of curiosity than concern. Aside from a burn from the chain and a bruised knee, she was okay. Ron held her hand and gently pulled her up. Her husband asked if she wanted to go to the hospital, but she declined.

Soon the small crowd dispersed and the manager began apologizing to Ron, all the while holding his wife's arm tightly. "I'm so embarrassed this happened, but sadly, it is not uncommon. I'm just so happy that you, my dear, are not seriously hurt. Anything could have happened. You could just as easily have been pulled into the street."

"I'm fine, really, I am; more embarrassed than anything else. I'll call our insurance company in the morning. They'll probably want me to go to the police and make out some sort of complaint. But, what can they do? I guess I'll write this up as a valuable lesson to never wear jewelry on a public street."

Ron asked, "Was the necklace expensive?"

"No, not really. It's just that was one of my favorite pieces. But I suppose I can buy another one," she said as she smiled at her husband.

He returned the grin. "Yes, my dear, I suppose so." Then he apologized to Ron again, trying to assure him that these types of incidents are scarier than they are dangerous. For Ron, however, it just reinforced that the streets of any major city are not without crime problems. He thought, *this could have just as easily happened in San Francisco.*

BUENOS AIRES, FLOODING AND CRAZY DRIVING

Ron's plane was, to his surprise, a nineteen-passenger turboprop plane. His seat was in the rear directly above the cargo door on the starboard side. When everyone was seated, the pilot came on the loud speaker and welcomed them. Then he added, "We'll be making one stop in Asunción, Paraguay for refueling. We'll be on the ground less than fifteen to twenty minutes, so I'll ask everyone to remain on the plane and stay in your seat."

True to his word, about ninety minutes into the flight, the pilot brought the small plane down and parked at one end of the runway, parallel to the main terminal with the starboard side facing away from the terminal building. Just as the plane came to a stop, Ron could see the fuel truck arrive and begin pumping fuel.

From his window, he also caught sight of four military-style Jeeps pulling alongside the cargo door. One of the passengers jumped out, ran over to the plane, and lifted the door directly below him. He then disappeared inside while three other men, each dressed in camouflage fatigues, stood near the open door. All four men were wearing bandoliers of bullets across their chest just like the Mexican bandits stereotyped in old Hollywood westerns. These men were not members of any country's established military.

A moment later, the man inside began tossing large duffle bags out, each being caught by one of the others, who, in turn, ran to their respective Jeep and threw them in the rear. Ron counted six bags offloaded and transferred to the Jeeps. This activity took less than ten minutes. They sped away across the airfield and disappeared into a nearby woodlot.

Soon afterwards, the plane was refueled and they were on their way. The pilot made no mention of the Jeeps and their business at the cargo hold. For a moment, Ron thought about asking one of the two flight attendants and then decided to keep quiet. No one else on the plane seemed to notice the activity, or, if they did, they didn't seem to care. And, just as the pilot had announced, they were back in the air within twenty minutes.

Ron was met by Steve Foote, the manager of their Buenos Aires office. "I do hope you had a good flight," Foote said before Ron had a chance to speak. "I'm certainly glad that the latest wave of our convective storms has passed. However, we are expecting a few more before they're over."

"Convective storms. What are those?" Ron had never heard the term before.

"Oh, my mistake. You chaps call them thunderstorms."

They walked up the loading zone, passing several cars without anyone being in them. After passing five of them, Foote stopped. "Here we are. I'll just pop the trunk and we'll give your luggage a toss, then we're off."

As they got in, Ron said, "I'm sorry, and please do not take any offense, but are cars allowed to be parked in a loading zone without anyone around? If I left my car at SFO in a loading zone, it would be ticketed and probably towed before I got back."

Foote gave a hearty laugh. "No, mate, everyone does it. The Policia de la Ciudad are very lenient about things like this. You can't just park your car and hop on a plane thinking it will be still here when you return, but if you're gone for a short while, it's no big deal."

As they exited the airport, Ron noticed that the streets were flooded, the water level just below the doors. Foote kept on driving. "It might get a little deeper as we go into the city, but I think we'll be okay."

Foote was pointing out various sites as they passed by, seemingly oblivious to his speed as water sloshed all around them. The traffic light ahead of them was red. Foote didn't slow down, instead looking both ways as he approached the intersection and continuing through. He looked over at Ron. "Don't worry about the lights, we don't stop for them. If you do, you'll likely be surrounded and they won't go away until you pay them—all of them. Most of the time there are only four, one on each side and front and rear. That's not so bad. But when there are six, seven, or even eight, it's better to just get out of your car and walk away."

Ron was dumbfounded. Foote just smiled and said, "You'll get used to it," as he plowed through the flooded waters. They were going up a slight grade and the water level was dropping fast. "Ah, I think we've made it. It never floods this high. Your hotel is just ahead. Our building is just around the corner."

HOW BUSINESS IS CONDUCTED THE BUENOS AIRES WAY

The next morning, Foote met him in the lobby and took him to a small café just up from the hotel entrance. Even though it was only bangers and eggs, Ron found the food very good. Even the dry, cold toast tasted good with marmalade.

"So, I understand you'll want to see how we do things down here. We don't do it quite like you might expect, but it's legal and it works for us and our customers."

"Okay," Ron responded. "This should prove interesting."

"I know you will want to be talking to your consulate and meeting with the Policia. Will you want to be meeting with Ackerman's man, or I should say woman, as part of your visit?" Foote asked, matter-of-factly.

Ron was caught off guard for a moment. "How is it that you know about the Ackerman Group? Do they work for you regularly?"

"I wouldn't call it regularly, but certainly several times a year."

Ron continued to be intrigued. "What for?"

"Mostly for background information. Buenos Aires seems to be where people trying to avoid being arrested in their home country come and try to set up a new life. That means loans for new businesses, money to buy a house or car. You have to understand, when they arrive, they come empty-handed and many of them have left their bank accounts either with family or just sitting in their home country bank. Often, in those cases, we work to get their money transferred here."

"Isn't that illegal? It certainly is in the U.S., not to mention the bank has policies against such transactions," Ron said.

"See, this is the kind of thing that we routinely do here that is different from the corporate office."

"Do our auditors know about this? What about our folks in International Banking?" Ron asked, incredulous.

"I suppose so. We've never been called on it. But we do have our requirements. No drug money allowed, no organized crime— money laundering, I think you call it, and no embezzled money either."

"That's interesting, but how do you know for sure that none of it is dirty?"

"That's where Ackerman comes in. If we get suspicious about a transaction, we have them investigate. They're really good. If they can't help us for some reason, they always send us to Control Risks. They're really good as well if the money is coming in from Europe or the Middle East. Do you know about Control Risks?

"Yes, they are under contract with us just like Ackerman. You're right, both are very good," Ron responded.

Ron spent the day with various unit heads learning how the operations worked and how they varied from what he was used to at the main office in San Francisco. That evening he had a quiet dinner and leisurely stroll through the area. For his tastes, he found the evening life vibrant and could understand why so many relocated there, despite the high crime rate.

The next morning, Foote took Ron over to the Ackerman office where he met both their local representative and a member of the American Consulate security staff. "Tell me, how is my friend Dan Holmes doing? I haven't talked to him in quite some time. Did he recover from the assassination attempt of his life? I heard it was quite worrisome for a long time afterwards," the Ackerman agent inquired.

"He's doing remarkably well. His former deputy director is as well. It took her much longer, but she's back working for him," Ron said. "I'll tell Dan when I return that you asked about him."

The consulate security officer asked what they were referring to and Ron gave him the Cliff Notes version. "Sounds like a close call. I'm glad he made it. I haven't met Mr. Holmes, but I hear a lot of good things about him. He's legendary around here."

Ron chuckled and said, "You'll need to fill me in later. I'd like to know more about that."

The two men and woman went to lunch and Ron was filled in on the current state of affairs regarding threats, scams, and employee protection. He found it interesting that American employees and their families lived in an area referred to as the American Compound. He asked if he could see it since it was described as a walled neighborhood with armed security at the gates. This was for their protection, given past kidnappings where they were taken as hostages for a ransom demand. The other employees lived wherever they wanted with no restrictions.

Ron made a special note to discuss this with Dan upon his return. In the meantime, he asked, "Do you report employee kidnappings to our home office? I don't recall ever hearing about any of them."

"That's because Ackerman always negotiates their release," Foote answered. "They're very good at this. We generally end up paying a few thousand dollars and they're let go. No one actually gets hurt or killed and we write it off as a cost of doing business."

"So, you don't report it to anyone?"

"Sure, we let International know when it happens and what the demands are and what Ackerman has negotiated as to what we will pay. They approve it, we pay the demand, and the hostages are released," Foote answered again.

"And do you ever report it to the police?" Ron asked.

The three laughed aloud. "The police? No, no, no, they are useless and quite candidly, they don't give a damn. They figure Americans can protect their own. They're too busy with other matters," the Ackerman agent answered.

Ron shook his head in disbelief. "I get it. And Dan isn't in the loop?"

"Sure, he is. When I file a report, it is forwarded to our office in the States and then on to him. Years ago, he was surprised, but when we explained how things work down here, he agreed and it's never come up again. You have to understand as well, the kidnappers don't want trouble. They just want the money, so their demands are always just a couple of grand in U.S. dollars."

"What's to stop them, or their friends and/or family, from returning?" Ron pressed on.

"Well, that's where we come in," the Ackerman agent responded. "Let's just say that as a part of our negotiations, they understand the consequences if they try it again."

"I'm not sure I want to go there," Ron concluded.

The meeting ended about thirty minutes later and Foote drove Ron out to the American Compound. It was as he described, a small, well-manicured neighborhood with American-style homes. It had its own fire department, schools for the kids, a retail center—complete with a large market and a fuel station. Uniformed armed guards were clearly present both inside and around the outer perimeter.

It was time for Ron to catch his plane and Foote drove him to the airport; of course, he never stopped for red lights, he sped the entire way, and was apparently oblivious to any remaining flood waters.

A NICE DAY FOR A SAIL ON THE SAN FRANCISCO BAY

As Ron was navigating his way through South America, John's good friend, Phil, had asked him to go sailing. Phil's wife, a stockbroker, had surprised him with the dream of his life. She worked for one of the larger day-trading firms in San Francisco and had had an exceptional year. Besides earned commissions on each of her clients' transactions, she had received a hundred-thousand-dollar bonus. What better way to spend it than to surprise Phil with a thirty-foot Hanse 315 sailboat? Albeit used—but by one owner only. She didn't quite follow that, but the salesman at the Oakland Marina made it sound like this was something important when it comes to purchasing such a sailboat.

With slip fees, registration, taxes, and inspections, the total cost would still be under one hundred thousand, though barely. But it was an adventure that she loved and she couldn't wait for their thirty-fifth anniversary, just a couple of days away. As for Phil's sailing experience, he was known to be an expert. He had been sailing since he was eighteen, achieving most of his experience sailing with his dad, another recognized expert.

The day had come when John and Abbey had run out of excuses. John always had an interest, but Abbey was not so nautically adventurous. Whenever the topic of sailing came up, she was quick to point out that fish don't live on land and humans don't live in the sea. And that was that; no need for any further discussion. However, knowing how much it meant to John and the fact that both of them got along well with Phil and Nancy, Abbey found the internal fortitude to commit. Commit, that is, so long as she could always see land, the wind wasn't too strong, and there was plenty of Chardonnay on board to keep her courage up.

Phil didn't have the heart to tell her that land was always within sight anywhere in the bay. As for the wind, that was a different matter altogether. Gusts could come out of nowhere at any time and die down just as quickly. That's why an experienced sailor always keeps a couple of blankets on board and rain jackets, even on sunny days. As for the vino, that was not a problem, especially if Nancy was in charge. She was personal friends with the Wente Wines family. This local vineyard had boasted several gold medals over the years. In short, Nancy would take care of Abbey very well.

The foursome met at the Oakland marina shortly before 11 a.m. and were out on the bay by noon. Abbey found the lower cabin more comfortable than she expected. Fearing she would get seasick, she had taken Dramamine just before she and John arrived at the marina. After an hour out, Nancy set out a few snacks and offered Abbey a glass of wine. Phil and John were topside taking in the view and talking golf. Meanwhile, a continent away Ron was headed to Chile.

SANTIAGO

By the time Ron landed in Santiago, it was after midnight. Just as he experienced in Bueno Aires, clearing customs and retrieving his bags felt like it took an eternity. He wasn't sure his driver would still be there, but to his delight, she was there holding a placard with his name. After exchanging greetings, she loaded his bags into her vehicle and started for his hotel nine miles away. The ride was quiet, the hillside dotted with lights. He saw the same along the median strip. After a short while, Ron's curiosity drove him to ask, "What are all the lights along the median strip and the hillsides?"

"That's where people live," the driver responded.

"What? I don't understand."

"It is hard to see at night, but you will see when the sun is up that many families live in tents and makeshift lean-tos. Some use large crates or even cardboard boxes for shelter. Because the hillsides are either too crowded or they are unsafe because the ground slides in the rains, many have their homes in the medians. It's not really safe, especially for the little ones, but they do it anyway."

"But the lights?" Ron asked.

"The government installs electric wires that are strung along the way. Where there is a shanty, you find a light bulb. That's why at night the hillside looks like a fairyland with all of the twinkling lights. But it's not safe. There are a lot of fires."

"And along the median?" Ron continued to ask.

"It's the same thing. Every few miles, you'll see an electric line strung over the highway to the median. They're high enough so the big trucks won't hit them."

Ron was speechless.

FIRE ON BOARD

Meanwhile on board, Nancy joined the men, telling them Abbey was feeling quite drowsy and was sleeping. After thirty minutes,

Phil noticed that smoke was coming up from the lower cabin. He yelled fire and John raced down the stairs to get Abbey. She was sound asleep and the smoke was starting to get stronger. Phil had sent out a mayday alert and Nancy was pulling in the trailing dingy tied to the boat so they could abandon ship if needed.

John couldn't wake Abbey up so he picked her up and started up the stairs, carrying her over his shoulder fireman's style. He soon found this wasn't going to work since the steps were too steep. He yelled for help and Nancy suddenly appeared. They decided to lay Abbey down on the steps and together, John and Nancy would pull her up into the cockpit. The dingy was designed to carry four adults, but that assumed everyone was awake and could sit up.

Phil could actually see flames now starting to engulf the cabin and knew they had to abandon ship right away. He made another mayday call and then Nancy and John climbed into the dingy while Phil pulled Abbey in and laid her on the floor. As he was doing so, Abbey began to wake up, bewildered and frightened.

Nancy, Phil, and John had their lifejackets on and Nancy struggled to get Abbey's on, all the while trying to help her sit up. Phil pushed off just as the flames broke through from down below and black smoke was billowing out. Moments later, John saw a Coast Guard helicopter approaching. It circled around them and then began hovering about twenty to thirty feet above them.

Suddenly two members of the rescue crew jumped out and landed in the water. They quickly swam over to the dingy to determine if anyone was injured. Nancy yelled that Abbey was sick and passing out. One of the rescue crew signaled the chopper and a basket was lowered. The two crew members, John, and Phil all worked quickly to get Abbey in and she was hoisted up to safety. John yelled that he was her husband and asked if he could go along. One of the divers signaled the pilot again and a safety line and harness was dropped. One of the Coast Guard divers assisted John and within moments, he too was airlifted along with one of the rescue sailors. The second crew member crawled into the dingy and asked if Nancy wanted to be taken as well. She declined and said she was staying with Phil, no matter the outcome. The diver waved the chopper off and it flew away.

Within a few minutes, a small Coast Guard Response Boat was on scene. As for the sailboat, it was totally engulfed and began breaking up. With everyone safely on board, the Response Boat stood by until Phil's dream slowly sank below the surface and disappeared.

Abbey was transported to the Kaiser Permanente Oakland Medical Center for observation. John accompanied her and spent the night in her room. Nancy and Phil were taken back to the marina to begin filing an insurance claim. On the way to the marina, Phil asked the skipper if this type of thing was common. He told him that where such fires were historically rare, with the newer electric-powered vessels, these types of incidents were dramatically on the rise, especially the older models. Just as with the battery issues associated with electric autos, the Coast Guard was finding the same to be true in the boating community. Phil would include those remarks in his insurance claim where it asked for the suspected cause of the fire.

SURPRISES IN SANTIAGO

Ron didn't have the best rest, he had too many things on his mind. As a result, he was up early and decided he would eat breakfast in the hotel's restaurant. When the elevator door opened in the lobby, Ron was amazed to see yellow police tape strung from the front desk to the main entrance. As he stepped out, the hotel clerk was standing there and asked if he was going to the parking garage. Ron said no, but others on the elevator said yes, so the clerk asked that they step aside for a moment and he would escort them.

As the small group of hotel guests passed by the front desk, they were guided through a door just on the other side. Ron could see that as each person walked through the door, they were stepping over something. He walked over, curious, only to discover that they were stepping over a man lying on the floor, blocking it from closing. After each guest disappeared into the garage, the clerk came over to Ron and asked if he could be of assistance.

"That man," Ron started, pointing at what appeared to be a dead person. He could see into the garage where there appeared to be several police officers. "What's that all about?"

The clerk explained, "There was a fight in the garage last night. When the night clerk opened the door to see what it was about, he was shot and killed. That's where we found him."

"Okay, but why hasn't his body been removed? There are guests walking over a dead man," Ron said, totally bewildered. "I saw some weird things when I was a Navy Seal, including a lot of dead bodies. But we never just let them lie where people had to step over them."

"I'm sorry, sir. But the police remove the body only when they are completely finished with the investigation. So, people must step over him to get to their car. It's sad, but they do it respectfully," the clerk explained.

Knowing there was nothing that he could do, Ron decided to get breakfast away from the hotel and then walk over to the bank's office. His visit to the offices in Santiago were tame in comparison to what he had encountered in his previous two country visits. His plans did hit a snag when he was told that he would not be able to meet with the head of the Investigation Police of Chile as originally scheduled. No reason was given; however, the meeting was moved ahead by three days and Ron was able to complete his business.

ALL ISN'T AS EXPECTED

He found the branch manager, a Canadian, to be friendly and interested in what Ron might have to offer by way of additional security, both in terms of physical assets and wire transfers. Ron discovered that Santiago was running their wire transfers on the bank's old software and breaches were common. Thus far, there were no major frauds, but Ron could see that it was a ticking time bomb waiting to happen. He called Dan that evening who agreed that there was a substantial risk. He would personally find out what the reasons were for Santiago's situation.

Since Ron was communicating daily with Dan, mostly by text

or email, there was little to update aside from the branch manager's attitude towards his employees. "When we were at lunch today," Ron said, "the manager leaned in and commented how good it was to see a friendly 'Yank.'"

"I understand, Ron. Do you think his prejudice is known to his employees?" Dan asked.

"I'm not sure. Of the employees that I have met, all of them seem to be friendly and professional. There's no doubt our manager runs a proverbial tight ship, but the employees seem to respect him. They do find that he has a couple of language quirks because of his Canadian background, but I think his Spanish is excellent since I speak it as well. It's more his accent, I believe."

"Well, keep me posted and I'll have someone from Wire Transfer get hustling. Things should move right along since they know I'll be monitoring their progress from here on out."

It didn't take Ron long to befriend the vault teller, who invited him to her house. She said that she was hosting a party and several of the bank's employees would be there. She thought this might be an opportunity for Ron to meet some of them and hear what they had to say about the operation and their manager. He agreed to go and said nothing to the manager.

Ron was picked up at the hotel and driven to her house. Even though he had no idea exactly where he was, his GPS was working and he could see that he was less than five miles from his hotel. As the evening progressed, he was approached by three of the employees. In Spanish, one asked what the bank's policy was regarding employees being kidnapped. Would they pay a ransom, and how much?

From his experience as a former Navy Seal, Ron's antenna for danger went up. Right now, the conversation was hypothetical at most. Were they planning something and was that something going to involve Ron? He thought for a moment and, in Spanish, he smiled and answered, "I'm not quite sure what you have in mind, but to answer your questions, first, the bank pays a ransom. Secondly, it's a scale set by our insurance carrier. Every employee, all the way to the top, has a value, and it's not very much ... and it's not negotiable. If the bank were to pay over and above what the insurance value is, the company would drop the bank as an insured and no other insurance company would pick them up. Do you follow me?"

One of them asked, in a menacing voice, "And exactly what is this scale? How much am I worth?"

"You're not going to like the answer," Ron answered. "We pay two thousands of your pesos, or about two U.S. dollars. Our bank president is worth less than ten thousand dollars and I'm worth about fifteen hundred. We're pretty cheap."

"You're shitting me."

Ron pulled out his phone and offered it to him saying, still speaking in Spanish, "It's about six o'clock San Francisco time. My boss is probably still in the office. Call him and tell him you've kidnapped me. He won't even hesitate for a moment. He'll tell you I'm worth about fifteen hundred and ask where you want the drop. If I'm not released immediately and call him to verify it, he'll be on the phone to the Carabineros. And since the branch manager knows where I am, it won't be long before your sorry asses will be behind bars."

"Fuck!" the man yelled loudly. "Fuck, fuck, fuck!"

Ron stood there, straight-faced. "I see my welcome has run out. I think I'll call the hotel and have someone pick me up. Don't worry, my GPS is showing the address here."

"What are you going to tell our manager tomorrow?"

Returning back to English, Ron said, "I'm not sure. I'll have to think about that. After all, there's no foul here. We were just discussing bank policies. Right?" Ron smiled, turned, and went up the stairs. As he passed the host, he said, "Nice party but I have to go. Maybe I'll see you tomorrow. In any event, I'm going to wait for my ride at the curb. Goodnight."

The next morning Ron reported what happened to him the previous night to the branch manager. The manager advised that the employees would be "taken care of" and thanked Ron. They said their goodbyes, and the manager thanked Ron for the information.

Ron's flight home would be long, just over eight hours to Miami and then another six hours to San Francisco. His first leg would be first class, so he knew he could sleep as comfortably as one can on a commercial flight. Through the bank's travel department, he would be flying the second leg on their corporate jet. As with many trips, the days seem to fly by in retrospect, but he was tired and changing times zones didn't help matters either. Regardless, by the end of the day, he was home and glad to be reunited with his fiancée. He spent his first day back sleeping, eating, and sitting poolside at his condo. By the following day, he was ready to return to 2nd National.

BACK IN SAN FRANCISCO

Ron's first meeting was with Dan. After recapping each office location, something that took less than twenty minutes since Ron had been briefing Dan all along, Ron asked what Dan had decided about the curious episode at the Asunción airport.

"We're going to sit tight for about a week. That way, no one will suspect that the tip came directly from you. Then I'll call our contacts and notify them as to what you saw. I've already had Unit 33 do a deep dive and it appears that the duffel bags most likely contained a variety of weapons. My assumption is that what you saw was a small group of radicals stockpiling guns and ammo.

"As you no doubt discovered, Paraguay is not without its problems both economically and politically, but overall, it's one of the more stable governments in the hemisphere. They're not afraid to crack down and when they do, it is hard and decisive. So, I think the national police will find what you observed of high interest, unless they are already aware. Either way, we'll pass along your observations as an anonymous tip."

Ron shook his head. He was satisfied.

ABBEY RETURNS HOME

Abbey returned home the following day. The doctors were initially concerned that complications might set in since her immune system had been severely impacted when she was shot a few years

127

earlier. But she proved to them that there was no reason for concern, even though she appreciated their caution and told them. By the time she got home, the twins and her father were waiting. They had been to the hospital the day before to make sure she was okay. Their feelings were still on edge from the time she was shot and nearly lost her life. This latest episode, for them, was all too real.

When she walked through the door, she could smell her favorites: matzo ball soup, kugel, and potato latkes. What surprised her more was to find out that John was the chef.

As they sat down to eat, Abbey smiled and commented, "Can you believe? A former Catholic priest turned Jewish cook. But I guess that it's okay considering Jesus was a Jew. What do you think was his favorite dish?"

They all laughed aloud.

"I'm not sure about his choice of food," John said, "but given that he could turn barrels of water into the best wine, he must have been some vintner!"

HOME AT LAST FOR RON

That evening several of Ron's people took him to dinner. They were anxious to hear about everything. As one of them said, "We want to hear it all. Blow by blow." Ron thought that was a little dramatic, but smiled and took it in his stride. When he recounted what happened along the way, his staff members found it incredible but believable.

That wasn't the reaction he had from his fiancée, however. She thought he might be embellishing the story, something that wasn't beyond him. Nevertheless, Ron wasn't put off. It was true. He had lived it and was glad he did. When he finished telling her everything, he kicked back in his favorite easy chair and thought silently for a few minutes. Then said, "Honey, if I ever fall dead in a doorway, will you have them move me? I don't want people stepping on me when I'm dead. I get a lot of that now and I'm alive."

She laughed loudly.

Commander Hines called Dan with the news. There seemed to

be a sense of peace, at least for now, on the streets. Dan told him the news was a mixed blessing, commenting that the true tragedy of war is so many innocent lives have to be lost before there is peace. As Dan contemplated, he recalled what his brother had said when they served side by side in war-torn Iraq: "Whether on the classic battlefield or in the streets at home, war is war irrespective of where it is … and it is just as deadly."

THE SHAW RESORT MURDERS

SATURDAY JUST BEFORE NOON

For the past twenty-five years, Brenda and Dan Holmes would drive up to Mendocino for long weekends away from everyone and, for them, everything. Even though it was less than a hundred and fifty miles between their place in Tiburon, California and the Albion River just south of Mendocino, the actual drive time was more than three hours. The roads were extremely winding in several places once you left Cloverdale, but the pace really slowed from the giant redwoods through Navarro State Park. It was Mother Nature's way of slowing you down and begging you to enjoy a little R&R along the journey.

They always stayed in the same condo high on the bluff, directly overlooking the Pacific's crashing waves on the rocks far below, even at low tide. There were twenty-eight condos in all, but only four were perched high at the cliff's edge, literally ten feet from being on solid ground and the precipice. The others were nestled far below. Of the four cliff condos, each had their own unique view and feel. Condo #3 was the Holmes' respite while in residence. Theirs was the crème de la crème that Shaw Resort had to offer.

Their secret passion was the oversized Jacuzzi in the bay window that looked directly out over the ocean where the evening sunsets were always awe-inspiring. Or, as Brenda often remarked, "It's as though God is gently pushing the sun down on another beautiful day." Dan would smile in agreement and toast the passing event.

This trip was going to be extra special since they had accumulated enough Frequent Stay Points that not only was this three-day weekend comped, but they had been given two additional nights. It was the resort's way of recognizing their fortieth anniversary. They arrived just before noon on Friday. As Dan drove in, he and Brenda saw numerous sheriff vehicles parked in front of the first condo. There was a paramedic unit as well, accompanied by the whirring of a rescue helicopter as it hovered close to the cliff in front of the condo.

"This doesn't look good," Dan commented as they exited their vehicle and walked into the front office. There they were met by Cliff Travis, the resort manager. "I'm so sorry that this has had to happen on your very special stay with us, Mr. and Mrs. Holmes," Travis began immediately, clearly shaken. "We tried to call you but with the spotty cell service up here, we were unable to reach you."

"What's happened?" Brenda asked, cutting Travis short.

"About two hours ago, our cleaning lady went to take care of the unit. She told me she found the front door was locked as usual. So, she knocked and no one answered. She thought they were gone. When she went in, she saw the bay window was smashed as though something had been thrown through it. Then she saw Mr. Martson lying on the kitchen floor, bleeding badly from the head. We called the sheriff's office. I rushed up to see things for myself. By the time I came out, the sheriff and paramedics were already arriving."

"Hopefully you didn't touch anything," Dan responded.

"No sir. The sheriff asked me the same thing. We didn't touch anything."

"Can I assume that we can still check in, though?" Brenda asked, showing her concern that Travis might suggest otherwise.

"Oh, most certainly, you can check in. I'm just concerned that this matter will ruin your anniversary getaway."

Dan could see Brenda wanted to stay. "Well, I must admit that it may appear somewhat callous, but we have really been looking forward to this getaway. Brenda, let's get checked in and go up to the condo. If we feel it's weird, I'm sure Mr. Travis will understand and accommodate us one way or another."

"Perhaps you would enjoy another unit much farther away from everything up there," Travis offered.

"That's your call, honey," Dan answered, looking directly at his wife.

"I have an idea. Why don't we go down to the resort's lounge, pour ourselves a glass of wine, and discuss it?" Brenda suggested.

"Sounds like a hell of a plan," Dan said.

"And put your drinks on my account," Travis joined in, trying to ease the tension.

SHERIFF BRETT WILMINGTON

Just as the Holmeses turned to leave, heriff Wilmington came through the office door. Mr. Travis asked what he wanted.

"My God, that was fast!" the sheriff exclaimed, seeing Dan.

"Brett," Dan acknowledged, smiling.

"I can't believe it. My office just got this call a little more than an hour ago. Were you in the area or something?"

"Hold on, Brett. First, this is my wife, Brenda. And secondly, we just arrived for a five-day extended anniversary getaway," Dan explained.

"Well, talk about coincidences. I take it you know something about why my people are here?"

"Very little. Mr. Travis was just filling us in. And what do you mean by 'coincidence'?"

"I mean, she's one of yours. Excuse me, she was one of yours. According to the ID in her purse, she worked for your bank."

"I'm confused, Brett, can you give me a little background?"

"Sure, I apologize for getting ahead of myself. There were two people killed in the first condo up on the ridge. We found a male bludgeoned in the back of the head in the condo and a woman on the rocks below."

"What's her name?" Dan asked.

"I'll do you one better. Here is her ID. I was just coming down here to see how the couple registered since the guy she was with has a different name." The sheriff laid two plastic evidence bags down on the counter, one containing a woman's driver's license and a bank ID card attached to a lanyard, along with two credit cards. The other bag contained the man's driver's license.

Dan carefully examined the two bags. "I've never seen the gentleman, nor do I recognize his name. As for the woman, I think I recognize her. Perhaps Brenda does."

Dan laid the bag flat on the front desk and Brenda leaned in to get a close look. "That's Maggie, Dan. She works in your Wire Transfer department. She's one of my friends from the book club."

Sherrif Wilmington picked up the bag containing the woman's identification. "Her ID and driver's license says Maria Nelson, not Maggie."

"That's because Maggie is her nickname. Everybody calls her Maggie. We have for years."

"What about credit cards? What name is on those?" Dan inquired.

"Funny you should ask," the sheriff answered. "There are two; one has the last name of Nelson, like her bank ID, and the other ID is listed as Margret Hudson." He then went on, "My guess is that Hudson is a maiden name. And, of course, Maggie is short for Margret."

"Brett, for what it is worth, I don't mind going up and conducting a visual ID on her based on how she is known at the bank."

"Thanks, Dan, but I'm not actually sure where she is. I mean, we have located her body. She was at the bottom of the cliff, washed up among some rocks. I'm just not sure if she is still down there or if we have transported her to the morgue. Let me check."

Sheriff Brett pulled his phone out and dialed a number. "I'm calling the on-scene commander."

A moment later, "Quick question, is the female victim still on scene? Okay. Sure, I've got a second. What do you have?" He listened for a few brief moments. "That's interesting. Well, sounds like you people are going to be there a while. Check in with me when you have anything else. Great. Bye."

Then to Dan, "She's on her way. Perhaps you can stop by the morgue in the morning if it isn't too inconvenient, what with this being your anniversary trip and all."

"I think I can slip away for an hour or so tomorrow, or I'm sure someone from the bank's security department will be here by then and they can do a positive ID," Dan responded, deliberately not looking at Brenda.

Cliff Travis asked to be pardoned and slipped away. As he was going, the sheriff called out, "Thanks and sorry for the intrusion. Someone will be down shortly to take the cleaning lady's statement—and yours. Wait, before you go, how did they register?"

"They registered under the name Howard Martson."

"Thanks." With that, the resort manager turned and left.

"Well, you might find this interesting. It appears that the woman was tossed out the window, but the window was shot out first."

"What?" Brenda exclaimed.

"Yeah, my folks tell me that the man was hit from behind with some type of blunt instrument and bled out. Meanwhile, she was apparently tied up and then the big window overlooking the cliff was shot out with several shotgun blasts. The casings are still on the floor. Then she was thrown out, still bound and gagged."

"Clearly, she was the primary target and someone was sending a message," Dan concluded.

"Well, listen, I want to get back up there. It was nice meeting you, Brenda. I hope we meet again under better circumstances," the sheriff said.

TO STAY OR LEAVE

As the sheriff made his way back up to the crime scene, Dan and Brenda walked over to the resort's lounge. They each ordered a drink and it was Brenda who approached the topic of staying or leaving first. "I've seen that look a million times before, Dan. If we stay, your mind will be working the murders continuously. You'll be on the phone a thousand times, calling someone to do one thing or another."

"I can't say you're wrong, honey. However, if I'm ever really going to retire, I suppose this is one of the best tests to see if I can let it go and turn it over to others," Dan suggested.

Brenda just stared and, after a moment, smiled. "Right, Dan. Would you like to place a small wager?"

Dan laughed. "Well, there's a part of me that wants to stay. After all, she was—as the sheriff says—one of ours."

"Sure, I can understand that, but your mind will be on it the entire time. It's weird, you know, being with a guy, not her husband. It's just so out of character. After all, she was a rather devout Eastern Orthodox Christian. I just don't see her cheating," Brenda noted.

"You raise a really good point about her character. Regardless of whether we decide to stay or not, I want to call Abbey right away. Unit 33 folks could prove to be very valuable."

As their drinks arrived, Brenda said, "I'm going to defer to you. I think you know my feelings. But right now, I realize that I'm pretty hungry and it's our favorite restaurant up here. What do say? Are you hungry?"

"You know, I am, come to think of it. Let's grab these drinks and see if they have a table available. Hopefully, our table."

Dan was referring to the table in front of the fireplace, which they always reserved whether it was burning or not. To their delight, it was free.

After they were seated, Dan resumed the conversation. "Let me strike a compromise of sorts. We stay tonight, but away from our condo. I call Abbey and get her started, and check with Brett in the morning to see if there is any update. That will give us a better idea about staying the rest of the time or not."

"Okay, but you know Abbey is going to send someone up here, which means you will have to meet with whomever."

"No doubt, but I'll ask Brett, as a favor, if he will allow one of his detectives to share info and answer any questions her person asks."

"And then of course, you'll pump her analyst," Brenda answered.

"No. Here's what I suggest. I'll meet with Abbey's analyst first, brief him or her on what we know, and then turn them loose, so to speak. I won't interfere. I promise. Besides, it's too early. With these types of investigations, you have to let them get a little steam going before you jump in," Dan responded.

After a nice lunch, they found Cliff Travis in the office and informed them of their revised plans. He said he understood and offered them a place overlooking the restaurant's garden. Once they were settled in, much to Brenda's surprise, Dan actually pulled a book from his luggage and went out on the deck.

Abbey suggested she send someone up the following morning since the drive was about four hours and the analyst would not get much information until the next day. Dan agreed and said he would call the sheriff in the morning and ask for the favor. Since he and the sheriff went back a long way and always got along, Dan didn't think this would be a problem.

THE FOLLOWING MORNING

The crime scene tape was still up around the entire condo and the Sheriff's Crime Scene Unit was back and still processing when Abbey, to the surprise of Dan and Brenda, arrived with her analyst. "I can't believe it," Brenda exclaimed as Abbey got out of the car.

"Well, I wanted to make sure what the dynamic was up here with us as outsiders, not even being law enforcement. Please don't take that the wrong way, Dan. But you know, these things can be tricky at the outset. By the way, this is Steve. Steve, this is Dan and Brenda. Dan is my fiancé's brother and, of course, Brenda is Dan's wife." The three of them shook hands.

"It's nice to meet you, Steve," Brenda said. "And don't let Dan give you a hard time. If he does, you can rat him out to me."

"Thanks. Good to know," Steve responded. He continued the

teasing. "I'm beginning to understand where my boss here gets her hard attitude from."

"Boy, have you got that wrong," Dan shot back. "Who do you think taught me?" They all laughed and Brenda affectionately put her arm around Abbey's shoulder.

"Abbey, tell me you're not going to be all business up here. I don't want to interfere, but can we at least get a cup of coffee or tea before you leave?" Brenda pressed.

"I don't see that as a problem. I would love to."

"Then I'll leave the three of you," Brenda said and, looking at Steve, added, "It was nice to meet you. And good luck." With that, she turned and headed for the deck.

The three of them went in and sat down in the living area. Abbey began. She explained that the night before, she had received a call from Ron Tyson, Dan's replacement at the bank, wanting to know what she knew before calling Dan. They talked briefly and Ron deferred to Abbey and Unit 33 at the outset since initially this didn't seem to be a bank-related incident. Still, they concurred that, given the female victim's position at the bank, his department's involvement was only a matter of time.

They also agreed that Unit 33, with their superior resources, might have better answers for some of the current outstanding questions. Meanwhile, Ron would advise the appropriate bank personnel, beginning with the bank president, his boss. Ron would simply say that she was a victim of what appeared to be some type of home invasion. He would then see if she had family that would need to be notified and pass it along to the sheriff.

Steve began, "We started working last night when Abbey got your call, Mr. Holmes."

Dan cut in with a smile. "I see you've been taking lessons from Abbey. It took her years, despite my pleading, to stop calling me Mr. Holmes. Actually, it took my brother proposing that threw her for a loop. She didn't know how to address me. Was I Mr. Holmes? Sir? Dan? She really struggled with that," he finished teasing with a short laugh. Then added, "Call me Dan."

"Okay, sir, I mean Dan." Abbey smiled as Steve continued. "Howard Martson is not the man's real name. He's actually been a CIA handler for nearly thirty years and Martson was his alias. For the past several years, he served as a handler for those in protective custody from Russia's Foreign Intelligence Service, or the SVR. So, what we can initially surmise is that they came here for some reason, most likely related to running from the SVR.

"Here's where it gets interesting," Steve continued. "Now remember all of this is very preliminary and things could change, as the saying goes, on a dime. Maggie Hudson, as she liked to be called, claimed that Hudson was her maiden name. Her husband is Brian Nelson, and has been for fifteen years. Nelson is the last name on Maggie Hudson's employee name tag. No problem thus far, female employees commonly go by maiden names these days even when their official ID has their husband's surname."

"But why is her first name different?" Abbey asked. "Typically, you would think that the name she goes by daily would be the same as on her ID badge. But it's not; she goes by Maggie and the badge name is Maria. The name Maggie could simply be a nickname, so no big deal. Right?"

Dan interrupted, "Maggie was a nickname she went by. I know, because she was a friend of my wife."

Steve responded, "Well, that clears that up. Thanks." He continued, "For what it is worth, we believe her driver's license is a fake. A mighty good fake, but fake nonetheless."

Dan just shook his head. "That is strange. The sheriff has taken the actual license into evidence. You should share this with his team when you see them. What about her husband? Where is he in all of this? Did he know Maggie was up here?"

It was Abbey who responded, "Right now we're not really sure, but one thing is for certain. Brian Nelson is dead. A single shot to the front of the head in front of his house."

"And I take it that the sheriff's office up here is aware of this?" Dan asked.

"Dan, we're not sure since we got the call about him while

enroute here. We'll certainly ask him when we meet up in a little while," Abbey answered.

"Where was home for the Nelsons?" Dan asked.

"San Francisco, near Coit Tower," Steve said. "Can I ask why?"

"I'm not sure right now, but I felt it should be asked," Dan said.

DAN'S RECAP

"Let me make sure I have the facts straight," Dan recapped.

#1:   Brian Nelson, the husband of the female victim up here was killed yesterday in San Francisco.

#2:   A CIA handler was found dead yesterday morning in Condo #1, here at the resort. His name is Howard Martson, only that was an alias. He was the one that registered the couple with the resort manager, Cliff Travis, at the front desk sometime the day before that.

#3:   The female victim was known as Maggie Hudson at 2nd National Bank, and by her friends and some members of the local Greek Orthodox community. However, her bank ID says her name is Maria Nelson. Her driver's license also identifies her as Maria Nelson. But the license is fake.

Abbey and Steve nodded.

"You're actually telling us a couple of things we're hearing for the first time," Abbey said, "but we can quickly verify them."

As Abbey and Steve headed to the murder scene, Dan joined Brenda on the deck. "Well?" she asked. "What do you think?"

"It's all very interesting. I haven't shared any of this yet, but here's my take. The Nelsons came to San Francisco as part of a witness protection program. My experience tells me they were hiding from the Russian spy group, SVR. If so, my assumption is that they must've have seen something or knew someone, or at one time they were Russian agents defecting to the U.S. Or, it could be something else, but it's sure as shit tied to the SVR. Shooting out a bay window and throwing a live body out is their classic signature. They were sending a message.

"As for Martson, he was her handler and was in the wrong place at the wrong time. These Russians are hardcore. They take no prisoners; they leave no witnesses. Her husband was probably tied to her through marriage. He probably knew things, but I don't think he was their primary target, otherwise he'd have had an equally horrific death to also serve as a message. As it was, a single shot in the head, no real message there.

"As for her calling herself Maggie Hudson, there's a story there. And, I'm sure by the time Unit 33 is done, we'll have the definitive answer. When we have it, it won't be any big thing. More like her grandmother's name or an aunt or somebody at their church; maybe even a name from a favorite novel. It's never anything romantic or cloaked in some spy thriller thing. As you know, I've always been a strong believer in Occam's Razor—the simpler the answer, the more likely it is the right answer."

THIRTY YEARS AGO

Thirty years ago, 12-year-old Arlin Volkof and her brothers would spend endless hours exploring the widespread tunnel system that ran beneath the streets of Moscow. For them, it was their playground. Even then the network was so complex at various points, the subterranean rivers would commonly be controlled by sluices redirecting the water into different channels.

Having a sense of balance was the first requirement the children discovered given the uneven brick and stone surfaces, especially those underfoot. One minute a person could be walking along and the next confront a steep shaft filled with rushing water. At other times, the sides would suddenly bank sharply upwards but be hidden because they would be underwater.

Little did Arlin know that such familiarity would prove the difference between life and death in the years ahead.

It was not uncommon for the children to wander near, or on occasion actually find themselves in a large underground military complex. Arlin would learn later that this was originally built during the Cold War and was supposedly insulated enough to allow the government to operate in the event of a nuclear attack. For now, however, these were children having fun and they were not seen as a national security threat.

TEN YEARS LATER

Arlin had recently completed her studies at Moscow State University in Materials Science and was looking forward to her advanced studies program. She would be specializing in the effects of polymers in Kevlar and Teflon used in bulletproof vests as enhanced protection from specialized high-power weapons. During her summer internship, her university professor invited her to join an elite research team to study the effects of these new vests on human subjects. He assured her that protesting had demonstrated that no harm would come to any of the volunteers.

She accepted his offer and after nearly a month in the laboratory she, along with several other students, was directed to meet the professor at a bench just outside the Kremlin's southeast wall. In front of the bench was a manhole cover. Having spent much of her childhood playing in the tunnels around Moscow, she readily recognized this type of manhole. When her professor arrived, he advised the group that they would be part of a highly classified program. He invited anyone who was uncertain about being a part of the program to leave. Three students voiced their concerns and left.

The others, including Arlin, stayed, and the manhole cover was pulled back, revealing a steep a rusty ladder that descended deep below. There were no lights so each student was issued a flashlight and instructed to strap it on their wrist. When everyone had gathered below, six in all, they were led under the Kremlin to a large room that Arlin estimated to be at least fifty feet under the surface.

Each student was issued one of the experimental vests and led into another chamber and then a second large room. When they entered, they saw that there were ten individuals lined up against a wall. Each were wearing prison fatigues and had their hands bound behind them. Their heads were covered with a hood. The students were directed to sit down on the opposite wall behind three soldiers, each holding what appeared to be a high-powered machine gun. On command, the soldiers discharged their weapons and each prisoner dropped immediately.

The students were horrified by what they saw, gasping and screaming. The professor calmly instructed them to remain seated. "You have just witnessed the power of these weapons. You should not feel bad; each prisoner was sentenced to die anyway in a matter of weeks. We will now bring in another group, but this time each prisoner will be wearing one of our currently issued vests. Whereas they will look like the ones you are wearing, they are what our brave soldiers are currently wearing on the battlefield and will probably not withstand the impact of these advanced weapons."

As the students remained seated, exchanging glances between themselves, it was clear to everyone that this was not only surreal, but their own lives were in danger. For the professor, this was nothing more than a research exercise. The second group was ushered in and forced to stand in front of the group, lying dead on the floor. A hood was placed over their heads and on command, the soldiers opened fire. Whereas each person fell, some were clearly still alive. One soldier stepped up and systematically executed each of them.

Realizing what awaited the students, Arlin jumped up, screaming loudly, "Get up, we're next!" She and the others rushed the surprised soldiers, knocking them to the ground. One of the male students kicked a soldier in the head and grabbed his weapon. He turned on the professor only to see that the professor had a gun aimed directly his head. He pulled the trigger as chaos broke out. Arlin ran towards the entrance, yelling over her shoulder, "Follow me out, I know the way!" When she found herself back in the tunnel, she turned to look back. No one else was there.

It was then that she heard the quick blasts from the machine guns. She knew the soldiers and professor were not aiming at the students' vests. She took off running as fast as she could. Even though it had been several years since she had last explored the tunnels, she was amazed at how much she remembered. The university was little more than three miles away. It would be longer for her since she knew she would have to use a mix of tunnels to confuse anyone who might be running after her. And then, of course, there were the tracking dogs.

As she made her way to the university where she had parked her car and taken the subway to the earlier Kremlin rendezvous point, her mind was racing. It dawned on her that many of the tunnel entrances would have soldiers and police waiting for her to ascend the ladder to make her escape. Having never discussed her childhood adventures in the tunnels with anyone, she felt confident that if she stayed in the tunnels with waist-high waters, she could fool the dogs once they lost her scent.

Something inside her made her decide that she needed to abandon her car. By the time she returned there, the professor would most certainly have sent out the alarm and her vehicle would be under surveillance. It was then she had a bold idea. No one would expect that she would turn around and make her way back to the Kremlin, only skirting the complex by a couple of blocks. She could make her way directly up a steep incline to the U.S. Embassy. Once there, she would plead asylum for what she had just witnessed. It was a long shot, but it seemed to be her only option.

Without further hesitation, she turned and started running. She could see where she and her fellow students had entered earlier. Just before this turn there was a small sluice that bore to the right. She remembered it was always wet and slimy, something as a kid she and her brothers loved because it turned an otherwise dangerous descent into a fun slide. She sat down on the edge and pushed off. Just as she did, she could hear voices and activity behind her, then the barking. Whether it was the police or the military, she knew they had K-9 units.

The sluice dropped her down about another twenty feet. At the bottom she stood up, turned and looked up. She could make out activity, but she wasn't sure what it was. She took off running as fast and as hard as possible then slowed, remembering that the tunnels ahead had always had waist-high water. She could not afford to slip and fall since the speed and volume was strong enough to knock a person down and carry them turbulently away. She saw this happen once to her brother and thought he was killed. He wasn't, but injured quite badly, leaving him with a limp for the rest of his life.

This tunnel stretch was approximately fifty yards long, fairly dark, and cold. Being wet didn't help either. Nonetheless she waded to the end where there was a t-shaped intersection. The right side was lower and carried the water away. The left was slightly higher, which meant it would be dry. She jumped up and began making her way slowly up what was now at least forty feet above, hopefully to the embassy.

As she walked carefully along, she smiled, remembering this section from her childhood days. It was not only the right path, but also her journey was nearing an end. About five minutes later, the tunnel passed by a set of wider than usual steps. If memory served her right, these steps led to a door that opened into a small tobacco shop directly across the street from the main embassy entrance.

She climbed the stairs only to find the door locked. *What now?* she asked herself. If she knocked, would it be friend or foe? Or, she could turn around, go back down, and figure out a new plan. She gently knocked. A moment later, she heard the lock turn and the door opened.

An elderly woman stared at her.

Arlin stared back.

The old woman smiled. "Hurry, hurry, they are looking for you. The soldiers were just here with their dogs. They say you are an enemy of the state, a traitor that must be caught." She took Arlin by the arm and led her into a small back room.

"You are trying to make it across the street to the U.S. Embassy. Right?"

Arlin nodded, silent.

"You stay here. I'm going to walk over there and tell the Marines that you are here and you need their help. Don't worry, I have done this many times before. They trust me. One of the Marines will come back with me and make sure you get across the street safely."

The woman left and within a matter of minutes, she returned with a U.S. Marine. Arlin barely had time to thank and hug the woman before the Marine coaxed her to the front door.

Suddenly there was a burst of gunfire from above. The Marine stopped and returned the fire. The Marine at the gate did the same thing. There was another burst from the roof of the embassy. Then all fell quiet. Arlin was laying on the ground, bleeding from the hip.

TWO HOURS LATER

Arlin sat up in a bed in the embassy's infirmary when a uniformed Marine Major came in along with a woman in a smartly dressed business suit. The Major began. "I take it you've had quite the morning. Our ambassador actually saw the shootout in the main quad earlier. You apparently made quite an impression," he teased.

"I'm sorry for causing so much trouble," Arlin responded.

"Hi," the woman began, "I am Agent Susan Mosher. I work with those desiring asylum. It's nice to meet you."

"Hi. You look more like a business executive."

"Well, thank you, but I assure you, I'm just an agent. Do you mind answering some questions so we can determine whether or not we can help?"

"No, I don't mind."

"First, your English is quite good. Where did you learn it?"

"My parents. My father was actually Canadian. I also took English classes at school."

"Well, why don't you start at the beginning."

Arlin went through her background and how she and the other students were invited to test out the new Kevlar and Teflon vests. She explained how their professor invited them to a demonstration earlier that day. When they arrived at the designated rendezvous spot, they were given a vest to wear and escorted into one of the subterranean tunnels under the Kremlin. She then briefly explained how she and her brothers used to play in the tunnels as children. As a result, she came to know her way around them.

She began to detail how the prisoners were positioned in the large room much like prisoners facing a firing squad. The first group wore no protective vests and the soldiers carried "very powerful automatic guns." She stopped momentarily when she noticed how the major's attention level piqued when she used the term.

A second group was then escorted in and they were told these prisoners were wearing conventional bulletproof vests. She described how she and the other students sat there stunned—horrified. They then witnessed the soldiers shoot each of them. A soldier executed those who didn't die immediately by shooting them directly in the head.

By this time, she understood that she and the other students were going to be the next group. She screamed to warn the others and the students rushed the soldiers and the professor. As she described, it was pure chaos. She tried to get the students to follow her out of the room and into the tunnel. No one followed and all she could hear were more rapid-fire gunshots.

Knowing her way around the tunnels, she originally thought about running back to where her car was parked at the university. As she was making her way there, she decided that they could well be waiting for her so she opted instead to take her chances at the embassy and plead asylum. When she finished, the Major asked, "Is this new type of vest the one that you wore here?"

"Yes, but I don't know how effective it is against the type of weapons the soldiers were using."

"Well, let me ask. Once you are feeling better, can I show you some photographs of weapons that we know the Russian military is developing? If you don't see a photo looking like the one the soldiers were using, that's okay, but we would like to test your vest against them. Okay?"

The embassy agent cut in, "You are a very brave young woman, not to mention gutsy."

"Thank you, but can you keep me safe?"

"If you continue to be as cooperative and informative as you have been so far, that should not be a problem. My government is indebted to you," the agent concluded.

Within six months, Arlin was secreted out of Moscow under the State Department's protective witness program and assigned a new identity, home, and personal background. Her handler out of the San Francisco office would be Howard Martson. Going forward, she would be known as Margaret Lynn Belltower, the daughter of Hungarian immigrants who arrived in the U.S. fifteen years earlier. She was a member of the Greek Orthodox Church. She was an only child and her parents had both died in a tragic boating accident several years ago. She attended schools in the San Francisco Bay Area and graduated from the University of California in Berkeley.

Eventually she would meet Brian Nelson, fall in love, and they would marry. They never did have children even though both of them wanted them. Now, going by the name of Maria Nelson, she worked in the Oakland School District for a couple of years. One spring day, while sitting outside a coffee shop on Martin Luther King Boulevard, she heard a young couple talking quietly at the table next to hers. After years of living in hiding, she had grown accustomed to not trusting her environment.

Maria could not make out most of what she was hearing but she distinctly heard the female mention someone by the name of Arlin and then added that she had defected to the U.S. a number of years ago. It was as though the woman was briefing the male. Arlin was shaken. The female said that her sources suggested that she was going by a first name of Maria and worked somewhere in the Bay Area as a school teacher. She added, "So, it's only a matter of time before we've scanned the school district records, thus limiting our search." For Maria, this was getting too close for her comfort.

Maria left as discreetly as possible. She went into a hair salon right around the corner and asked that her hair be cut short and dyed a musty blonde. As the stylist began working, Maria called her handler, Howard Martson. They agreed to meet later that night. It was then that they decided she would take ill and request a medical leave for a few weeks. This would allow her and her husband time to decide where they wanted to relocate.

In discussing their options, it was her husband who offered, "I hear that often the best place to hide is in plain sight. Why don't we simply move over to San Francisco, you change your name, and get a job downtown? I'm sure Martson will do whatever is needed to get you a great job, maybe even in the financial district; you've always liked that area. And, we could change the names on the title of our home and turn it into a rental. Given today's housing market, the rent we collect in Oakland can go a long way towards paying a mortgage in San Francisco."

Maria liked the idea and called Martson. "Even though I'll officially be Maria Nelson, can I use a nickname, sort of like an alias?" She thought that overtime people would come to know her as Maggie and not pay too much attention to Maria Nelson. If it were possible, she wanted to use the name Maggie. "I've liked the name ever since I discovered an author by that name. She writes really good books about real people. She's become my kind of a heroine."

Martson moved fast and the Nelsons were relocated across the bay into a small bungalow near Coit Tower. Before her "sick leave" was up, Maria, now going by the name of Maggie, was offered a position at 2nd National Bank as an international commercial wire transfer operator. It was an entry-level position, but she was told advancement was steady if she proved herself. As for her employment record as a school teacher in Oakland, it was totally expunged. To the educational world, Maria Nelson with her date of birth never worked in Oakland, nor lived there. It never ceased to amaze Brian, as he once satirically confided to his wife, "You got to love all of this spy crap. The underworld can create a person or make them go away with a couple of keystrokes and no one is the wiser."

SATURDAY MORNING

Dan and Brenda decided that they would leave Saturday and Abbey would join them, leaving her car available for Steve. That afternoon he would meet Detective Casey and compare notes.

Steve began. "I appreciate you taking the time to meet with me. I've heard some good things about you. You are very experienced."

It was clear to both of them that the police detective could possibly have the same number of years of experience as Steve had been alive.

"No problem. The sheriff and your boss have quite a history together. He told me that you might have information that we can discuss. If it is as he said, you can probably help me shave a great deal of time off my having to run around to gather it."

As Steve listened, he quickly assessed that even though the detective was following his boss's orders, he didn't have a great deal of confidence in Steve. Detective Casey suddenly asked, "Just how old are you and how long have you been doing whatever it is you do?"

Arrogant prick, Steve thought, all the while smiling. "Well, this is actually my first job since graduating a couple of years ago with a Master's Degree in IT."

"No offense, but you got to be kidding," Casey shot back. "Oh, what the fuck. What have you got, and what do you want?"

"Well, perhaps I can build a little credibility by you asking me what questions you have and seeing if I can answer them."

"Fair enough. We need to identify these guys. What have you got?

"I don't have names just yet, but we're fairly certain they are members of the Russian spy group, SVR. The woman was most likely trying to outrun them and the man that was with her was her CIA handler."

"That's interesting. What's your source?"

"That will come. First I need to clear that with my people."

"Just know, I can get a warrant anytime."

"I understand."

"What else?"

"Are you aware that her husband has been killed at their home?"

"I just found out earlier this morning. Anything else?"

"Not for now, but we're working on identifying the vehicle they used and where they went after leaving here."

"Are you saying that you may be able to determine where they went?"

"And where they might be right now," Steve calmly responded.

"You got to be shitting me. Are you fucking real? I'll believe it when I see it," Casey snapped indignantly. He continued, "As with all of these types of cases, I need a motive, I need to show intent, and most importantly, opportunity and means. That's what a California prosecutor needs to get a conviction."

"Okay," Steve came back. "If I'm right about the SVR, I think you have everything. We have motive: paid assassins. We have intent: to shut her up. And clearly, by the evidence at the scene, we have opportunity."

"Say we go with your spy theory, we still have to prove all of it," Casey pushed back, trying to save some face. "And then, we can't rule out that this could be something else entirely. Maybe this is an ugly domestic dispute gone really bad. She was having an affair with this guy up here. Her husband finds out and has someone follow them here and kill them."

"You really don't believe that, do you?" Steve asked. As soon as he asked, he regretted it. Casey just glared and Steve knew he had a lot of rehabilitating to do to save this already tenuous relationship. "I'm sorry, I didn't mean for it to come out that way. Yes, what you say is possible, but who killed the husband?"

Ignoring Steve's apology and question about the husband, Casey said, "You gotta watch what you say and when you say it and to whom you say it. Or you won't make it in the real world of police investigation."

Steve silently asked himself, *Whoever said I wanted to be cop, let alone a dick?*

"I've been told that they have been hunting her for years. And, the SVR never stops hunting someone down until they are dead. Her husband was most likely killed by the same people, earlier in the day." Steve looked at the detective with a poker face.

"Well, I'm hungry. Who is taking whom to lunch? I want to know more about how you are going to find them."

"Okay, I'll pop for it."

"Good answer, kid."

At lunch, Steve wanted to set the record straight. "Listen, again, I'm sorry for popping off like I did. I'm just an analyst. I'm not bragging, but my team and I are really good at what we do. Who knows, when we're done, the sheriff may promote you. You can have all of the credit. As for me, my job is to simply provide provable intelligence. It will be up to you as to what you may want to do with it. Just know there are others already working this case. You can either trust me and stay ahead of the curve or come in second and watch others get the credit and promotions. As I say, it's up to you."

"You're either the biggest bullshitter I've ever run into or you're one hundred percent legit. You better be the latter."

"Do you think Mr. Holmes would set himself up with your sheriff on a case like this? You need to understand one thing. You may be old enough to be my father, but my organization has been around a long time, probably longer than you've been a police officer. And I have full access to everything they have. So, I don't need bullshit like so many detectives rely on; my job is simple. Get you the info to make a provable case, and have some fun doing it."

"Alright, you've sold the shoes, so to speak. How do we proceed?"

"We begin by me feeding you info not unlike one of your confidential informants. You do have confidential informants, I think you call them CIs, correct?"

"Here in pot heaven for the past one hundred plus years? You got to be kidding yourself. We live and sometimes die by what they tell us."

"Well, let's hope no one gets themselves killed unless they really screw up and then it's probably best. Not unlike Darwin's theory of the survival of the fittest," Steve responded.

"God, kid, that was cold."

"Yeah. I suppose so. But it's better someone else ends up the cold one and not me. It's this way, you have your CIs and I have my computer and colleagues at Unit 33."

"Perhaps before we go any further, you can tell me a little more about this Unit 33. Like, is it legal?"

"Not only legal, but we're fully funded by several legal entities. If you need more, and I understand that you may want that, that is something you'll have to discuss with my boss."

"Well, tell me how it works. Or, is it something you can't talk about?"

"There was a time until fairly recently that we were a deep ops organization known by only a select number of people, and these were people who truly had to prove they had such a need. Now we're a little more open and many organizations are discreetly employing our services."

"Can I hire out your services, or perhaps the county?"

"We're expensive," Steve answered.

"We've got some pretty well-known wineries. Perhaps that might sweeten the pot," Casey feebly tried to counter.

"Mr. Holmes might accept a bottle or two as a sign of gratitude, but we are a cash-only business, in U.S. currency. We don't even take checks or money orders. And no, we don't accept Bitcoin or any other virtual cash medium. Nope, my boss accepts cash only. She's kind of funny about that as well."

"Can we get serious and see what takes us where?" Detective Casey asked, trying to get their investigative interview back on track and keep it there.

"Great idea. Let me ask a couple of critical questions. When did our victims sign in and did they go directly to the condo?" Steve asked.

"The victims arrived and signed in at 5:43 p.m. on Thursday, according to the front desk camera. They then left and drove straight to their condo, 1."

"And, do any of the security cameras pick up what time the assailants arrived? What kind of vehicle was it?" Steve pressed on.

"At 6:15 p.m. the resort cameras picked up an intermediate size SUV, medium-gray in color, coming onto the property and driving straight up the cliff to the parking area in front of the four condos. Since it was getting dark, you can't really make out the type and model; perhaps a Toyota, a Kia, a Honda. Upon arrival, they actually parked next to the victims' car. I think this was to make our victims believe that they were just another guest arriving. They both exited the vehicle at the same time. One appears to go along the side of the condo where there are no windows and then out of sight. He was carrying a shotgun. My guess is he went to the back. The other was carrying what appears to be some sort of bedding and went directly to the front door. You can barely hear it, but he yells something like, 'Extra bedding,' or perhaps 'Extra blankets.'

"There's some hesitation. Then he puts the bundle on the front porch about three or four feet away from the door and walks away without turning back. He gets in the driver's side of the vehicle. Meanwhile, you can see the second assailant coming back to the side, just standing there waiting. When the door opens, the assailant rushes the door and pushes his way in. You can see he is still brandishing a shotgun. Then the first assailant jumps out of the SUV and races into the condo."

"Any license plate?"

"Nothing definitive. We have a partial as it is leaving the property. We got that from the camera on the porch of the guest house. It exited and headed north."

"I wonder if we're dealing with a rental or a stolen vehicle? The good news is we should be able to identify it, vehicle make, year, color and where it is right now," the Unit 33 analyst said matter-of-factly.

"Wait a moment," Casey insisted. "You're telling me again that based on what I told you about the SUV, you can not only positively identify the car used in this double murder, but also where it is right now?"

"Yeah. Based on everything I've heard, these guys are one of two types of assassins. The first kind is full of themselves—a sort of hubris thing. They have plans for moving on once they get their next assignment. When they do, then and only then will they ditch the car. Probably some chop shop sort of thing. Our window for identifying the vehicle is fairly limited; maybe a week at most since these guys don't hang around long, but that should give us sufficient time. We might get lucky and identify it and its location in a matter of hours.

"The second kind are paranoid, but they want to make a quick buck. Greed trumps fear. So, they'll try to actually pawn it off or sell it on one of those internet sites. You know, Facebook Market, Amazon, Craigslist, those sorts of places. They believe no one can tie the vehicle to the crime so they run around trying to sell it to the highest bidder.

"These are the dumb shits but so much more fun to bust. You should see the look on their face when the police arrive. 'Hey, how did you find us? You can't prove a thing.' Then we show them the photos and a lot of them just stand there and wet themselves. It's actually pretty cool," Steve said, showing his youth and lack of actual street experience.

"Alright, but how? How do you do it? And, I'll only believe it when I see it," Casey responded, a true doubting Thomas.

"I don't blame you. When I was first hired and the others told me, I thought it was some sort of bullshit initiation rite of passage thing. But, it's not only real, we've used it a number of times, all with amazing success.

"We'll be using two methodologies. The first is our vehicle-mapping AI software. As for the how, I can only tell you it's all about our latest version of AI. You can't believe how much artificial intelligence has progressed in this area of criminal investigations. This much I can share. The concept is based on the same principles as facial recognition. We take an area, separate it into grids, type in select criteria. The more specific distinguishing characteristics— you know, dents, scratches, signage, tires and/or wheel covers, etc.—the greater the likelihood we can scan a grid quickly. So, one of the first things I'll do is send copies of all of the camera videos taken during the suspected timeframe. My team is really good narrowing down the likely suspect vehicles to three or four.

"Since we can do multiple grids at the same time, we'll start by going north. That's their last known direction. It should not be that difficult since we know the day and time. It's largely a two-lane highway so we don't have to try and pick it out among hundreds. If they happen to turn around on us, we'll grid Sacramento and North Bay. Then, if we need to, the South Bay, San Jose, and the Peninsula. We'll start with those metro areas and if we strike out, we'll go smaller until we have a hit."

"But what makes you so sure they're still in the area? Why are they not headed for LA, or north into Oregon, and wherever else?"

"Right now, we don't. They may be. But our satellite imaging along with another of our AI software capabilities should confirm if they stayed north or at some point turned around and went south, or headed east. One thing's for sure—they didn't go west," Steve joked. "Today there are so many imaging satellites up there, it's difficult to say what each one's capabilities are. Trust me when I say that there's some pretty weird Star Wars stuff going on, and not just on our side."

"Alright, I agree some pretty weird but exciting stuff. But what happens if they took the car back to their place, put it in a garage, closed and locked the door?" Casey asked.

"They might, but nine out of ten times, they don't. If they do, we can track them right to the garage. It may be a day at most, but we'll be there. Besides, you may want them to think they've outsmarted us. But as soon as they back out of the garage, we'll laser-tag them. They won't even know it. Wherever they go, we'll be just above them, albeit at sixty thousand feet. It's to our advantage that they will still need transportation until they're given instructions for their next assignment. One thing I've already learned is that being an assassin for hire is kind of boring. You sit around a lot waiting for the phone to ring. That of course is in our favor."

"Okay, I think I'm getting some understanding, but since they have a good head start on us, how do we ever catch them, unless they stop?"

"Great question. First, our AI vehicle recognition program is lightning fast. This means we can cover where they have been and project where they are headed. If they stop to spend a night at a motel or stop to eat, we can ping them. With enough pings, our algorithms can create a projected route. It goes something like this: we ask our computers where a vehicle with identifiers one through ten has been over the past so many hours and where is it now or where it is headed. In a matter of seconds, if there is such a vehicle, we know where it's been and where it is."

Casey was, as the saying goes, blown away. "Brilliant, absolutely brilliant. How many satellites do you have?"

"Actually, we don't own any. We piggyback on over fourteen thousand of them from all over the world."

"Fourteen thousand. You have agreements with the owners of more than fourteen thousand satellites?" the detective asked.

Steve looked at him without saying a word.

"Forget that I asked that. I'll just accept it and we can move on," Casey said. He was starting to submit to the data nerd.

"So," Steve continued, "we focus on heading north out of the resort. This becomes our ground zero. They have a two-to-three-day head start. Further, let's assume that they switched vehicles shortly after leaving the resort. We'll be able to see all of this. We now have a new suspect vehicle and allow it to take us where it goes."

Casey interrupted, "Aren't you just talking about some sort of glorified GPS?"

"Well, there is certainly a global positioning feature in our system. However, we can go anywhere in the world, enter a vehicle description, and ask where it is. Besides, we're only talking about two of its features. Trust me, there is a great deal more."

"It seems to me that you might be sharing some of your organization's intellectual property and I dare say you have some sort of nondisclosure agreement."

"As for the NDA, I have one. However, what I've described is readily available to our customers, so there is little I'm sharing with you that's confidential. And let's not forget, you are going to have to have a working knowledge of this when you are called to testify in open court. Can I tell you something on a personal note?"

"You haven't held back thus far. Sure. What is it?" Casey responded.

"If you were to just drop your attitude about geeks and nerds, you might find that you have a powerful ally, not only now, but also down the road."

Steve waited for Casey to comment. The police detective remained quiet.

"So let me get this straight," Steve continued. "We got your intent—professional killers hired to kill, leave no witnesses. We have your motive—killing is what professional assassins do. Third, you want opportunity. They drove to the condo unimpeded. Isn't that opportunity? And finally, the means. I'd say a combination of surprise, brute force and, of course, the shotgun."

"You make a strong case, but we still have a lot of work to do, such as the weapon that killed her CIA handler as well as establishing the link between her husband's death and the murders up here. And let's assume it was the SVR, how much help will we get from the CIA or will this just become another one of those spy versus spy tit-for-tat things?" Casey complained.

"The politics of this is way above my pay grade. That's something for your sheriff, Mr. Holmes, and the police investigating her husband's death to strategize about. All I can tell you is that we can lead you directly to the assassins. We can give you a complete profile of them and a direct link to the SVR, thus their culpability," Steve concluded.

"Well, I must admit that if you can find the vehicle and the assassins, you have my awe and admiration. But how can we use what you will give us? I can't go the prosecutor and say we're using apparently top-secret spy photos."

"Detective, that's your characterization. I never said anything about top-secret spy photos. For that matter, they may have come from a weather satellite that just happened to be passing over at the time," the analyst said with a devilish grin. "Don't worry about our source right now. When the time comes, an anonymous source will lead you to where you need to go and what to do. You know, something like a conversation overheard in a bar, or you got lucky and were able to identify the car from traffic cams, etc. We'll know the exact strategy when we nail down the car. Mr. Holmes is actually quite good when it comes to explaining how things like a missing car was found. Who am I to question a highly regarded and respected investigator like him?" Steve chuckled.

"Okay," Casey said. "We have each other's phone numbers. If either of us needs something, we can call one another. You take care of the car and I'll start looking into firming up if it was the SVR that actually put the hit out on them and who exactly our assassins are."

"Works for me. Wait, there's still a big question hanging out there," Steve began. "How did they know that the victims were going to be up here and when? It seems strange that they drove in with bedding to serve as a decoy. Was there actual spare bedding? I think my boss was told that neither the resort manager, nor the cleaning lady, touched anything and you didn't say anything about the assassins coming out carrying anything."

"I guess it might be my turn to play detective. I've been wondering about the bedding myself. Originally, I thought that someone up here at the resort had to be in on the murders. The bedding made me think it had to be an inside job. When I checked with the resort manager, he told me the victims called the morning of their arrival asking if he had a vacancy. They apologized for the short notice, but he told them they were in luck because the resort literally reopened the four cliff condos after undergoing renovations. And with the exception of the Holmes, the others were available. They said great and the man gave his credit card to hold the room.

"So, that seemed to put a hole in the theory of this being an inside job because the room request came in randomly and with little notice. That left me with two possibilities. First, the cleaning lady did touch something. In fact, she took something; e.g., the sheets. Maybe it was just out of habit that she picked them up when she left since they were in a pile on the floor and looked like they were used. Or, she wanted them for herself. Either way, we should have her on camera when she exited the condo. I've got her lined up for an interview Monday afternoon. If she took them, we'll find out," explained Casey.

Casey then continued, "That begs the question, why did the assailants arrive with them? If they are from the resort inventory, then we're back to the inside theory, which really doesn't make sense. The more I thought about it, the answer came. These are professional hit men. They were going to use the sheets to carry the victims away. Hotel sheets make great tarps, so to speak, and they don't have the hassle of tearing them off a bed. They were hoping that someone would open the door. If not, they would simply leave the bedding behind as though it was something the resort commonly did.

"But who carries sheets around with them? Answer: someone who is transient. Someone staying at a hotel or motel waiting for an assignment. That person gets a call and has to leave right then and there. They know what they'll need when they get there. And if they are going to need some sort of tarp, how perfect but to take the sheets from the hotel you're staying at. My bet is that when we find them, they'll have some identifier as to where they came from. And it will not be from the resort here," Detective Casey concluded.

"I like the way you think, Detective. Any theories about how the assassins knew where the victims were and when they would arrive?" the analyst inquired.

"For now, it remains part of the mystery."

"Care for a friendly unsolicited suggestion?" Steve asked.

"Sure."

"Search the woman's house. The answers to both of your questions are there."

"Interesting, though I think I would have eventually come to the same conclusion."

"Perhaps, but your case is only hours old and you have so much. Remember, we aren't just a group of pretty faces. We have our methods."

"You're scaring me, kid."

"If I can be of any additional help in nailing your theories down, don't hesitate to call."

The two men shook hands and parted. After Casey left, Steve

called Dan to ask if Abbey was still around and whether he, Dan, wanted to be debriefed. "Actually, they're still here and were just about to leave. What's your status? Do you want me to ask them to hold off until you arrive back here at our condo?"

"I'm not far, I should be there in less than fifteen minutes. Why don't you ask Abbey what she wants because I'm ready to head back."

Dan left for a couple of minutes. When he came back on, he said, "We'll be waiting here for you. See you soon."

MARTSON AND HUDSON MAKE A RUN FOR IT

It was Wednesday evening when Maggie's phone rang. She was at home with her husband and they were just putting dinner on the table. The caller ID showed that it was her handler, Howard Martson. "Hello, Howard, what's up?" Maggie asked. And then teased, "If you are calling to beg a place at my dinner table, you know you're always welcome."

"I think I'll pass, as much as it pains me. But we need to talk ASAP. Something has come up. Can I come over?"

"Absolutely, should I have coffee or tea on?"

"Either will do, but I suspect you may want something a little stronger."

"Shit. Are we moving again?"

"I'll be there in thirty minutes or less," Martson answered.

It was just thirty minutes later when the doorbell rang. Brian opened the door and hustled Martson in, looking up and down the street to see if there was any indication that he might have been followed. A bottle of good vodka was sitting on the coffee table alongside three glasses.

"I see that you have set the table for me. What are you two drinking?" he teased.

The Nelsons glared. Clearly, they were in no mood.

"I'll get right to the point. We believe you have been compromised."

Both Maggie and Brian knew what this meant and what lay ahead.

"I think you know Alexa Morozov?"

"Yes, we are in the same church choir. We sing every Sunday and practice several times during the week. Why?"

"She has a mother who is an SVR agent. Has she ever discussed her mother with you?" Martson asked.

"Not that I recall. Are you suggesting that Alexa is SVR?" Maggie stammered.

"No, but she has a picture of the two of you on her mantle. When her mother came for a visit, she saw the photo and commented that you look like a little girl she knew years ago, Arlin Volkof, but she thought Arlin died years ago trying to run from the military.

"Alexa's mother was very clever. She took a photo of Alexa standing at the mantle and over her right shoulder is the picture of the two of you. She sent her photo to her SVR contact who, in turn, sent it on to the SVR headquarters in Moscow. They ran a facial scan of you and wonder of wonders, you popped right up as the wanted Arlin Volkof who defected, taking with you not only intel on some their experiments but also one of the protective jackets that was classified.

"When the Defense Department received the jacket, they reverse-engineered it and produced our version. Our soldiers are essentially wearing the vest you turned over to protect our men and women against their high-end close-range weapon systems. As you have known all along, the SVR will not give up hunting you until they have you," Martson summarized.

"What's the plan?" Brian asked.

"We're going to move you fast because they'll be moving fast. I say we move you into a hotel for tonight and leave early tomorrow. You call in sick. Say nothing to anyone. The same goes for you, Maggie. When it's safe, we'll arrange for your stuff to join you. We'll take two agency cars, one to serve as a decoy. Neither agency car will have a GPS for them to track us. Our mobile phones operate on a highly secured network, so our people can use them to track us. When we are traveling, I need to have both of your phones off. Understand?"

"There's only one problem," Brian said. "I'm sponsoring a young boy at a juvenile court hearing tomorrow. If I don't show, they'll throw the boy into juvie hall. It'll crush him. I can't just up and leave him. He's a great kid; I'm literally his last bridge. I'm not running from him to save my own hide."

"Fuck, you're not making this easy. I understand though. Quite admirable. Let me think about it and talk to some people. I'll leave you two to pack. Remember, one medium-size bag apiece. We'll backfill with anything else you'll need once we get to wherever we're going. I suspect Seattle. Maybe even Canada; we have a new mutual aid program."

With that, Howard left.

"I have a crazy idea," Brian began. "We go to the hotel tonight and you leave with Martson. I'll go to the hearing. I'm sure Martson can arrange security so I should be fine. After the hearing, if I'm successful, the court may be open to putting him in my care. He might enjoy the change of pace and see that there are those who care for him. We won't be able to leave the country, but do you think the SVR would be looking for a threesome instead of just the two of us?"

Maggie responded, "I understand where you are coming from, but a life on the run is no way for a juvenile to live. You know, asking questions all the time. And if the SVR does capture him, it will not be nice. Let's rethink this once we're settled again."

THE NEXT MORNING

Maggie and Martson headed out of San Francisco without breakfast knowing they would pick something up along the way. Two agents arrived and stayed with Brian until it was time to escort Brian to his hearing.

"For God's sake, this looks like one of those mobster movies that you see on TV!" Brian exclaimed as the agents all but pushed him into their vehicle. Once inside he observed, "This only underscores what Oscar Wilde expressed, 'Life imitates art far more than art imitates life.' Let's hope this an example of that. If it is, we'll all get out of this with our lives."

And then he asked one of the agents, "Do you know if your agency would be open to me adopting my ward if I'm successful today?"

"It's not that we would oppose your idea, Mr. Nelson. Just know we can't turn him over to you right away. If you're successful in your petition today, we'll take him into protective custody and keep him safe until he is properly vetted. Then we can transfer him to wherever you folks settle. In the meantime, you cannot say anything to the kid. Once we know his fate this afternoon, we can move him quickly and safely. If you say anything in advance and your petition is denied, it will likely crush him. Trust me. If all goes well, he'll be in a safehouse this afternoon," the agent explained.

"Great," Brian said. "When is breakfast? I know it sounds weird, but I'm really hungry."

"Now. Let's hit something with a drive thru. It's public and probably the safest."

THURSDAY, 10:30 A.M.

By mid-morning, Brian's hearing was over. The judge ruled that his request was reasonable, all things considered, and that she would take it under advisement. In the meantime, the juvenile was remanded to a home for wayward youths. Sentencing would not be for another three weeks. Everyone was devasted, but no one talked about the plan to move him into protective custody.

"Listen, don't lose hope," one of the agents encouraged. "We've run into this before. By the end of the day, I suspect the judge will be getting calls from our State Department. If she refuses to cooperate, the State Department and Homeland Security may forcibly intervene, explain the situation, and take the youth. In short, they'll slam the door of justice in her face if they need to. For now, let's wait a few days and then we'll step in."

"I want to talk to my ward one last time and make all the necessary assurances that despite what it may seem, he has people working, powerful people, on his side. Who knows, maybe he'll be released soon. Trust me, that is all I will say. But I want him to hear it from me."

NOON

It was noon by the time Brian and the agents were on their way to his hotel to gather his belongings and then it was time to head north. On the way, Brian said, "Wait. We have to stop by my house. I need my meds. I'm a diabetic and need my insulin."

The first agent said, "Okay, but you stay in the car when we arrive and one of us will retrieve them. Where are they kept?"

"In the medicine cabinet above my sink in the master bedroom."

"If you have a key to the front door, I'll dash in and get them," the passenger agent said.

Brian gave him the key and when they arrived at his house, the agent made a dash to the front door, unlocked it, and stepped in. A few minutes later, the driver agent received a text. "My partner says your meds are not in the cabinet."

Brian loudly responded, "They got to be." He instinctively jumped out of the car and ran towards the front door. The agent in the car jumped out. The agent inside yelled, "Get back to the car." Brian turned to go back to the vehicle. Before he could, a shot rang out. A mailman pushing a mail cart had stopped, extracted a rifle, and discharged one shot, hitting Brian in the head. He dropped immediately. The two agents drew their weapons. As the one in the house exited, he was firing his Glock. Similarly, the agent behind the car emptied his weapon at the assassin. He fell over his mailcart lifeless.

5:30 P.M.

Once they passed Cloverdale, they discovered that the cell service was spotty, at best. More often than not, there was nothing. Even though this was bothersome, they kept heading north, assuming that once at their destination full service would be available. They were soon to discover they were wrong.

From the moment they pulled away from the hotel, Maggie and Howard were being tracked by a drone over twenty thousand feet in the air. It followed them North to Cloverdale where they stopped for lunch and then westbound on Route 128. Traffic over the Golden Gate Bridge slowed them and then again construction near Santa Rosa took its toll on their travel time.

A short time later, Highway One was just ahead and they saw an advertisement for the Shaw Resort. They pulled in and, after a few minutes, Martson emerged, waving a set of keys and smiling. It was Condo 1 at the top of the property overlooking the ocean with an uninterrupted view.

A few minutes later, Maggie dropped the keys on the coffee table, unlocked the door to the deck, and sat down on one of the deckchairs. Meanwhile, Howard had brought the bags in and was getting them settled in the two bedrooms.

About ten minutes later, unexpectedly, there was a knock at the front door. Maggie came in, closing and locking the deck door behind her. By this time, Howard was cautiously looking through the front door peephole. He yelled at the man standing on the front porch with what looked like a bundle of fresh bedding.

The man yelled back, "Sorry to disturb you but we don't think one of the beds is made-up. If you would like, I'll just leave them here on the stoop and you can get them when you want. Okay?"

"Yes, that would be fine," Howard Martson yelled back through the locked door. Neither of the occupants were aware that there was a second person standing nearby at the edge of the front porch.

"Howard, who was that?"

"He said he was from housekeeping and that he had a set of fresh sheets for one of the beds. He seemed legit. Besides, he left."

"Okay, but give it a minute or two before you step out to retrieve them. You never know," Maggie insisted.

A few minutes passed. Martson looked out the front windows and the front door peephole. The coast was clear. He slowly opened the door, checking both ways before stepping out. He picked up the bedding and turned to go back in. As he did, the SVR assassin rushed from the side of the condo and pushed Howard back inside with the butt of a large shotgun. Moments later, the second one rushed in. Maggie's screams went unanswered.

The second one pushed her into a kitchen chair and quickly tied her arms behind her back, aiming a revolver at her. "Just sit there, don't make me have to tie you down." The other one ordered Martson to pull out the other kitchen chair. He then went behind him. With all his force, the assassin slammed the back of his head with the butt of the shotgun. Blood gushed out. Martson gurgled a few times and his head fell forward. And then the assassin said coldly, "I never liked you, you SOB. It's taken me years to track you down, you haughty prick."

He blasted two rounds into the bay window overlooking the ocean. The casings ejected onto the floor. The assassin reloaded and pumped two more into the window. What was largely left of the window fell to the floor along with the last two shell casings.

The second assassin looked directly into Maggie's eyes. "I must admit, you've been one of the tougher ones to track down. How long? Twenty years? But, people like you know that this is how it's likely to end. You should just relax. You fought a good fight, but it's over."

The shotgun-touting one barked, "You always give the same stupid speech. I don't know which you enjoy more, the actual kill or your little speech. Sometimes I think you do this just to get your jollies. Let's stop with the talking. You grab the left side, I'll grab the right." That's when they realized that Maggie had passed out. "On three we lift, go to the window, and throw her out." As though they were throwing out a bundle of dirty laundry, they executed the exercise flawlessly.

MONDAY MORNING

Detective Casey's phone rang just as he was walking into the sheriff's office. He answered. "What do ya got?"

"Good morning to you too, Detective," Steve responded. "I hope you had a pleasant night, but it won't compare to the morning you are going to have."

"Fuck! Don't tell me you know where they are."

"I can probably tell you what they are ordering for breakfast," Steve teased back. He was loving this.

"So, you're telling me that your 1970s technology has won the day?" Casey shot back, laughing out loud.

"Tsk, tsk, tsk. It was my 1960s technology, just a little upgraded," It was Steve's turn to laugh.

"Okay, okay. Where are they?"

"They're at a small diner on the north end of Fort Bragg on Highway One. The place is called Granny's and you better move quickly because they will not be there long. And, not to be a smart 'I-told-you-so,' but from the number of cars in the lot, we estimate there may be twenty people inside. If you want, we can stay on the line until your people are on scene," Steve offered sincerely.

"Hold on, Steve, I'm going to put you on a three-way conversation. The two of us and our dispatch center." On the second ring, Steve heard, "Good morning, Detective, this is Operator 24."

"Hi, I have a third party on the line. He's going to give you a vehicle description along with descriptions of two men. These guys should be considered armed and dangerous. They are currently eating breakfast at Granny's in Fort Bragg. While he's giving you the descriptions and any other info you need, I'll be turning this over to the Watch Commander. Do not release any of this info until you hear directly from the W.C. Got it?"

"Yes, sir," Operator 24 responded. "We'll be standing by."

Then Casey said, "Steve. Fantastic job. Give us the vehicle description. My partner and I are headed there now."

"It's a 2020 Silver Gray Kia Sorento with California tags JP 974."

"Will you be at this number?"

"Sure."

"Great. I can't say exactly when, but I'll get back to you shortly. Operator, this is Steve, treat him like gold. My partner and I are out the door and enroute. I'll call the W.C. now."

Stave said to Operator 24, "Bear with me a moment." And then to his own console operator, "Can you put a hold on that satellite for another hour?"

"No sir, but not to worry, we have another two satellites coming into position if we need them."

"Great. Push the feed to my monitor. Do you know if Abbey is in yet?"

"She should be here in about ten minutes. I'll ask her to stop by your desk."

"Thanks," he said, "Sorry about that, Operator 24, I'm all yours. What do you need?"

"Right now, we have the vehicle and location. All that's left is a description of the perps."

Just as Steve finished giving the sheriff's operator descriptions of the two men, Abbey walked in and quietly sat down across the desk from Steve. When he finished, he smiled. "We have our first win of the week."

"That's what I understand, let's see what you have."

Steve picked up his phone, dialed a number. "Can you put our Cron File #846 on my Monitor #2?"

A Cron File was Unit 33's designation for a Chronological File of Events associated with one of their cases. Within a matter of seconds, Steve's monitor began displaying a video of the Sorento leaving the resort's parking lot, turning left, and speeding away. It was date- and time-stamped indicating Thursday, 18:04 hours. From there, Steve fast-forwarded the vehicle's movement until Monday morning at 07:40.

"I'm not sure what the police plan is, but you can see several units arriving and taking up positions around Granny's."

"Let's hope it doesn't end in any more bloodshed." The two of them watched as events unfolded live. As Steve continued to monitor, Abbey stepped out and called Dan.

"Good morning, Dan. The Shaw Resort murders are drawing to a conclusion. The police have surrounded a diner on the north side of Fort Bragg."

Just then Steve yelled, "Abbey you got to see this. The patrons are running out the front while the kitchen staff is running out the rear."

Abbey said to Dan, "Let me call you right back, things are beginning to break."

Abbey and Steve watched as two men ran to the Sorento. They began to exit when police vehicles, marked and unmarked, seemed to come out of nowhere and everywhere. It was only a matter of minutes before they were being pulled out of the vehicle, forced to lay on the ground, with handcuffs applied. "Nice start to a work week indeed, Steve. Great job. Let your team know I'm proud of their efforts," Abbey said, smiling broadly.

That evening, the local news reported on the arrests. Detective Casey, the lead investigator, would only say that it was an ongoing investigation. However, he wanted to thank the members of his department for their hard work and, using his words, "good old-fashioned police work" to bring about a speedy arrest.

Steve is still waiting for Detective Casey's call.

THREE PAINTINGS, FIVE MURDERS

MONDAY, 4 P.M.

When your phone rings at this time of day and caller ID says it's a police commander, you know this is not a social call. Nor is it likely to be a solicitation for the police officer's ball. But for Dan Holmes, receiving this type of call was not unusual. Besides, he and Commander Hines were long-standing friends and over the years had exchanged favors.

"It's the commander," Dan said to his wife, Brenda."

"Were you expecting his call?"

"No, but I guess we'll know shortly what this is all about." With that, Dan answered his phone.

"I'm sorry to bother you at home Dan, but I am hoping you can help me."

"No problem. How can I help?"

"Do you have any of your father's old case notes?"

"Yes. They're far from complete. However, some cases that really flummoxed him are here."

"Can you check to see if he left behind a case dealing with a series of homicides and some missing paintings by three master artists? They all involve the O'Reilly family."

"I don't have to look. I know he left several files on that case. He was actually working on it when he passed away. I do know, however, that his official case notes are with you guys. What I have are his abbreviated notes; you know, like a couple of words on separate sheets of papers, some photos, and hand-drawn floor plans. There's a list of the family vault's contents. I know because I was just looking them over as Brenda and I were sorting what to save and what to throw out. This stuff is in a box labeled 'Open Cases.'"

"This is great. Can I send one of my detectives over to retrieve them?"

"Sure, no problem. But why? You've tweaked my curiosity."

"A few days ago, we found a body hanging in the shower of an apartment. At first we thought it was a suicide, but it didn't take long for our CSI folks to find a rather unusual note. It suggests that this was not your typical suicide, more like a plea for help since the victim thought people were after him. He still had his wallet in his back pocket and the driver's license identified him as Nelson O'Reilly. The search of his place also led us to believe he was the son of the O'Reilly shipping family.

"When my detectives notified the family, they discovered that the only living relative was his brother, Edward. He told them that they were not estranged but that it had been decades since they last talked to one another. As a result, he didn't seem to be upset to hear about his brother's death."

"Well, after several decades, I can see this. Just how old are these guys, anyway?"

"The victim was eighty-two and Edward is eighty-seven. Apparently Edward is wheelchair-bound and has memory issues, having suffered a couple of strokes, according to his valet. My guys tell me the valet may even be older than O'Reilly, but appears to be very sharp and remembers Nelson well. Your father's notes could prove to be very useful. You say there are floor plans and a list of contents in the family vault?"

"Yes, though I'm not sure how helpful the floor plans will be. They appear to have been sketched out by my dad. From what I can determine, the house was actually built in the late 1800s, not unlike many of the others on Billionaire's Row."

"Well, anything you have will undoubtedly help. Thanks."

About an hour later, San Francisco Homicide Detective Sullivan arrived and, after a few pleasantries, retrieved the files. He shared little else about the case except to say that besides Edward O'Reilly being in his late eighties and the valet over ninety, there was a cook, along with her husband, the landscaper. "Both are in their late seventies, possibly even early eighties. I've never had a case where everyone is so old. Not that it is a bad thing, I'm just worried one or more of them could kick off anytime and set our investigation back," he joked.

Just as he was leaving, he received a text from Commander Hines. It read, "Our victim is not Nelson O'Reilly."

"Well, here's a twist, Mr. Holmes. Commander Hines just texted that the victim is not who we thought he was."

"That's interesting," Dan responded.

"Yeah. What's stranger is the fact that I compared the man hanging with the picture on the driver's license and they matched. And, when I showed the license to O'Reilly and his valet, both men identified him as Nelson O'Reilly."

"A doppelganger, do you suppose?"

"I don't know. What I do know is that this case just keeps on getting more and more intriguing."

"Listen, Detective, I know this may seem a tad unorthodox, but do you have the note that was left behind? And if so, can I read it?"

"I don't see why not, since you are technically a part of this investigation. Here, I took a picture of it."

Dan read the note aloud: "I know they are on to me. No one wants to believe me. They want the paintings, but I don't have them. I've never had them. Mrs. O promised to give them to me, but she didn't. That was the deal, but she cheated me even though I trusted her. I promised Hans that he would have them. Now even he doesn't trust me. I love Hans, I would never cheat him. I told him they were in the vault. All this, and I'm not even the person everyone thinks

I am. I should have never trusted her. It was his mother's idea and that butler of theirs. It's been a good life, but it is all a fake. I don't know where I can go. Who can I turn to now? I owe them so much. They'll kill me for them. It's just a matter of time."

"Well, that's somewhat morbid," Brenda commented.

"It will be interesting to find out who this guy was, not to mention where the real Nelson O'Reilly is hiding," Dan said

9 P.M.

Dan's phone rang a second time, only this time it was Ron Tyson, his replacement at 2nd National Bank. "I'm sorry to bother you this late, Dan, but I just got off the phone with a homicide detective. He wants to inspect one of our customer's family vaults. He said you were aware and on board. He wants to do it tomorrow morning—catch this, before the bank opens. What gives?"

"Ron, I'm aware that SFPD is conducting a rather strange homicide. Commander Hines called me earlier and a Homicide Detective Sullivan stopped by a few hours ago to pick up some case info my dad left behind. I knew they are interested in the family vault, but I can only guess why they need to do it so early."

"What do you think the reasoning is?"

"My hunch is that there will be a number of uniformed officers there as well as Sullivan. He wants to downplay this as much as possible. So, he's likely under orders to do it soon, but not during business hours in front of employees and customers."

"Well, the joke is on them. The family vault in question is not even here. A number of the family vaults have a hundred-year lease, paid in advance. When we moved from One Mongomery to here, several families opted to stay there. So, we have an arrangement with West America Bank to allow them to stay until their lease runs out. For the O'Reilly's, that's another couple of years."

"Did you tell this to the detective?"

"Sure. He just laughed and said he would meet me there since I'm the Chief Corporate Security Officer for 2nd National, and this vault is leased by one of our customers."

"Actually, Ron, he has a point. I'm just not sure he's going about it the right way. Do you want me to call the commander?"

"God, no. I can call him. I just wanted a little clarification. I'll call Commander Hines in the morning and blow the detective off for now. I don't think waiting a day or two will jeopardize their investigation. And, they sure as hell don't need uniformed officers just to look in a subterranean family vault. Between their security chief and one of my agents, I think we can give the homicide dicks what they need without bringing out the goddamn fucking calvary."

"Sounds like you got it covered," Dan answered—chuckling aloud. "Need anything else from me?"

"Not now. Say goodnight to Brenda and apologize for my calling you guys so late."

"I will."

THE NEXT MORNING

True to his word, the next morning Ron was a no-show at One Montgomery. He had called West America's Corporate Security Officer, Charlie Chesterfield, after he hung up from Dan and explained the situation. The CSO thanked him and said he would take care of it, and not to worry, no one was going to the O'Reilly vault without a family member present and/or a search warrant. Ron smiled and thought, *Those arrogant homicide pricks. There's actually a part of me that would love to be there and see the expressions on their faces.* But, the more politically correct side of him kicked in and simply said, "I figured you would like to handle this on your own. If you do need any assistance, don't hesitate to call."

"How about I text you since this is now the twenty-first century?"

"Okay, smartass."

TWO DAYS LATER

Having been put off by West America's CSO, Sullivan showed up, armed with a search warrant and flanked by two uniformed officers. When served, Chesterfield knew all too well that his only option was to cooperate. Hence, his attitude was suddenly very cordial. The group stopped by the branch manager's office. The CSO explained the situation and the branch manager said he understood. "One question, however," the branch manager began. "We typically have a family member present when these vaults are opened. I'll have to call Mr. O'Reilly first."

"Please do," Detective Sullivan responded. "I called Ed O'Reilly last night. He said that because he is wheelchair-bound and isn't that much interested, he gave me his personal okay. I told him that someone would most likely call for verification and he said he would be waiting."

The manger put through a call and less than two minutes later, the group was enroute to the subterranean family vault.

While they were going down in the elevator, the branch manager commented, "Here's a fun fact. The bank was founded by one of the city's early tycoons, Charles Crocker, back in the late 1800s. I think it was 1883. He was one of the early railroad barons. The original bank was destroyed in the 1906 earthquake and rebuilt, only this time on bedrock. This allowed them to install a number of these iron vaults for the city's rich. So, this particular vault has been in the O'Reily family ever since then."

No one seemed to be all that interested, let alone impressed.

When they arrived at the vault, it was the branch manager that spoke up once more. "When you see inside the vault, don't wet yourselves because you're going to see a couple of four-by-four pallets—one with gold and the other silver. Don't even try to count it all, it will take a while. Besides that, you'll discover paintings just leaning against the walls with a tarp over each of them. The same type of covering can be found on sculptures, figurines, and whatever else they have put in there."

"Do you have some sort of inventory we can review prior to opening the vault?" the CSO asked.

"Yes," the branch manager answered as he was pulling a document out of a file folder. "The last time it was opened, there were twelve frames covered by individual tarps. These cover a number of different artists. Originally there were fifteen, but since 1975, three have been missing. It is believed they went missing when a number of items were taken by the family to be displayed in their mansion. When someone inventoried the items there, that is when the loss was first discovered. My record shows that we did a re-count here and there were only twelve, as expected."

"So, in short, we should count twelve tarped frames along with a variety of other valued antiques and two pallets, one holding gold bars and the other silver ingots. Right?"

"Correct. So, if you are ready, I'll open the vault."

Everyone watched. The giant door swung effortlessly open once the last combination number clicked.

"They don't make doors like this anymore," the branch manager commented as he swung the door open.

Detective Sullivan walked by him and stepped into the door-way. He quickly turned on his phone's flashlight and scanned the room. Leaning against the right wall was a tarp clearly covering something bulky. It was shaped like the other tarped frames. He passed the light across the middle of each wall. When he finished, he observed aloud, "There are twelve tarped frames; all about the same size. And then there is this one up front here."

As he spoke, he pulled the tarp away revealing three framed paintings. "Well, this is interesting. If all of the others have only one masterpiece and this has three, then either new ones have been added, or these are the three supposedly missing ones."

He was about to add something else when CSO Chesterfield, who had entered the vault on the opposite side, gasped, "Fuck! There's a dead body back here!"

The detective walked the rear of the vault. "I'll be damned! There is. Okay, everyone back outside and away from the door." Then he asked, "Is there a way to close the door without it locking?"

"No. However, I'm sure we can find something, even if it is something from inside, to prop it open," the branch manager sug-gested.

"Good idea." Then, turning to the two uniformed officers, he asked, "Are your body cams on?"

They both nodded.

"Great. I'll call for the CSI unit. Until they finish up inside there, no one else goes in. Got it?"

"Wait," the CSO said. "Somebody should take an inventory in here before a lot of others start coming and going. I'll have my CCTV technician rig up something temporarily to record everyone coming and going. We'll also need to figure out a way to protect the gold and silver."

The branch manager quietly suggested, "I have what may seem to be a wild idea. Why don't you have two of your security officers literally sit on each tarp? That way they can manage them accordingly and be out of the way."

"That's actually a great idea. Sounds a little unorthodox, but is anything about this otherwise?" Sullivan asked. "Officers, work out the logistics when his people show up. Just understand, I want everything and everyone filmed as they come and go. The last thing we need is for gold and silver bars to go missing."

"I have a count from the last time they were inventoried. So, if you inventory them first, that will create a baseline for when we count them a second time when everyone is finished," the branch manager suggested.

"Again," the detective smiled. "I like it. We'll do it. Everyone, listen up. The mission seems rather simple. It may take a while, but let's find out who our victim is. We'll have CSI bag the three masterpieces as evidence. And, finally, let's not fuck this up or our commander will go ape-shit all over us."

"A tad crude, but the point is well made," the branch manager whispered to his CSO.

TWO DAYS LATER

Dan had just finished his morning exercise routine and was looking forward to a relaxing cup of tea on the back deck with Brenda when Ron called.

"What's up?"

"You sitting down?"

"Yeah, with Brenda. It's what a lot of retirees do at this freaking time of the day. Do you have any idea what time it is?"

"Whoa, sorry. When can I call you back?"

"God, Ron, I'm just yanking your chain. What's up?"

"Well, I just thought you might enjoy an update on this whole O'Reilly case. It's proving to have some rather interesting twists."

"Brenda, Ron wants to update me on the latest involving that case. You remember, Detective Sullivan stopped by a short while back and picked up my dad's case notes."

"I'll let you two have it. As for me? Roscoe needs a long walk."

"Thanks, honey. Okay, Ron, let's hear it."

"The coroner has identified that the dead guy I told you about in the back of the O'Reilly vault is none other than Nelson O'Reilly. The three masterpieces covered by the tarp are the ones supposedly missing. It seems as though the family's insurance company paid nearly twenty million for all three and, of course, want either their money back or the paintings. Here's the strange part, though. The sole survivor, Edward, has told them they can have the master-pieces. He says that if he kept them, he would donate them to the DeYoung Museum along with everything else."

"How did they go missing and now are found back in the family vault?"

"Beats the hell out me. Old man O'Reilly says he is in his late eighties and really has no use for them. He thinks the insurance company should donate them to some museum, be it the DeYoung or whomever. He apparently told Detective Sullivan that he never missed them before, so why would he miss them now? This guy must really be loaded to just give away over hundreds of millions in fine art."

"So, do you think everyone is just going to drop the whole mat-ter since no one can prove they were ever stolen in the first place? And, the insurance company is apparently going to make one pot full of money on their appreciation?"

"That's what it looks like to me."

"Okay, and what about the fact that Nelson O'Reilly was found dead in a vault that is leased by your bank and not West America, even though the vault is on their property?"

"That too is intriguing. I suppose the banks' attorneys will argue over liabilities for some time and then come to some sort of shared responsibility. At least that is what you taught me in the past."

"And I don't see any reason to suggest otherwise. But what does Detective Sullivan have to say about having two dead Nelson O'Reilly's?"

"He's going back to the family. Obviously, there are a lot of unanswered questions. He wants to know if I want to join him since he believes that the vault is technically ours and he died on either your watch or mine."

"Well, I can't fault him for coming to that conclusion. Besides, I think you might enjoy cranking up your ol' investigative juices."

"Candidly, that is what I've been thinking. I'm going to a have a go at it."

"Good luck. But, first, tell me. In the beginning, Commander Hines told me the homicide division was investigating a series of murders in addition to the theft of the paintings. Have you picked up on any of that?"

"I have and I can't help but believe the murders are tied to our two Nelson O'Reilly's. Shortly after the masterpieces went missing, the youngest daughter was found mysteriously dead behind a tool shed. No one was ever caught, but the police—especially your dad—was closing in on either her parents or the old man's valet.

"Then a few years later, 1977 I believe Sullivan said, the O'Reilly's were hosting a dinner party on their yacht when supposedly one of the missing paintings was spotted hanging on the main deck by an art critic. The next night, he and a private detective snuck on board, intent on stealing it and exposing the O'Reilly's. However, shortly after boarding the yacht, it blew up, killing the two of them and sinking several other boats moored nearby. The bodies were eventually recovered but there was no trace of the painting."

"Talk about bizarre," Dan responded. "Someone was clearly out to embarrass the O'Reilly's or one of them was pretty arrogant to think they could get away with so blatant a display. Really stupid."

"And then there is the proverbial icing on our cake of bizarreness. Right after the yacht incident, Nelson went missing. His mother always claimed that he wanted to go to school somewhere in Europe and began sending him money on a regular basis. From what SFPD can put together, Nelson returned sometime later, but no one knows for sure. Sullivan wants everyone in the mansion interviewed again. So, whereas they don't know now, tomorrow Sullivan is bringing everyone in to the PD and asked me if I'd like to sit in on the interviews."

"I assume you're going?"

"Wouldn't miss it."

8:30 AM THE NEXT MORNING

By the time Ron arrived at Sullivan's office, Ed O'Reilly was in one interview room, door open, being watched by a uniformed officer. It was the same with the valet, Olsen Parsons. It wasn't long before the two saw both the cook and her husband pass by. Ron found Sullivan in his office just finishing up his notes and prepping for a day of interviewing.

"Good morning Ron," Sullivan greeted him pleasantly. "I have a really good feeling about this case. I think we're going to tie up some loose ends and get some resolution to a lot of our questions."

"That sounds great. Do you expect any arrests to come out of this?"

"Not sure. I think that once we rattle old man O'Reilly, he may fold. After all, what does a nearly ninety-year-old extremely rich guy have to lose? As a first-time offender and with his connections, I think he'll throw his parents under the bus without hesitation. And why not? They're dead and he'll likely get some type of accessory after the fact and probation. Or, worse-case scenario, home detention, which in essence appears what he has been doing for several years. So, no big deal."

"Okay, so how's all of this going to go down?"

"I want to interview O'Reilly. My best interrogator will take the valet; she's very effective and has a high closure rate. Another of my other experienced interrogators will be handling the cook and her husband."

"Where do you want me?"

"Which one sounds the most interesting? Your choice."

"If you don't mind, I'd like to see how the valet reacts to all of this."

"Go for it. Here's the timeline. I want to hold off interviewing O'Reilly and Parsons for about fifteen minutes. That should allow the other two interviews to reach a point where we will tell them we have to change rooms and march them by the other two a second time. As they pass by, one of the interviewers will tell them how much we appreciate them coming in and what they have said will be very helpful. It's an old trick designed to put O'Reilly and Parsons off their game. Of course, we'll start each interview advising them that the cook and landscaper helped us a great deal."

"And what do we do if someone wants a lawyer?"

"I suspect O'Reilly might want one from the get-go. I'm not sure about Parsons. As for the other two, hopefully they'll feel as though they're here for information only and open up. Let's see how it goes."

With that Sullivan walked to Ed O'Reilly's interview room. "I'm sorry, Mr. O'Reilly; this delay will only be a matter of a few minutes. I'll be back shortly. In the meantime, do you want something to drink?"

"I don't suppose you offer martinis this time of day, do you?" he quipped.

"I'm sorry, but our coffee isn't half bad and then there is always tea."

"I'm fine."

Sullivan went next door to where Parsons was and apologized for the delay, making the same offer to him as to whether he preferred coffee or tea. "I'm fine, I suspect we'll be leaving shortly, anyway."

After initial introductions and admonishments, the cook and landscaper were asked if either or both recalled the little daughter, Jennifer. The cook, despite her advanced age, clearly recalled not only Jennifer, but also there being a loud and angry argument between Mr. and Mrs. O'Reilly as to what to do with their daughter. It was shortly after some paintings had turned up missing. Given her mental retardation, the father wanted her institutionalized. He thought that way, no one would take seriously anything she might say. Mrs. O'Reilly, on the other hand, wanted her sent away to her aunt's home in Ireland.

As the two of them argued over their daughter for the next few days, it was suddenly discovered that Jennifer had gone missing. According to her husband, the landscaper, he found the little girl's body a couple of days later behind a tool shed in the back of the residence while he was gardening. "It was like she was just tossed back there in a fertilizer bag," he said. "She wasn't laid out, or anything. The way the bag was laying there on its side, I thought, at first, it was one of the open fertilizer bags that had fallen over. When I looked closely, I could see a body inside the bag and a wire around her neck."

He went on. "My thoughts were that Mr. O'Reilly paid to have someone kill her and throw her out in the trash, but when he found out about her death, he seemed genuinely surprised."

The cook added, "Then my husband and I began to suspect that it was Olsen Parsons, the valet. He was strong enough to throw her and he really didn't care much for her. He always thought she was coming between Mr. and Mrs. O'Reilly."

Just then a uniformed officer stepped in and whispered something in the interviewer's ear. "Thanks, I'll move them right away." Looking at the couple, he said, "I'm sorry, but it appears that we have to find another room. There is one just down the hall."

They gathered up their belongings and papers and made their way to the new room. As they passed by the room with O'Reilly and Parsons, the interviewer said loud enough for them to hear,

"Well, I can't thank you enough for all that you've told us. It will help us a great deal."

Once in the new room, the interview continued. They were asked if they knew anything about the paintings. Neither could remember much about them, only that they were missing and Mr. O'Reilly was upset. As for Mrs. O'Reilly, she didn't seem to be terribly concerned and agreed with the valet when he said that the insurance company would pay out. They were then asked if there were any secret places in the mansion that could hide the paintings, maybe even a secret tunnel. Neither of them admitted knowing anything about that.

"What do either of you know about the son, Nelson, going missing?"

The cook hesitated at first and looked at her husband. It was the husband who spoke. He told the detective that a long time after Nelson went missing, he overheard Mrs. O'Reilly and Olsen Parsons quietly discussing what they should do with his body. He was listening through the library door while supposedly fixing one of the shelves. He told his wife and together they decided that it was best not to say anything to anyone for fear of being deported since they hadn't applied for citizenship. It was then that they were advised that they were now considered, at the very least, material witnesses and they would be contacted later.

The cook broke down crying while her husband silently held her hand and kept his head down.

THE O'REILLY INTERVIEW

Sullivan started by telling O'Reilly that there was no need to be admonished since this was an exploratory interview and not an accusatory interrogation. It didn't take Sullivan long to conclude that even though Ed wanted to cooperate, his memory was severely limited due to the stroke he had several years ago. Whereas he remembered his parents and Nelson, he had difficulty recalling Jennifer, let alone her suspicious death. The two of them discussed the three paintings. Here again, he had trouble recalling specific details about them, however, he was aware that at one point they were stolen—he thought from the family bank vault during the war.

As before, O'Reilly said that he could not recall a time he had ever been to the family vault at One Montgomery Street. He said he was not much into art and had made arrangements to donate all of the artwork upon his death.

As for his brother, Nelson, he explained that there was enough difference in their ages that when they were growing up, they had different friends. Besides, he explained, Nelson was known as one of the local playboys and was heavily into alcohol and drugs, particularly cocaine. He told Sullivan that as best he could remember, it was his father who kicked Nelson out, telling him he was cut out of the will. He added that his mother was strongly opposed to this and secretly made arrangements to have the valet pass money along every month. Ed O'Reilly said that he hated his brother for the confusion he had sown in the family and never forgave his mother.

When asked about one of the missing paintings being seen on the family yacht the night before it was blown up, Ed O'Reilly chuckled aloud. "Yeah, I remember that. That was Nelson's doing. The dumb fucker thought he could get away with doing something outrageous and embarrassing my parents. He did it on a bet that he could get away with it and then right after the party he took it down. I think he put it in his bedroom, but wasn't sure."

O'Reilly chuckled a second time. "Do you know that stupid ass actually came to me and told me about it and wanted twenty thousand dollars to cover his bets? What a fucking idiot. It really didn't much matter since he was gone before the week was out and I never spoke to him or saw him after that."

Detective Sullivan shifted gears, "Tell me about the secret rooms and tunnels."

"What do you want to know?"

"Well, according to your cook and landscaper, there are several in the mansion," he bluffed. "I'm thinking that any one of them would have made for a perfect hiding place to stash anything—say, three masterpieces—and then file an insurance claim after the police concluded they were stolen. Hide them, file a claim, and later sell them. Nice scam and a quick way to get double their value."

O'Reilly responded, "First, there are these so-called hidden rooms as well as a tunnel. I was told that during the war, many of the neighbors had the tunnel system put in. It interconnected all of them so they could move from house to house without being caught by the Japanese. Several of the mansions already had secret rooms from when they were first built in the late 1800s. At the time, it was all legal and the city actually used some of the rooms for their own artwork and sensitive documents."

"So, all of this is interesting, but you haven't actually answered my question. Were the three paintings hidden in one of the secret rooms so as to collect the insurance?"

"I honestly don't know. That would have been something between my parents. They never discussed it in front of me and I never asked. The first I heard about their so-called return was just the other day when the family vault was opened. Say, how much longer are you going to keep us here?"

"Let me check a few things with my colleagues and I'll be right back."

"I suppose it still isn't martini time?"

"I'm sorry. No."

PARSONS' INTERVIEW

While Sullivan was interviewing Ed O'Reilly, his investigator and Ron were interviewing the valet, Parsons. Just before they entered the interview room, the investigator briefly stopped Ron and expressed, "I'm glad you will be in there. I've heard some good things about you. Since I was just assigned this case, I could use all the help you can provide. So don't hesitate to jump in anytime."

Parsons was admonished and told he could leave anytime. However, to do so would cast doubt on any future discussions, a simple but subtle threat intended to keep a suspect off guard. The investigator began asking Parsons for a brief background of himself and his relationship to the O'Reilly's. The valet started by explaining that sometimes people get confused, since over the years there have been two Parsons who have taken care of the O'Reilly's. He explained that his father originally served the family, he was Olsen Parsons Sr. And, that when he died, Parsons Jr. took the helm. He then added that his family had a long-standing tradition of serving as valets for wealthy families and the nobility in Ireland. His father principally took care of Mr. Bryson O'Reilly, but also catered to Mrs. Katy O'Reilly and occasionally their children.

When his father died, Parsons assumed the role of personal valet to his son, Edward O'Reilly. He found Mr. O'Reilly to have a "gentle heart," but he was always distant from the rest of the O'Reilly family and staff. Ron found this difficult to believe since Bryson O'Reilly was head of the local longshore union for years and eventually had his own shipping company. He was known for his hard-heartedness. Parsons went on to say that Jennifer was rarely talked about, especially her mysterious death, but for some reason, he always felt that his father was somehow involved. When Ron pressed him, he could not offer anything concrete. As he said over and over, "My dad said that he was ferociously loyal to the family and would do anything to protect them."

And then Parsons asked, "Has anyone told you that my dad served in the Second World War as a sniper and small ordinance officer?"

Ron was puzzled and asked, "No, and how does this relate to young Jennifer or any of the other O'Reilly's?"

"Why, everything. He was very kind to them but he could be fierce in defending any of them if they were threatened."

Then Ron asked, "Parsons, let's just say, hypothetically, that one of them asked your dad to kill another member of the family because that person was a threat to everyone else. What would he have done?"

"I suppose it would depend on who it was doing the asking. If it were either Mr. or Mrs. O'Reilly, he would do whatever they wanted. If it were one of the children, he would ask one of their parents first. He was loyal like that."

"Did your father ever say or implicate that he was involved in young Jennifer's death?" the detective asked.

"He never said as much, but one time I asked him and I'll never forget what he said. 'Son, the Navy has a saying, "loose lips sink ships."'

"I told him that I need help in understanding what he was trying to tell me. That's when he said that the O'Reilly's youngest, Jennifer, had some mental problems. She was always going on about something. Once she said she saw paintings in a secret room and she knew who took them and hid them. She thought it was a sort of game. Regardless, that made her parents very nervous and they were discussing what to do about her. A couple of days later she was found behind the tool shed dead. Even though the parents were suspected, nothing could be proven and no one was ever arrested."

"Let's talk about those paintings for a minute," Ron began. "Can you tell us anything about their disappearance and then somehow, at some time, they ended up back in the family vault?"

"Times were financially rough then. My father told me Mrs. O'Reilly put them in one of the safe rooms—that's what she called them. She told her husband what she did and it was him who got the idea to report them as stolen so they could get the insurance money. My dad told me that Mr. O'Reilly always intended to have them magically appear once their financial situation improved and claim it was always a mistake and wanted to make the insurance company whole.

"It was sometime after their daughter died that the O'Reilly's hosted a Christmas party on their yacht and Nelson got this bet going that he could hang one of the missing paintings in plain sight and no one would even notice. According to my dad, Nelson hated all of his parents friends and business associates. He thought that if they got caught it would embarrass them a great deal. Well, he hung the picture somehow before the party started and it was apparently recognized by some art critic. Nelson lost the bet and tried to hit up his brother Edward for twenty grand to cover his bets. Mr. Edward told him to go to hell. A day or so later the yacht blew up, killing a couple of men and it was assumed that the painting was destroyed. It was much later that I found out the painting had actually been removed before the explosion."

"Who set the bomb?" Ron asked.

"I've never known for sure. Some say it was my dad, others say it was Nelson."

"But, isn't it true that your father worked with explosives during the war?"

"True, but he would only have done it if someone asked him. Mr. O'Reilly loved that boat. Mrs. O'Reilly maybe. Nelson had no use for it and couldn't have cared less and Edward was gone at the time—somewhere off to school. As a kid, I remember him calling and I answered the phone. He was shocked to hear the news and thought that the men may have been Mr. O'Reilly and my dad."

"So, you think Mrs. O'Reilly put your dad up to it?"

"Like I said, my dad never admitted to anything and no one could ever prove it was the lady of the house. You have to understand the culture of the house. If no questions were ever asked, no one need ever give an answer that could come back on them or someone else in the house."

"Interesting family code," the investigator observed.

"So, tell us about Nelson's disappearance," Ron pushed.

"Here's what I can tell you. Shortly after the yacht incident Nelson was shipped out. Please excuse the pun, I didn't mean to make it. I don't know where, but he only came back a couple of times and then not for very long. His dad always got mad; scary mad and Mrs. O'Reilly had to step in and calm the waters. On those occasions when he did return, he wasn't allowed to eat with the family. He always ate with the cook and her husband.

"When he was there, it was always somewhat awkward. His coming back always put everyone ill at ease. Mr. Ed even said that the cook told him that the man looked like Nelson, but he wasn't Nelson. I remember one time running into him late one night. He appeared to be lost. I wrote it off as him being drunk so I took him to his room and put him to bed."

"How do you think the paintings made their way back into the vault and Nelson was killed?" the detective asked, keeping the pressure on.

"Good questions. I'm not sure but I suspect the Mrs. I'm just throwing this out there, but perhaps Nelson comes back one time, and wants more money. She says that they can get something of value from the family vault; gold and silver, you know. Anyway, they take the paintings back after all those years for some reason. In the vault, they get in an argument, perhaps over the gold and silver and in a rage she pulls out the gun she always carried and shoots him. She leaves, closing and locking the door.

"She finds and hires a lookalike and sends him off somewhere. She arranges to pay him monthly to pretend he is Nelson and no one is the wiser. It's a theory."

"Sounds like a damn good theory, Mr. Parsons. It's almost like you were there." Sullivan said as he entered the room. He had finished with Ed O'Reilly and was listening to their interview from the adjacent observation room.

PERSONS OF INTEREST RELEASED AND A DEBRIEFING

From the outset, Ron had contacted Unit 33 and requested a full report on each of the principals in the O'Reilly family and any information they could find relating to the death of the young girl, Jennifer. When Sullivan's interviews for the day were complete, he released Ed O'Reilly, Parsons and the cook and landscaper. He admonished each of them that they remained persons of interest and advised they were not to leave the country.

Detective Sullivan asked the others to join him in the conference room for a debriefing.

"Let's start with you Ron. Where are you at?"

"Well, based on what I heard you guys talking about just now in the hallway, let me tell you that I have asked Unit 33 to conduct a full intelligence report on the O'Reilly's. Can I assume all of you at one time or another have heard about Unit 33 and what they do?"

Everyone nodded.

"Well, I'm waiting for their report. It may take another day or two. When I get it, you'll have it; complete and unredacted. Having said that, based on what we have so far, here's where I am at:

"First, Parsons Jr. is lying. He knows more, but for now isn't talking. He says that Mr. O'Reilly had a gentle heart but we know he was ruthless as a union boss and shipping magnate.

"Second, Parsons believes, but cannot prove, or so he says, that the young daughter was probably killed by his father acting on his own, or on request from Mrs. O'Reilly.

"Third, it was Mr. O'Reilly that hid the paintings so he could collect the insurance.

"Fourth, Nelon apparently knew about the missing paintings and wanted to embarrass his parents by hanging one of them on the yacht just before a party. He made a bet that it wouldn't be noticed, but it was. Shortly afterwards the yacht blew up with two men on board who were attempting to retrieve the painting. Unbeknownst to the two men, the painting had been removed. They were killed when the boat was destroyed.

"Fifth, Nelson was forced to leave and apparently Mrs. O'Reilly was the only one that actually knew his whereabouts.

"Sixth, it appears that at some time Mrs. O'Reilly hired a doppelganger—a lookalike—to play the role of Nelson.

"Seventh, this doppelganger got in over his head, promising someone he would give them one or more of the paintings. But he never received any and was hung for essentially nonpayment.

"Eighth, the real Nelson was recently found dead in the family vault along with the three missing masterpieces."

"Well, that was rather thorough. Thanks Ron. What about the cook and her husband?"

The primary interviewer recapped:

"It was the landscaper that found Jennifer. He originally thought that the father killed her. But, later began questioning that.

"They believe that Mrs. O'Reilly and their valet took the masterpieces and hid them for the insurance. Mr. O'Reilly apparently knew this and had reservations, but went along with the scheme.

"They claim no knowledge of any secret room or tunnel. We suspect they are lying.

"Finally, it was the landscaper who overheard Mrs. O'Reilly and senior Parsons talking about how to dispose of Nelson's body."

"Interesting, especially about the secret room and tunnel since Mr. O'Reilly, in my interview of him strongly implied they were aware of them," Detective Sullivan added. He then went on to outline his interview with Ed O'Reilly.

"He claims his memory is severely limited due to past strokes several years ago.

"He claims he had difficulty recalling Jennifer, let alone her suspicious death.

"He said he has trouble recalling specific details about the theft of the masterpieces; however, he thought they were taken from the family vault during the war. Moreover, he has never been to the family vault at One Montgomery Street. He said he was not much into art and had made arrangements to donate all of the artwork upon his death.

"He wasn't close to Nelson and his brother was known as one of the local playboys and was heavy into alcohol and drugs; particularly cocaine.

"He said his father kicked Nelson out, telling him he was cut out of the will. He added that his mother was strongly opposed and secretly made arrangements to have the valet pass money along every month. He said that he, Ed O'Reilly, hated his brother for that and never forgave his mother.

"He remembered the yacht explosion and blamed Nelson. He said that Nelson bet he could hang one of the masterpieces in plain sight on the boat and no one would notice. Nelson tried to hit up Ed O'Reilly for twenty thousand dollars to cover his bet. Ed said no.

"He admitted to the secret rooms and tunnel and said

they were commonly known among everyone, including the neighbors.

"He said he never knew what exactly happened to the paintings and it was only a few days ago that he heard they were in the family vault at One Montgomery Street."

Detective Sullivan then concluded, "I think we're pretty far down the road here, but we need some additional evidence if we are going to arrest anyone. At most, we have some possible material witnesses and/or persons of interest. For now, let's see what the coroner can tell us about the body in the vault. We'll also wait to hear from Ron's Unit 33. Until then, folks, thanks for a great job."

UNIT 33'S REPORT

The next day Ron received the Unit 33 report.

It detailed how Mrs. O'Reilly was making payments to her son for years leading up to her death. It also revealed that just prior to the masterpieces being taken, the O'Reilly's were asset rich, but getting cash poor.

Their investigation into Jenniefer's death hit a dead end. However, there was a strong circumstantial case that Olsen Parsons was culpable. It appears that the masterpieces were most likely not stolen and a false insurance claim was filed by the O'Reilly's.

The coroner would be releasing a report within the next forty-eight hours stating that DNA testing would prove that it was Nelson O'Reilly who was shot in the family vault.

The gun used remains unknown. However, Mrs. O'Reilly was known to always carry a .38 Smith & Weston snub-nose police special. The coroner will also verify the bullet that killed Nelson O'Reilly came from the same make and model.

DNA extracted from the body, found on the inside of what remains of the waistband, indicates that of a male.

The male body found hanging in his apartment is a probable homicide which is being actively investigated by the homicide division of SFPD.

Recommendations:

- A search of the mansion be undertaken to possibly locate the weapon Mrs. O'Reilly was known to carry.
- DNA samples be taken of all living and past residents of the O'Reilly mansion.
- Despite the amount of time lapsed, another search of the tool shed be undertaken for latent prints and/or materials where DNA may be present.

After reading the report, Ron called Detective Sullivan and briefed him. "This is all very good stuff, Ron. You need to send along my appreciation to the Unit 33 specialists."

"Well, when things settle down, a letter of appreciation from the PD would be happily received."

"Consider it done. I'd still like to know how they come up with the stuff they find. Perhaps that's something I'll be privy to down the road."

Ron did not respond.

TWO DAYS LATER

At eight o'clock in the morning there was a knock on the door of the O'Reilly mansion. Parsons answered to find Detective Sullivan and several uniformed officers standing on there. "We have a search warrant to look for the weapon described herein. If you know where it is, it will save all of us a great deal of time. The warrant also states we will be taking DNA samples from everyone as well as items that Mr. and Mrs. O'Reilly handled, along with anything similar your father may have left behind that would contain his DNA."

Parsons invited the police into the library where Ed O'Reilly was sitting. He then explained the purpose of the police and Edward said he would gladly cooperate. O'Reilly asked Parsons to have the cook and her husband join them.

As Parsons left, Detective Sullivan said, "Mr. O'Reilly, it would save all of us a lot of time if you were to tell us how many secret rooms there are and where they are located. The same is true regarding the tunnel."

"I don't have anything to hide. When Parsons returns, I'll have him show you everything."

"Do you know if Mrs. O'Reilly's handgun is still around?"

"Yes, I believe it is in the bureau drawer behind you."

Detective Sullivan opened the drawer and the gun was there. He signaled to one of the uniformed officers to retrieve it and bag it for evidence.

"Anything else?" Ed O'Reilly asked.

"Nothing for now, but you should know that your brother Nelson is the individual we discovered in the vault. He was killed with a gun matching the description of the gun we just pulled out of the drawer."

"Are you suggesting my mother killed him?"

"I'm suggesting nothing for now. We're here just to gather evidence. Once we have analyzed it, we will notify you accordingly."

Sullivan turned to the cook and her husband who had just entered the room. "Whereas you told us in your last interview that you didn't know anything about secret rooms and a tunnel, we know you lied. Would you like to correct the record now since it will help you later?"

The two of them lowered their heads. Ed O'Reilly said, "Tell them what you know. Don't worry, I don't think you're in any serious trouble for lying. I assume you were just trying to protect me."

The cook responded, "Yes, we know about the rooms and tunnels. We were just trying to protect Mr. O'Reilly and Mr. Parsons."

Several hours later, having searched the entire mansion and collected everyone's DNA, Sullivan advised that they were finished for the day and would be in contact shortly. He admonished them not to leave the country.

Once everyone was on their way, Ron called Dan and briefed him accordingly.

"Well, it looks like this thing is drawing to a close quickly," Dan said. "At least the aspects of the bank's involvement with the family vault at One Montgomery. So, who killed Nelson?"

"I think that when things shake out, we'll discover that Nelson,

Olsen Parsons, and Mrs. O'Reilly were in the vault altogether. I suspect that Nelson was getting greedy and wanted any number of gold bars and silver ingots. An argument broke out, Mrs. O'Reilly shot her son and Olsen Parsons dragged the body to the rear of the vault behind the pallets of silver."

"And what of young Jennifer?"

"That depends on what, if anything, they find in and around the tool shed. I know that the PD is petitioning to have the body exhumed, but I'm not sure what that will accomplish unless they can somehow tie Olsen Parsons to it directly."

"So, how do you see this whole thing playing out?" Dan asked.

"I think Ed O'Reilly is in the clear. Besides, if there are any charges filed, his high-priced lawyers will keep him out jail. As for Parsons Jr. and the cook and her husband, I'm not sure. They might get some degree of accessory after the fact and everyone is put on probation. I don't really see jailtime for any of them since the killer or killers of Nelson are dead. The insurance company will get the masterpieces at an obscene value. And the doppelganger death is in the hands of SFPD."

"I suspect your boss, President Sands, will sleep well tonight. As will Commander Hines."

"All in a day's work," Ron teased. "I have to call Abbey and have her thank the folks at Unit 33 for their help."

A WEEK LATER

Ron was wrapping things up for the day when he received an email from the Unit 33 manager, Abbey Gentry. It read:

Here is some supplemental information for the O'Reilly case. We will be closing our case file tomorrow. However, this report contains additional information that may or may not be known by SFPD.

A review of the archived files concerning the family vault being leased by the O'Reilly shows that the last access was by Mrs. Katy O'Reilly, Nelson O'Reilly, and Olsen Parsons Sr.

Forensic evidence shows that the body of Nelson O'Reilly was dragged from on top of the tarp covering the silver ingots to the location where he was found, six feet away. There were DNA traces belonging to Nelson O'Reilly and Olsen Parsons on both the silver tarp and on the floor under the body.

A search for DNA at the location of Jennifer O'Reilly's death was negative.

The named insured on the three masterpieces were Mr. and Mrs. O'Reilly. However, retrieval of the archived claim files shows that Edward O'Reilly submitted the claim.

Senior O'Reilly filed the claim on the loss of their yacht. There was no claim for a lost masterpiece. Given the total destruction of the boat, no forensic evidence was gathered to suggest who the perpetrator might have been. Like the death of Jennifer O'Reilly, to date, there is no physical proof of culpability.

SFPD ballistics lab report identifies the gun belonging to Mrs. O'Reilly was the same weapon that killed Nelson O'Reilly.

Forensic evidence collected by SFPD shows that latent prints and DNA belonging to two hired assassins typically contracted by the DeAntonio crime family were found at the crime scene where John Akers, aka Nelson O'Reilly, was found hanged. These individuals are wanted by several law enforcement agencies for a number of similar hangings and remain at large. They are considered armed and dangerous.

The line at the end of the email read, "Not sure you are aware, but Ed O'Reilly has been admitted into hospice. He is expected to live less than a month."

Ron responded with an acknowledgement of its receipt and called Detective Sullivan.

"Hi, Ron, what's up?"

"I'm sending a supplemental report from Unit 33. They are closing out your case. I believe you are aware of most of the information but there are a few surprises."

"Like what?"

"Did you know that it was Ed O'Reilly who filed the insurance claim on the missing masterpieces? And the vault records show that it was Mrs. O'Reilly, Nelson O'Reilly, and Olsen Parsons who last entered the family vault?"

"We know about the access records to the vault, but have been frustrated about who actually filed the insurance claim on the masterpieces. Can you send a copy over of the claim?"

"Not a problem. Did you know Ed O'Reilly is in hospice and expected to die within the month?"

"Fuck no!"

"Check it out."

"Well, crap. To file for an arrest warrant seems a tad academic."

"Not to mention goonish. I think I'll call Dan and update him accordingly. In the meantime, you need anything else regarding this, just let me know."

"I will, Ron. And thanks. I like working with you guys."

"Same on this end."

ELLEN RETURNS
AND RON'S FRIEND NEEDS HELP

WEDDING BELLS AND THE SFPD

Abbey Gentry's big day was only two days away. She and John had been engaged for some time now and her wedding was less than forty-eight hours away. It wasn't going to be a traditional big wedding as Jewish weddings go, just family and a couple of close friends and work colleagues. Of course, Dan and Brenda Holmes were among the invited. After all, Dan was John's brother and until recently, he was her boss and mentor. And now, soon he would be part of her family. *Wow!* she thought, *That is going to take some time to get used to!*

Recently, Dan had arranged with 2nd National Bank to spin Corporate Security's somewhat clandestine intelligence gathering group, Unit 33, away from the bank. The caveat, however, was that Dan would serve as a sort of executive emeritus with full access to the unit through Abbey. Abbey was the managing director and Unit 33 was now officially a non-profit organization.

Abbey found the demands on her personal life hectic as she wanted even this small wedding to be a joyous occasion for everyone. That included her dad, who lived with her, and her twin boys, both of whom were now college sophomores at Cal Berkeley.

Abbey had lost her husband in the Iraq conflict and as a Jewish widow she was nervous about marrying John, a former Catholic priest. They had met just prior to his announcing that his Bishop had granted him leave from his ordained vows, but Abbey couldn't shake the feeling that somehow she played a part in John's decision to step away from his vows. Despite his insistence that he had arrived at the decision well before he met her, she always wondered; and could not fully shake her guilt.

The wedding was going to be held at Temple Sinai in Oakland, California. Much to her surprise, John's bishop accepted their invitation to the wedding. Such a high honor was simply indicative of the amount of respect the bishop had for John and his work, even after leaving the priesthood.

He wasn't the only one with an interest in Abbey and John's marriage. Though not invited, Commander Hines of the San Francisco Police Department had arranged for two of his detectives to serve in an undercover role as a bartender and waiter.

Hines had always suspected that Abbey's best friend, Ellen Fischer, a trained Mossad sniper, was responsible for assassinating Chaval, the leader of the 5th Streeters Gang. Even though his death was ruled a gang-related killing between the 5th Streeters and another gang, the Wah Ching crime organization, Hines always suspected that it was Ellen either acting alone or as a hired sniper. Since both Dan and Abbey were unconscious in the hospital at the time, neither were ever suspected of putting their own hit out on Chaval.

He knew that Ellen and Abbey were very close. He also knew that Ellen was good friends with Dan. Hines therefore suspected that she acted out of revenge for his ordering the assassination of both Abbey and Dan, along with one of Abbey's supervisors. Whereas the supervisor was killed, Abbey and Dan were critically injured. The police commander's experience led him to understand that as a Mossad trained sniper, Ellen believed she had a duty to avenge the attempt on her best friend's life.

Within an hour of the assassination, Ellen and her spotter, Peter, were on a Mossad jet headed for Tel Aviv and out of U.S.

jurisdiction. To Hines' knowledge, Ellen had yet to return to San Francisco; however, the wedding of her best friend, he reasoned, might be the impetus for coming back. If so, he wanted Oakland Police plainclothes detectives in a position to discreetly bring her in to the station as a person of interest. Hines knew the detainment was dicey at best since it involved potentially embarrassing his long-time friend, Dan. The plan was simple. If Ellen was there, she would be followed once she left the venue and taken into custody. Just as added insurance, Hines had arranged with the Oakland Police Department to have each entrance surveilled with a uniformed officer. Hines had vowed that if she was there, she wasn't going to get away this time.

Much to the commander's surprise, she wasn't there. He had sworn to himself that Abbey's wedding would draw her back. At about nine o'clock, however, Abbey was slipped a note from one of her bridesmaids. It was in a sealed envelope and looked just like all of the other wedding envelopes that the couple was receiving. As Abbey looked at the handwriting, she recognized it immediately. It was from Ellen. Abbey calmly folded it and asked John to put it in his pocket until she asked for it. No problem.

About an hour passed before Abbey excused herself to go to the ladies' room. As she stepped away, she passed by John and asked for the envelope. Once inside one of the stalls she opened it. There was a note that simply read: T, 2, RH, 617/820. Abbey understood right away. She and Ellen oftentimes would send these types of cryptic notes to each other when they were assigned to Military Intelligence in Tel Aviv years ago. It simply meant, Tomorrow at two o'clock, the Roosevelt Hotel, pass by Room 617and meet in 820. Abbey tore the note into as many small pieces as possible and flushed them down the toilet. She waited and flushed again. She stepped out of the stall and returned to her new husband and guests.

A CALL AT 3 A.M.

It was close to three o'clock in the morning by the time Ron Tyson and his fiancée made it to his place from the wedding. They were both exhausted and all he wanted to do was sleep. He had no sooner laid down when his phone rang. He couldn't believe it. *Whomever it was, it sure as hell better be important*, he thought to himself. Caller ID showed it was Al Sloane, a close friend—perhaps even his best friend— for years.

"Who is that?" Catherine asked as she slipped into bed.

"It's Al," Ron answered. "Something must be wrong, really wrong, for him to call at this hour."

"Hi Al," Ron began.

"I know it's late, but I think I've fucked up. Fucked up really bad. Anyway, can I see you tomorrow night?" Al blurted.

"Sure. Are you in town?"

"No, I'm in LA, but if we can meet, I'll fly up to Oakland, or wherever, tomorrow afternoon."

"Are you okay?"

"Physically, I'm okay. Mentally, I'm going crazy. Really crazy."

"Slow down, Al. Text me your flight and I'll meet you at the gate in Oakland. If you need, you can spend the night with us."

"Great, Ron, I really appreciate this. See you tomorrow afternoon. I'll text all of my arrival info. See you then." He hung up.

"Sounds like he's really desperate, Ron. What do you think it is?"

"I haven't a clue, honey. This is so out of character. I guess I'll have to wait until tomorrow. You okay with me inviting him to stay the night, if he needs it?"

"Sure. God yes, Ron. He's a part of who you are."

"Thanks." And with that, Ron slipped into bed. He was no longer as tired as he thought he was. He lay awake for what seemed like hours with his mind racing.

TWO O'CLOCK THE NEXT AFTERNOON

The newlyweds' honeymoon didn't officially start until they boarded Flight 645 to Lima, Peru at 11:55 p.m. That would give Abbey plenty of time to meet Ellen at The Roosevelt and still catch the flight. She would go alone so as to draw the least amount of attention. Just as the reception was ending, Abbey had pulled Dan aside and told him about the note and what it meant.

He advised, "Listen, Abbey, you know Hines still thinks Ellen killed Chaval. I wouldn't doubt that he had the wedding staked out. Just be careful. If you go, go alone and you'll have to have some sort of plan."

"Don't worry, we've done something like this before. I think we've got it dialed in. Trust me," Abbey responded.

"Well, it's short notice, but if you want, I think I can get it set up to create a distraction, if you need it."

Shortly before two o'clock Abbey arrived at the front desk of The Roosevelt. "My grandmother and her nurse checked in earlier this morning. I think it was Room 617. Can you call and see if they are still in their room?"

"No problem," the clerk responded and dialed the room.

In Ellen's room, she could see that it was the front desk calling. "Yes," she answered.

"There's a lady here just checking to make sure you're in your room."

"Great. Please send her up."

Abbey thanked the clerk and as she turned to walk away, she stopped and turned. "Listen, Grandma always likes her afternoon tea at three. Can you have someone deliver some along with some sort of pastry?"

"Consider it done. It would be our pleasure. I hope you have a good visit." With that, Abbey turned back to the elevators. She never looked around until she stepped in. A quick glance into the lobby revealed that there was a couple standing nearby the front desk looking totally out of character. Just as she suspected, she was followed.

She exited on the sixth floor and walked to the end of the corridor. She noticed there were no cameras. She walked past Room 617 and exited via the stairway and walked up to the eighth floor. As prearranged via coded text, she then went to room 820 and knocked on the door. A moment later, it opened and Ellen was standing there, smiling. She quickly grabbed Abbey's arm and pulled her inside.

The two embraced. It had been so long since they had seen each other in person. Sure, there had been the occasional Zoom meeting, but those things are never the same. They both softly giggled just like sisters would. Theirs was a special relationship and despite their quite different lives, they never stopped loving each other like close sisters.

"So, how did it go? Were you followed?"

"Oh yes. They aren't very good at their jobs," Abbey answered, laughing out loud.

"I've ordered tea and crumpets for three o'clock. I'm sure they heard me. If these detectives are anything like the ones in Paris and Barcelona, they'll wait and follow the room service cart up. So, that should give us, hopefully, an hour."

"It's never failed before. Let me introduce you to the first of my partners-in-crime," Ellen chuckled. "This is Agent Moorehead. We've worked this type of scam before. She makes a great grandmother. At the appropriate time, you'll meet the second, posing as her nurse."

"Hi." Abbey smiled and shook her hand.

"Here's a small gift for you." Ellen said, handing Abbey her wedding gift. "Congratulations. I hope he'll make you happy for the rest of your life. You deserve it."

"I must say," Abbey said as she took the gift, "I just can't believe you would risk coming back, even if it were for my wedding. I very much appreciate it."

"Well, for us, it's not all pleasure. Are you familiar with a guy called Rodney Witherspoon?"

"You mean the self-avowed antisemitic who goes around stirring people up against us?"

"That's the one. As you may have heard, he stirs up crowds and leaves just before someone torches a temple. Even though he's been arrested several times, his lawyers are slick and he's always managed to avoid your criminal justice system."

"I'm not sure I like where this is going, Ellen."

"Like it or not, after ten of our own have died as a result of this guy's hate, the decision has been made to make sure he doesn't have another opportunity."

"God, Ellen. You're here to do what I think you're going to do. Right?"

"Listen, I'm a soldier. I go wherever I'm sent. For me, it's more than duty. I'm proud to take scum like him out. He is an enemy of our people. We need to strike back. I simply carry out my orders. Besides, I asked for this assignment since it gave me a chance to see you. When will I get a copy of the video?"

"That's going to take a few days. Can I leave with the Segal brothers like before?"

"They're always there for me."

"So, when and where?"

"He's putting together his next rally in Cincinnati in about a week. That gives me time to be ready. Actually, I should say 'we'. Right, partner?" Ellen looked at Agent Moorehead.

"Can you talk about something else? We have so little time. Tell me, are you still seeing that Adonis?" Abbey asked.

"Oh yes. We're actually getting serious." With that, the conversation shifted dramatically to lighter topics as the two dear friends talked about what was recently happening for both of them. The hour started to slip by quickly.

"Ellen, we got to get you out of here. Agent Moorehead and I will go to Room 617."

Abbey then turned to Agent Moorehead. "Are you good at faking a heart attack or stroke?"

They all smiled. Abbey and Ellen made it a quick goodbye and left by way of the stairway. About five minutes later, Ellen could hear the paramedics arriving. She looked down on the street and watched the action below. With that, she slipped down the stairs and out of the hotel. She wore her favorite shawl over her head to avoid the cameras and disappeared up the street.

Meanwhile, in Room 617, the paramedics arrived to find

Abbey's grandmother having "a great deal of trouble breathing". As they began to treat her, a man and a woman slipped into the room.

Looking at Abbey, the female detective identified herself.

A few moments passed when a woman stepped inside the room. "Oh my God! What is going on?"

"It seems this woman is having some sort of stroke or heart attack. Who are you?" the male detective asked.

"I'm her nurse. I needed to step away for a minor family emergency. I can't have been gone twenty minutes. And you are?"

"We're the police," he answered.

Abbey looked at the group and commented, "I have to go. I'm off on my honeymoon. Gramma, you're in good hands, but I'll be checking in on you daily. If things get any worse, John and I will be back in no time. Listen to your nurse. Okay?"

Moorehead waved back weakly. Abbey bent down, gave her a quick kiss on the cheek and thanked the paramedics. She then turned and left. As she made her way to the elevators, she smiled. "Works every time."

LATER THAT DAY

Ron did not have a long wait at the gate. Al's plane landed right on time and he was one of the first to exit. He spotted Ron right away and picked up his pace. "God, it's great to see you, Ron." They gave each other a brief hug and then shook hands.

"Have you booked a flight back?" Ron asked.

"Yeah, but it is not until after nine. I think that'll give us enough time."

"Okay. There's a small café about a ten-minute drive from here. You can get most anything there if you are hungry," Ron suggested.

"Well, if you don't mind I think we'll need something a little stronger."

"Oh, yeah. You're probably right. What was I thinking?" Ron asked rhetorically. "There's a pretty good bar in the hotel just before you come into the airport. It's always quiet."

Fifteen minutes later, they were settling into a table near the back. There were only a few other customers and they were sitting at the bar. They ordered their drinks and Ron began.

"So, what's up, Mr. Risk Adverse?" Ron teased. Between the two of them, over the years, Al had come to call Ron Mr. Swashbuckler. Ron was always taking risks operating on the belief that the higher the risk, the higher the reward. As a result, Al said that Ron reminded him of an old pirate on the high seas—always out for the next adventure. As for Al, he had earned his nickname because he never took big risks. He once told Ron, "Listen, you do it your way. But for me, I have always found that if you operate at the forty-nine percent level when it comes to organizational politics, you'll never get caught on management's radar. Slow and steady, always the corporate way." Hence, Mr. Risk Adverse.

"Ron, I've really fucked up. I mean big-time fucked up. I don't see a way out. I'm pissed at myself, I want to kill my wife, and I'm on the verge of losing everything," he said, starting to choke up.

"Hold on, old friend," Ron pleaded. "Start at the beginning. I've been in many a scrape over the years thinking there was no hope. And yet, look at me now. Trust me. I don't know what you've done, but there is a road out of your mess. So, slow down and start at the beginning."

Al began. "About four or five months ago, I was in Las Vegas on business with a couple of guys. One guy wanted to hit Ladies' Legs. It's a strip joint in town and there's a lot of lap dancing. You know the kind of joint."

"Let me stop you there to say that I've never been in one of those places. So, if I ask what may seem like a stupid question, please excuse my lack of experience."

Al smiled. "Duly noted. Anyway, you know me; I never take chances. Well, there's this one dancer, her name is Candy. I know, I know, but it's her stage name. She comes down from her pole, comes in front of me and asks if I'm interested in a lap dance. The guys I'm with are going crazy and pushing me to say yes, so I did.

"Ron, I thought I was going to, well, you know, right there. She's a 34-Double D and she's got them buried in my face. All the while, she's gyrating like hell over me."

"Al, I don't need this kind of detail. I get it. How's this getting you in big trouble?"

"I know this sounds crazy, but I fell in love."

"You mean you fell in lust."

"No. Seriously, I thought so at first, but then I met her as we were leaving. Her shift was over, we got to talking, and the next thing I know, we're at her place."

"Oh boy. I think I can see where this is going."

"Listen, Dan, Las Vegas is less than three hours away. Not that far. We have a great night and she taught me things I never knew. In the morning, we agree to see each other that night since she has it off and I was leaving the next morning. That night, it was just as exciting. The next morning, I tell her I want to see her again and we agree to meet in a week. That's when it started."

"Al, please don't take this the wrong way, but did she ask for money?"

"God no! Well, not that time. Let me go on. So, we meet a couple more times. My company is building a new facility, so it's easy to tell my wife that I need to spend time over there. About a month later, Candy asks if she can borrow five hundred dollars. She told me she has an eleven-year-old and no insurance, but needed the money for his dentist appointment."

"So far, aside from the affair, I don't see what has got you so upset."

"Two weeks ago, my wife's sister found out. Don't ask me how, I don't know. But you know these hotheaded Latin types. Once Louisa finds out, she blows up at me. Telling me she is going to put it on Facebook, on X, write to her family in Caracas and tell them what kind of cheating bastard I am. Then she tells me she is going to sue for divorce and take everything—the house, my 401K, the IRAs, my stock options, everything. She says she won't be happy until she sees me broke. She even said that if she could take my company car, she would. And Ron, she's the type that will do it all!"

"Wow, after how many years? Forty-five, if I'm not mistaken," Ron quietly acknowledged.

"But it gets worse," Al continued.

"How can it get any worse?" Ron asked incredulously.

"Three weeks ago, I bought Candy a new house and a car. I had to dig deep into our savings, but I thought I would divorce Louisa and sell the house. I figured I would use my half to secure a loan on her house—our house—we'd move in together and eventually things would settle down. But if Louisa gets everything, I'm in big trouble."

"Hold on, your wife might threaten to take everything, but California is a fifty-fifty property right state. She could never get more than half. It may take you a while to recoup, but it is doable."

"You don't get it. I put everything in Candy's name. And now, she says she's questioning if she wants to continue. She's dumped me because she doesn't want to go through another messy divorce. And, if I try to get anything back, she'll sue me for mental cruelty and physical pain."

"Where's the physical pain come in?"

"We practiced S&M, only about half of the time I was the masochist and she was the sadist."

"Goddam, Al, what the fuck were you thinking? Other than Louisa and now Candy, have you ever been with a woman?"

"No."

"Not even when you were a merchant marine? What about shore leave?"

"Nope. I was engaged to Louisa at the time and promised her I would be faithful."

"Boy, did this Candy woman ever see you coming. Have you ever even seen her son?"

"No."

"My money is on the fact that she doesn't have one. Or, if she does, he's probably with his father."

"What am I going to do? I feel like blowing Louisa's brains out."

"Hold on, I know you're upset, but that's just you being angry and scared. Right? You aren't thinking about doing something stupid, are you?"

"No. I'm just pissed-off at the whole world and I want to hurt someone. Hell, maybe that someone is me!"

"Okay, where are you staying now?"

"She threw me out. I'm renting some dive near work."

"Well, here. It's close to six hundred dollars. I was going to deposit it. I just sold my old bike yesterday. You take it and use it until things settle down. I know you're good for it. How did you pay for your airline ticket?"

"I put it on a credit card."

"I'll go to the ticket counter with you and buy your ticket home. Just try to keep your head low at work until Louisa is off the warpath. God only knows what she is capable of. Got it?"

"I will if it's not too late."

"What the fuck does that mean?"

"My work performance hasn't been quite up to par since this whole thing started. I've missed a couple of critical deadlines and my boss has put me on notice."

"Shit. Anything else?"

"No. I think that pretty much covers it."

"It sounds like we need to get you a lawyer, a really good lawyer, and sooner rather than later. Let me poke around and see what I can do. If nothing else, maybe my former boss, Dan Holmes, might be able to help. He's been around a long time and knows a lot of people. For that matter, I think he knows your bosses' boss. He mentioned it one time. Perhaps he could put in a call for you and buy you some time." Then as an afterthought, "Do you want to spend the night? I can get you to the airport first thing in the morning."

"Thanks anyway, but I think I need to get back sooner rather than later."

JUST OUTSIDE CINCINNATI

Ellen and her spotter, Peter, were sitting outside Café Alma not very far from Golf Manor Synagogue. They found that the restaurant's commitment to serving certified kosher menu items was a huge plus for them. Despite its name, the synagogue is a long-time member of the Orthodox Jewish community that just so happens to be located in Golf Manor neighborhood near Cincinnati, Ohio. It had been less than a week since Ellen slipped away from The Roosevelt Hotel in Oakland. While she perused the menu, Peter was busy checking out the nearby buildings, traffic, and neighborhood.

"It looks like they have quite a variety of pastries. You interested in anything in particular, Peter?"

"Not really. Just something sweet that would taste good with this rather bold cup of java."

Ellen made her selections and went inside to place their order. Peter kept on assessing his new environment. When she returned, Peter looked at her and said, "This place is no good. There are too many ways to get bogged down," which was his code word for getting caught. "The street is too narrow in the first place. There are too many homes, which means too many cars and people on the street. I understand that the rally is going to be in front of the synagogue, but I don't like our odds for getting out."

The rally Peter was referring to was the one Rodney Witherspoon was boasting about. He claimed that in two days' time, he and his followers would be amassing as many as ten thousand protestors in front of Golf Manor Synagogue. The purpose was ostensibly to protest the ongoing conflicts between Israel and Hamas. In reality, it was just another excuse for him to continue spreading his message of Jewish hatred.

"If this venue isn't going to serve our purposes, perhaps the next one will," Ellen offered.

"Let me call our cell. Those guys should not only have his itinerary, but also tell us modes of travel, places they're staying at, and so on," Peter suggested. He was referring to one of several clandestine cells that operated throughout the U.S. These groups tracked anyone deemed a threat to the security of the Jewish state and Jewish communities. Once someone was identified as such, in this case Witherspoon, a unit was dispatched to eliminate them as a threat. Israel's Prime Minister had secretly approved the plan a few years ago and despite its controversy within his administration, no one was arguing about the results. Prior to the project's initiation, twenty innocent Jewish people had either been killed or seriously wounded in just the previous year.

Peter called his contact and within a few minutes, he turned to Ellen. "Here's an idea. Apparently Witherspoon and his entourage are traveling from one place to another via a touring bus. They are currently staying at a nearby hotel. On the morning of the rally, if they follow their typical pattern, they'll exit the front of the hotel and board the bus. What about positioning ourselves on the roof? As he is about to board the bus, you take him out? We should have plenty of time to exit the roof and get away before the what few police officers will be there can react."

"I like it. Give the cell a thumbs up and we'll go over right away and case the hotel," Ellen replied.

Within two hours, Ellen and Peter had made their way onto the roof. Peter was assessing the landscape and considering a number of exit strategies. Ellen, on the other hand, was doing her own assessment. She was determining which roof location would work best. All she would need is one clear shot to take Witherspoon out. Since the hotel was only six stories high, she would have more than enough firepower. She found the best vantage point and let Peter know. By this time, Peter had also completed what he needed to do.

"We'll leave our rental car a few blocks away. I see that there is a large parking lot across the way and about a block down. If anyone sees us arriving, they most likely will give a vehicle description to the police. We'll have one of the cell member's cars in the rear at the loading dock. It should take less than a minute to exit the roof and go down the fire escape adjacent to the loading dock. We'll be out of there well before the rest of any police contingency arrives."

Two days later, the plan was executed flawlessly. Just as Witherspoon put his foot on the first step of the bus to enter, a shot rang out and he fell to the ground, dead. Ellen and Peter scrambled from the roof with Ellen retrieving the spent cartridge in under a minute. The trunk was open, waiting for Ellen to put her weapon in, and the rear doors were open as well. The vehicle exited from the hotel as the responding police were arriving at the front. By the time the police had set up their command center and begun searching the building, the cell car was miles away.

FOR AL, FROM BAD TO WORSE

In 2010, Ron had wanted to express his appreciation for Al having taken time to help him out of an organizational jam that looked as though it might cost Ron his job. For some time, Al had expressed his desire to own a Detective Special, but Colt had stopped producing them ten years earlier. This made the weapon extremely difficult to find, especially one with a stainless steel frame and a .357 Magnum caliber. To make it even more difficult, Al wanted the rare three-inch barrel as opposed to the standard two inches.

Ron certainly had his work cut out for him. However, after one of those "a friend of a friend" type of situations, Ron was able to track down the gun of Al's dreams. Both men were licensed to carry concealed weapons due to their respective jobs—Ron worked for a large bank and Al was a precious gems courier—so it was only a matter of negotiating a reasonable price. Given its rarity, Ron agreed to pay eight hundred dollars. Al couldn't believe what Ron had done when he received it. But they were close friends and Ron was making good money at the time.

It didn't take long for Al to find a comfortable shoulder holster. He carried the gun with him at all times. His permit allowed him to carry it across state lines since he was frequently carrying thousands of dollars' worth of jewels from one jeweler to another. Even though his employer had provided him with one of their weapons, Al had locked it in his desk and carried the Detective Special.

A week following his meeting with Ron, Al was called into his boss's office. "Listen Al, I'm worried about you. Hell, we're all worried about you. That stunt you pulled last night was the last straw." His boss was referring to the fact that Al had been stopped the previous night for drunk driving. He barely passed the field sobriety test and was issued a written warning since he was carrying his gun. The police had notified Al's employer the following morning.

His boss went on, "I'm sorry, Al, but we can't have one of ours driving around drunk, or even near drunk. For God's sake, man, you're driving a company car and carrying a weapon, not to mention thousands of dollars in diamonds and rare gems."

Al tried to counter but realized soon enough that they were little more than empty excuses. Finally, "I know you don't want to hear it, but I'm going through a real rough patch. It's all of my own doing. I'm sorry."

"I appreciate you not trying to defend your actions, but you still remain a risk."

"I don't suppose there is some type of inside job, maybe a desk job, even if it at a lower pay grade? Anything to just hold me over until I get things settled," Al pleaded.

"I'm sorry, Al. We discussed that and the top dogs don't want to set a precedent. I do have a small severance package. It's not much, but perhaps it will hold you over for the short term." He handed Al an envelope. There was a check for three thousand dollars. It was generous, all things considered, but far short of what it would take to cover even the most modest costs of living. Leaving without a vehicle would mean some sort of short-term rental. That alone would take a good chunk out of the three thousand.

The company offered him a ride to wherever he needed to go, but he declined and opted to take the city bus. He knew he would be too embarrassed for anyone at his company to see where he was living. While waiting for the bus, he called Candy. She was cold and impatient. She threatened to have a restraining order put on him, even though they both knew it was his money that bought her the house and car, draining his life savings. "What a fucking bitch," he said aloud when she hung up on him. He felt lost. For the first time in his life, he honestly had no idea what to do. The more he thought about, the angrier he got.

After he got on the bus, he began to think that he had to call

Louisa. After all of their years together, maybe there was some hope. He called her and she agreed to meet him at their home. At least this was a first step, he hoped.

The next day he knocked on the door and found it slightly ajar. He stuck his head in and called out. A moment later Louisa appeared wearing her robe and carrying a butcher knife. Al stepped back. "I ought to stick this in your heart, you worthless bastard!" she yelled. "The bank tells me that you mortgaged our house to buy your slut a house! Where's our retirement money? No, don't tell me! That whore has it, doesn't she? You big-ass prick! The more I think about it—think about you—I want to run away to Caracas and never see your ass again!" And then she added, "Have you seen my Facebook page this morning? What about X and Instagram? Well, no need to; I've let everyone know what kind of miserable prick you are!"

Al turned and literally ran from the house and down the street. He had no idea where he was going. All he knew was that he had to get out of there. And, for the first time in his life, despite all of their previous heated screaming matches, he thought, *What a fucking cunt!*

Later that night, Ron caught up with him. He was in a bar not far from where he was staying, but told Ron he was in his room. When Ron asked how things were going, Al told him about getting fired and the latest blow-up between him and Louisa. Even though he thought about it, he decided Ron didn't need to know about being stopped for drunk driving.

Ron began, "Well, I found a lawyer that might be able to help. He's up here and a lot of cops have used him through their own sticky divorces. He's expensive, but I'll try to help out."

"Thanks, Ron, but I'm going to pass," Al said.

The words and the tone told Ron that Al was defeated. "What do you think you're going to do?"

"I'll think of something."

With the money he received as his severance, Al took a bus to Las Vegas. One thing was for sure. If he wasn't going to be able to enjoy the house he bought for her, she sure as hell wasn't going to either. He knew that she would be working by the time the bus arrived in Las Vegas. It wasn't that long of a walk between the bus station and the strip joint. When he arrived, she was on stage and didn't see him. He made his way to the rear where the dressing room was. He waited.

Ten minutes went by and Al found her purse. He took her car keys, emptied her purse of money and credit cards and the keys to the house. He noticed that one of the credit cards was in his name; no surprise there. She came into the dressing room and was genuinely surprised to find him standing there. "What are you doing here?"

He looked at her coldly. He looked at two of the other strippers and politely asked, "Can we have some privacy?" They nodded and left. "I assume your car—my car—is where you always park it? Right?"

"What the fuck are you talking about?"

"Let's take a walk."

This was the first time she noticed Al had his gun on her.

"Hey, Cowboy, slow down," she said nervously.

"Just walk out the door and to the car. No need to bring your purse, I have your keys right here." He reached into his pocket and pulled them out. They both exited the rear of the building, crossed over the alley, and stopped at her car.

"What now, loser?" she asked him with detachment.

Al looked around and pulled the trigger three times, each hitting her in the chest, ensuring she was dead. Then he calmly got into the vehicle and drove off. At first he thought about going to the house then thought better of it. He wasn't sure how many people actually knew what kind of car she was driving since he had only recently bought it for her. He knew it wouldn't take long for the police to run her name through DMV, so he had to put as many miles between Las Vegas and his home in Ontario, California as quickly as possible.

As he passed by the bus depot, his mind raced. He pulled into the loading zone and asked when was the next bus to Ontario.

"In about ten minutes," the window attendant told him.

"And the next one?"

"Well, that isn't until morning, but there's one leaving in about twenty minutes to Long Beach. From there, you can always catch a bus to Ontario."

"I'll take the one to Long Beach." He bought the ticket and raced out to the loading zone. There he saw a young couple sitting on a bench waiting for the next bus. He approached them.

"Say, you by any chance heading west?"

The young man answered, "Yeah, LA. Why?"

"Well, tonight is your lucky night. I just hit it big. I'm waiting for my fiancée. This is her car. Take it, it's yours. I'm sure the title is in the car. When she arrives, I'm going to buy her a Mercedes. Take the car, it's yours and good luck."

The young man looked at the girl. She responded, "What the fuck. Let's grab it and get the fuck out of here." They jumped in and drove off.

Al knew that the police would be looking for him and most probably the car. By the time they caught up with the young couple, he'd be on his way to Long Beach and the police might be looking for a new Mercedes. It was a long shot, but he had to take it.

It was after two o'clock in the morning when Al's bus rolled into Long Beach. During the ride, he came to realize what he needed to do next. He remembered that Louisa had an Uber account under his name. He called and asked if they took credit cards. They said they did and he ordered a ride. He would use Candy's card; the one with his name on it.

Shortly his driver pulled up and Al gave him his home address. He knew it would take about an hour, which meant he would be home sometime after three o'clock. Along with a car fob, he still had a house key on his key ring. He paid the Uber driver, tipped him handsomely, and quietly made his way to the front door. He unlocked it and walked in. He walked into the kitchen, laid down a note that he had written on the back of the envelope his boss has given him earlier. In less than a minute, he found her fast asleep in the bed, laying on her back and gently snoring. He walked up and stood beside her. He pulled his gun and put a bullet in the middle of her head. Blood went everywhere, including all over him. He didn't care.

He slipped into his side of the bed. He pulled the covers up and placed the gun in his mouth. He had two bullets left but knew he only needed one. He pulled the trigger.

ABOUT NOON THAT DAY

Ron's phone rang. "This is Ron."

"Hello, Mr. Tyson, this is Lieutenant Simeon, Ontario Police. Have you got a minute?"

"Yes," Ron answered.

"Do you know Albert Sloane?"

"Yes," Ron said, his mind racing, wondering what Al had done.

"I assume he is either a friend or relative?"

"A friend. Can I ask what this is all about?"

"Sure. I have some rather bad news. He and his wife are dead. It appears that Mr. Sloane shot her then shot himself. I'm sorry to have to be the one to tell you. But there's more."

"Oh my God. What else?"

"The Las Vegas police are requesting our assistance. He's a prime suspect in the shooting death of a call girl earlier in the evening."

"You must be talking about Candy. I'm sorry, but I don't know her last name," Ron replied.

"I believe that is the stage name she goes by, according to LVPD. Let me ask. Do you know anything about Mr. Sloan owning a Detective Special?"

"Yes. I gave it to him more than ten years ago. It was a gift. It was registered and he has, or had, a permit to carry it. Why?"

"He left you a note on the kitchen table."

"A note? What kind of note?"

"It simply reads, 'Give this Detective Special to Ron Tyson, Corporate Security, 2nd National Bank in San Francisco. He always said that when I no longer had any use for it, he wanted it back. Take care, dear friend. Al.'"

Ron gulped as tears began to roll down his cheek.

Later that same day, Abbey received a text. It read, "Home safely."

SAN FRANCISCO'S OLYMPIC CLUB

TWELVE YEARS AGO

Jonathan Johnson, or JJ, as he liked to be called, had a natural eye for spotting pure silver. It did not matter if he was looking at someone's heirloom silver tray set, a silver ingot or rare coin, or even a trophy. Just by glancing at the item, he could tell if it was silver plating or solid silver. He first discovered this gift when he was in high school and a group of his buddies were looking at the trophy case. They were admiring not only the number and size, but, as one friend exclaimed, "Look at all of that silver. We ought to steal a couple of them. I know a guy who could melt them down and we could split the difference with him."

"You'd be wasting your time. And then there is the risk that you'd probably get caught and be arrested. Most of these trophies are anything but silver. Maybe a few are made with some silver plating and then polished. Shit, man, some are probably plastic or stainless steel and highly polished."

"What makes you a goddam expert?" one of the group challenged.

"All you have to do is look at them, and I mean really look at them. If the damn case wasn't alarmed, I'd pull one out and show you. Besides, just look it up online."

"I still don't see how that makes you Mr. Know-It-All Silver Man."

"You know what, Marv? You're a fucking idiot. I work in my old man's pawnshop every day after school. I've seen dozens of these things come into the shop. It was one of the first things Pops taught me. He said I had a natural eye for spotting the fakes from the real McCoys."

With that, the group moved along and it wasn't long before they were arguing among themselves about something else. This time it was the latest NFL football champion. "Hey, now there's where you can find some real silver trophies. My old man says a professional football trophy can go as high as a hundred thousand or higher. Now, that would be something worth stealing," JJ informed the rest.

SKIP AHEAD TO TODAY

Dan Holmes had just returned from lunch with Brenda and her brother, Maurice DuPont. Maurice was spending the summer with them, having recently retired as a homicide detective with France's Police Nationale. Maurice's reputation extended well beyond France's borders for his ability to solve the most difficult cases. It was not uncommon for other countries to seek him out as a consultant when they encountered what seemed to be unsolvable crimes. He never disappointed.

Dan's phone rang just as he was about to step out into the rose garden. Brenda had been after him for three weeks to help her prune the nearly forty different varieties. It was a task that wasn't high on his list, but he had finally run out of excuses.

Matthew Osborne was calling. He was the managing director of the Olympic Club's golf courses, or simply The Club, as the members referred to it.

"Hi, Mathew. What a pleasant surprise."

"I hope I haven't caught you at a bad time, Mr. Holmes."

"Far from it. You have rescued me from one of the more dreaded tasks a retired corporate guy is required to perform. I was just about to begin pruning our roses, and by our roses, I mean Brenda's. What can I do for you?"

"Well, I'm afraid I need your help on a rather sensitive matter, something the Board of Directors and I would not like to see in the local media, which means no police, if that is possible."

"I see. Why don't you tell me what it is and then we can discuss whether we should involve the local gendarmes?" A nod to his brother-in-law who was standing nearby and well within earshot.

"We have been experiencing a number of thefts of late. Most of it we can actually live without. However, lately, whoever is taking our items has graduated to stealing several expensive silver items. Last night, our prized PGA Trophy was taken from a secured and alarmed display case."

"I think I know the one you are referring to—the one on display in the Main Hall as you enter. Right?"

"That is the one indeed. It means a great deal to us. For many, it is our signature piece. It is nearly three feet tall and over two feet wide, made of solid silver. Since it is a one-of-a-kind, we bought a million-dollar insurance policy, but because of the sentimental value, it is priceless. Who do you think would want such a thing? To display it properly, one would need a very large room, a grand ballroom for example or a large library room perhaps even a wide and tall hallway."

"Or none of the above if it was melted down and the silver sold to a jeweler or silversmith."

"God forbid!" Osborne responded in a loud voice, clearly shocked at what he just heard.

"Listen, I know your reluctancy about bringing the police in, but they have experts in this area and they can be very discreet, *very* discreet," Dan added for emphasis.

"I appreciate your point, Mr. Holmes, and perhaps we may have to resort to asking them for their professional expertise. But not now. Do you think you can help us?"

"Well, not directly. However, I have a few contacts. I can call them and see if they can help us out. You know, of course, they are not cheap."

"Oh. That would be so wonderful. You are going to make several of our board members very happy, very happy indeed."

By late afternoon the next day, Dan had contacted JJ and asked if he could assist, at least initially, in helping to determine the value of the items taken. He thought the project was interesting and readily agreed. Dan also asked his brother-in-law if he might have an interest even though this was not his usual forte. Nonetheless, he seemed to have a God-given talent for investigations irrespective of the type of case. Besides, Dan was convinced that after their initial meeting with Osborne, the case would be forwarded to the San Francisco Police Art and Antiquities Theft Unit, or the PAT Unit.

THE TEAM AND THEIR INITIAL IMPRESSIONS

The next morning Dan met Matthew Osborne at the club house and introduced him to his colleagues. He began by giving Osborne a brief synopsis of each man's background.

"Jonathan Johnson is the proprietor of one of our city's upscale consignment retailers"—Dan's way of skirting around the issue of Jonathan being known more for his pawnshop. "Typically, he goes by JJ and specializes in what he calls himself—a proprietor of all things silver, among other things. Maurice, on the other hand, happens to be visiting here from France where he is an internationally renowned police detective." Dan thought that both men, for quite different reasons, would enjoy his description of his brother-in-law. For Osborne, hearing about Maurice's reputation appealed to his snobbish demeanor. Dan also knew the Board of Directors would give Maurice instant credibility. As for Maurice, he took pride hearing Dan describe him this way. He respected Dan a great deal and to hear Dan call him internationally renowned boosted his already somewhat oversized ego.

Osborne explained that for the past few months, he began noticing certain items were missing. Most of them were small items like the twelve gold miniature salt and pepper sets given to the club by the winner of the first U.S. Women's Open Championship at the Lake Course, Yuka Saso. "That was recently, in 2021. What a memorable event. She won over Nasa Hataoka who came from behind to force the playoff. She said she could not see any of the salt or pepper shakers at the winner's dinner because the silver ones were 'lost' among all of the other silver settings. She joked that the gold shakers would stand out." In addition, Osborne told them of other stolen items given by the local charities for the club's sponsorship of events over the years.

As he explained what was missing, Dan and his colleagues could see Osborne was beginning to choke up. In particular, he explained the loss of two framed portraits. Holding back his emotions, he said, "One was of club president, William F. Humphrey, the driving force behind rebuilding it after the 1906 earthquake and fire. He held that position for nearly half a century. The other was a collage of those who upset some of golf's legions on the club's Lake Course, earning it the nickname *Upset Lake*." He listed each player as though their victory was just last month.

The men could feel his pride. "These were Jack Fleck beating Ben Hogan, Billy Casper over Arnold Palmer, Scott Simpson edging Tom Watson, and Lee Janzen, who won over Payne Stewart. In the center was Nasa Hataoka even though she lost to Yuka Saso. As I explained, she, too, upset the favorite, Lexi Thompson, to force a playoff. Since this was a collage of upset tournaments, she earned her spot in the middle. We just received the painting in 2023. Both oil paintings are far more sentimental in value for club members than their probable monetary worth."

Despite Osborne's show of sentimentality, JJ kept asking himself, *All of this might be interesting to a golf enthusiast, but what about the silver items?* Maurice, on the other hand, listened carefully to Osborne's enthusiasm in describing both paintings. Dan enjoyed the anecdotes, but, like JJ, wanted to move on.

It was then that Osborne took them into the dining room where they saw a room right out of the Middle Ages, complete with large wooden beams that stretched from one end to the other, over forty feet long. The walls were paneled with dark oak and the center table was cherry and walnut. The table sat twenty guests on each side and one setting at both ends. Along one wall was a massive breakfront that William Randolph Hearst donated from his famed San Simeon collection, which housed all of the fine china, Murano glassware, and silver serving sets along with the solid silverware sets for fifty guests. On the opposite wall was a ten-foot-long buffet that was used to serve food, as well as store linens and extra dishes.

"The cabinet and buffet are always locked and there are only three of us that have keys: myself, Stanley our head porter, and dining room manager, Miss Jennifer Hudson. Stanley has been with us for more than forty years and even though Miss Jennifer is still in her thirties, she celebrated her twentieth anniversary with us just last week. Both are very upset about the thefts, especially several missing items from the serving sets."

One couldn't help but be amazed. The room certainly caught the attention of JJ and Maurice, who quietly asked Dan, "Have you ever dined here?"

Dan smiled and answered, "I've been known to do so." He then looked up and saw Matthew Osborne smiling. He clearly had heard the exchange.

"I take it that you are saying that items are missing from the china cabinet. Do you have a list of these items?" JJ asked.

"I personally do not, but I am sure Stanley and Miss Jennifer do and will cooperate in providing you anything you need."

"Speaking of lists," Dan interjected, "can we get a list of employees, vendors, and workmen who regularly have access to this room day and night, especially on the weekends?"

"That is something my office will need to address. If you can give me a couple of days, I'm sure we can produce such a list. Anything else?"

Osborne then suggested they step into the trophy room and library. The walls of the trophy room were lined with display cases.

All of them were filled with trophies made of silver or gold. JJ walked from case to case, looking over each trophy as he went. Maurice, on the other hand, was more interested in the room itself. He slowly walked from one end to the other, admiring the wooden paneled walls, the oak flooring and here, too, the wooden beams on the ceiling.

When they entered the library, Maurice stopped in the doorway and examined the room, going from wall to wall and from floor to ceiling. Everything was a deep, dark wood, not unlike the dining hall and trophy room. The shelves were overloaded with books on golf. There were history books, instructional books, old catalogues, even rolled-up posters. Where there wasn't a bookshelf, the wall had an oil painting. Most were of other U.S. golf courses such as Pinehurst, Pebble Beach, Oak Hill in Rochester, New York, and the Presidio under the Golden Gate Bridge.

The wooden floor was worn and there were a number of Persian rugs of varying sizes spread out across the room. There were several writing desks, each with its own vintage green banker's lamp. At the far end there were three seating areas, each with at least two large leather recliners and a coffee table strewn with magazines and books that had not been put back. In the corner was a fireplace, once wood burning, now converted to natural gas. As the group stepped out of the library, Osborne suggested they proceed upstairs.

JJ cut in and said, "If there are no items of silver up there, I'm anxious to start looking at the pieces in the dining room. Is that possible?"

"Most certainly. If you wait right here, I'll call Miss Hudson and she can assist you. Before I forget, though, I took the liberty to make color copies of our missing trophy. Hopefully, they will be of help. As I explained to you on the phone, Dan, we need to find it and get it back on display. It is our signature for visitors and professional golfers competing in our tournaments, one of which is scheduled for a month from now. Need I remind you that it is solid silver and worth a fortune."

He handed the photos to Dan who, in turn, passed them over to JJ.

"Thanks. Will you be needing these back?" Dan asked.

"No, they are yours to help you in your inquiry."

"Thanks."

The other three left and went upstairs. A few moments later, Jennifer Hudson arrived, introduced herself, and escorted JJ to the dining room.

There were eight fully furnished master bedroom suites upstairs. It reminded Dan of the hunting lodge in Oregon where he and his family spent many vacations. They never went hunting; they just enjoyed getting away and sitting on the large front porch overlooking the nearby lake at night, which they swam in by day. As Maurice walked along the hallway, he would stop, step inside, and look all around. In one room, he went over to the windows and tried to open one. It slid right up.

When the tour was over, Osborne asked if either had any more questions.

"How about you?" Dan asked Maurice.

"Yes, I see that you have a number of security cameras both outside and inside. Is there someone who monitors them all of the time? And, how many security personnel are on the property at any one time?"

"Well, no one actually monitors the cameras. We look at them when there is a need. But, you should know we use the same tapes over and over. We record over them every week. As for the number of security officers, I'll have our Chief of Security provide you with that number."

"Wait, are you saying that you are still using VCRs and video tapes as opposed to digital recordings?" Maurice asked with a tone of amazement.

"I'm afraid that I am."

"Please don't tell me that the cameras record only in black and white and not color."

"I guess you can see that we don't have the latest technology," Osborne admitted.

"My guess is that you have the nightly janitor change out the tapes. Right?" Dan asked.

"No, that is one of Stanley's duties."

"Oh, I see," Maurice remarked. "I see. Mr. Stanley takes care of changing the security tapes because he can be so trusted, I assume?"

"Hold on, Maurice," Dan jumped in trying to calm what was rapidly escalating. "I'm sorry, Matt. I guess the three of us are just used to a more up-to-date approach to security systems and procedures. But don't feel like you are alone. We run into this sort of thing frequently. Sadly, small businesses and organizations don't pay much attention to security threats until they've been hit. And why should they? It's not like this type of thing happens all the time." Dan, ever the politician, glared at Maurice as he tried to calm Matthew Osborne down. "I apologize for my colleagues."

Maurice was quick on the rebound. "Yes, Dan is absolutely correct. I sincerely apologize for my unprofessional responses."

"Thank you, gentlemen," Osborne said, graciously accepting their individual apologies.

DAN AND MAURICE GO FOR A WALK; JJ EXAMINES THE REST OF THE SILVER

"Anything else at this time, gentlemen?" Osborne asked.

"I guess we would like to take a tour of the grounds."

"No problem, I'll get my security chief and he can show you around."

"That would be great."

Dan and Maurice didn't have to wait more than five minutes before the chief arrived. He introduced himself as Chief Donald Armstrong. Dan reciprocated and introduced Maurice and himself.

The security chief commented, "I understand that you gentlemen would like a tour of the club house and the exterior buildings."

As they walked along, the chief pointed out a number of maintenance buildings and asked if they were interested in looking inside any of them. They declined. The men proceeded to the cart barn where they saw a man working on one of them while the rest were hooked up to individual charging stations. From there, the chief took them to the Pro Shop and introduced them to the resident golf professional. Just as they were about to leave, Dan spotted an empty table in the corner and asked if he had time for a couple of questions prior to them going back to the club house.

"Sure. Fire away."

"How many security personnel work here?" Dan started.

"We always have one at the gate. That's 24/7/365. Then we have a rover on duty 24/7/365. He uses a golf cart to get around. He checks the club house, the facilities around here, and then of course he patrols the two courses and adjacent property to make sure no one has tried to compromise the fence line. And then we have one officer on duty in the club house during the day—that's typically me—and then another on the afternoon shift. Since the club house is closed and locked at night, we use the midnight shift rover to check on it and make sure it is secure. He does this at least four times a night."

Maurice asked, "Tell us about the cameras and alarms."

"Well, the gate officer is responsible for changing out the tapes every night. We have two four-screen monitors. So, he or she changes them and files them away in the cabinet inside the guard shack. We keep them for sixty days and then reuse them. It's not ideal but we have a very limited budget. You know how it is; security is always seen as the runt of the litter."

"Before you go on, Mr. Osborne told us that Stanley changes out the tapes," Maurice commented.

"Mr. Stanley hasn't done that for at least the past three or four years. I don't want to talk behind my boss's back, but this is an example of how little Mr. Osborne knows about how things work around here," the chief added.

"And what about Miss Hudson, does she know much about your security operation?" Maurice gently pressed.

"A great deal more than Osborne, especially how badly we need new cameras or at least repair the ones that have been broken for months. If we had a decent security camera system, we probably wouldn't have lost the big trophy," the chief answered in an indignant tone.

"Why is that?" Dan inquired.

"Simple. The cameras in the lobby are down more than they are up. On the big night in question, they were down. And the same can be said for the cameras at the loading dock and in the management office. We're always—how does the saying go? Oh yeah, robbing Peter to pay Paul. I'm always complaining, but it gets me nowhere. You know, sometimes I feel as though they don't want to fix or replace the cameras. In a way, I'm glad they lost their precious so-called solid silver trophy. Maybe they'll see it as a wake-up call." And then he added almost inaudibly, "But I doubt it."

The chief's comment caught Dan's attention. "What exactly are you saying, Chief?"

"Oh, I don't know. It's more a feeling than anything else. When I complain that the cameras in one location are down, nothing happens. Then there's a theft and everyone seems so shocked. Take for example the other night. I'm not a big believer in coincidences. As I told you, several key cameras were down, not to mention that the dock exterior lights are down. I reported all of this to Miss Hudson and she tells me she'll get right on it, but she doesn't. And then, wham! The next day, the trophy is gone. I guess I've said too much already, we should get back to the lodge, as a number of our members like to refer to the club house."

Meanwhile, JJ had been shown into the dining room by Jennifer Hudson who unlocked both cabinets. Together they put several pieces on the dining table and JJ asked if it was alright if he could take photos. She said she was comfortable with his suggestion, then added, "You've caught me on a rather busy day. Do you think you are going to need me here? I'll just be across the hall and down a bit, the second door on the left."

"I think I can handle it from here." He sat down at the table. She smiled, and put her hand on his shoulder as she left. He looked around as she left the room and could have sworn that she smiled back at him somewhat provocatively. *But then, it's probably just her way of being friendly*, he thought. "Strange," he said aloud softly. "I'm old enough to be her father. Well, maybe an older, more experienced uncle."

JJ began taking photos of everything and making notes. He was well into his task when Dan and Maurice walked by with the security chief.

When Dan and Maurice finished their tour, they found JJ sitting in the parlor in front of a large stone fireplace with a brandy in his hand and talking to Stanley. "You look like you've settled right in, JJ," Dan commented, smiling.

"I have. I'm thinking about becoming a member," he joked.

"Well, I hate to break things up, but we need to be heading back."

"When will we see you again?" Stanley asked.

"I'm not sure right now, but I'll let Mr. Osborne know tomorrow," Dan concluded. "Please pass along how much we appreciate all of you taking the time to accommodate us."

As they drove out the main gate, Maurice waved goodbye to the female officer. She returned with a smile and waved back. Despite being on the phone, she watched them pass her and out of the gate.

"JJ, do you have time to debrief us over another brandy?" Dan asked.

"Sure. I'm anxious to hear about your little tour."

"I know a quiet place not far from here."

THE DEBRIEFING

Once they ordered drinks, Dan sent Brenda a quick text to update her and said he hoped to be home within a couple of hours, just in time for an evening cocktail with Maurice and then off to dinner. "So, JJ, what do you have?"

"Matthew Osborne is full of crap or very naïve if he believes his precious trophy is anything but a cheap knock-off. The same can be said for many of his so-called centuries' old silver antiques and flatware. It's not all fake, only about half. It's almost as though someone has been systematically replacing the real stuff with cheap crap. Oh, it all looks genuine enough, but then you pick it up and realize it's not real. My guess is that someone has been doing the ol' switcheroo for some time. Or, perhaps at some point the club was running short of funds and were selling off the good stuff with hopes of buying it back at some point in the future.

"Stanley told me that they have put in several insurance claims in the past, but lately they have been denied until a full audit has been completed and a police investigation undertaken. He believes that they are going to lose their insurance underwriter very soon. From what I've seen today, I'm surprised the insurance company hasn't already been out.

"And if that weren't enough, I think Stanley is holding something back. I'm not sure if he is involved in anything, but he sure as hell knows a lot more than what he's letting on. Then there is Miss Hudson. She's either a hell of flirt, a horny young lady, or likes to use her lady charms to keep you distracted. After showing me where the silver was, she left me alone. Initially I thought that strange, but she kept coming back to check in on me. Candidly, I think she was coming onto me. I'm not kidding, it started when she left me for the first time. Within an hour, she checked in three times. Each time she got friendlier and friendlier. On her last visit she stood directly behind me—real close like, if you understand where I going with this."

"She sounds French," Maurice joked.

"French or not, she's got a nice rack. Almost makes me forget I'm a loyal married man."

"Alright," Dan came back. "Nice work. Now we've got to figure out what we are going to do with this info."

"That's easy," Maurice started.

"I know. I know. Call SFPD, I know," Dan said, agitated.

Dan began his inquiry. "What did you walk away with, my august police detective?"

"Tease, if you must. However, my first question is, 'How many hidden rooms are there in the place?'"

"What are you talking about?" JJ asked.

"Simple, there are at least three that I counted. I suspect there may be more. There is one large hidden room in the library, one in the dining hall, and another upstairs in the hallway."

Both Dan and JJ's jaws dropped slightly. It was Dan who asked Maurice to explain.

"It's all a matter of simple observation. In the upstairs hallway, one of the panels jutted slightly out at the floor. The reason is because whoever went through the secret door didn't make sure it latched completely. While you were in one of the rooms with Mr. Osborne, I kicked the lower panel and the door opened into a stairway with spiral stairs leading up and down. I assumed going up probably ended in the attic, but going down would require actually descending into, for now, an unknown room.

"As for the library, did you notice that there was a slight gouge in the floor, less than two meters into the room on the left side? It extends out about a meter and a half. Someone has tried to repair it on numerous occasions over time, but to no avail. I assume that the gouge is made by the bottom of a perpendicular wall sliding in and out from the inside. It comes out just far enough for someone to come and go from inside the hidden room. What appears to be a molding strip running from the ceiling to the floor is actually the back of the retractable wall. I'll gladly show you the next time we are in the room.

"There is a second door next to the corner fireplace. It swings open from left to right about a meter and a half as well. If my observations are correct, this is very large room. Such hidden rooms are typically not that large. Regardless, there are two doors in and out of the library aside from the windows.

"Like the others, the trophy room has its own secret room. JJ, after spending some time in the room taking out silver sets and returning them, perhaps you noticed that mirrored wall behind the primary trophy case was actually a two-way mirror suggesting, of course, the presence of a room behind the case?"

JJ just sat there. He didn't know what to say.

"Why do you think it has so many hidden rooms?" Dan asked, incredulous.

"My guess is that this lodge was formerly a private home. Probably built sometime in the mid-1800s during your famous gold rush era. As I understand, times then were, as you say, 'rough and tumble.' Absent of any type of formal police organization, the wealthy had to come up with ways to hide their valuables and even their lives."

"And what of you, Dan?" JJ asked. "What are your takeaways?"

"First, I'm calling my friend, Commander Hines of the SFPD, in the morning to brief him accordingly. As you suggest, there's more to this than some thefts of silver commodities."

"If I can interrupt, Dan?" Maurice asked. "Whereas I agree that you should call your police commander friend, be careful. Thus far, we have nothing to suggest that any theft has actually taken place."

"That's an interesting observation, one which will require some explanation. For now, however, allow me to continue. My take is that there is something between the young golf pro in the Pro Shop and Jennifer Hudson. Whereas you two had your backs to him, I couldn't help notice that he was taking a keen interest in what we were discussing with the chief, especially when Jennifer Hudson's name came up.

"Secondly, I don't think Matthew Osborne is involved in any of the thefts, but he seems to be out of touch with the daily operations, leaving that to Stanley and Jennifer. I think he might make a good PR person for the club, but not necessarily a good manager. As for the other two, I'm beginning to develop a theory that I'll explain in a minute. I'm not so sure about Chief Armstrong. He seems more than just your typical frustrated guard. He knows what should be done, but he's beaten down. He strikes me as more of a sad sack with a gun than a competent loss prevention specialist, which means he needs more of our attention.

"For example, Maurice, did you notice that when I mentioned the thigh pockets on his uniform pants, he gave a small laugh and said that they were good for carrying a number of things? He reached into the right pocket and took out his phone, wallet, and some loose change. But he never took anything out of his left pocket. At first, I didn't pay much attention. However, as we walked around, he kept his left hand in the pocket. It was like he was trying to hide something."

"I find it interesting," Maurice began. "Mr. JJ, you focused on the physical items. For my part, I looked at the environment and Dan, you concentrated on the people involved. I think we make a good team."

"Well, before it slips away, Maurice, what makes you think we may not have a series of thefts?"

"There is no doubt that several items are missing. However, I can think of at least two reasons, both of which are not necessarily related to theft. First, if the club is experiencing a decline in revenue or unable to keep up with operating expenses, what better way than to begin slowly replacing real items like place settings and flatware for fakes? They can sell off the real stuff and use the money for other things and their guests would not know the difference. If so, then the furniture and other furnishings could be used as they are with the silver."

"Intriguing," JJ quipped. "And this strategy might actually go right to the top. Stanley and Jennifer Hudson might actually be aware of this and given their approval. That would help explain why they are not keeping the security systems up and running. They don't need prying eyes prying."

"Or," Maurice continued, "they could simply be storing the items in any one of several secret rooms for now to reappear at a future time for any number of reasons."

"Your first assessment makes sense," Dan countered. "But, I'm not so sure about the second. Can you give me an example of something in the future that might cause them to bring out the 'good stuff,' so to speak?"

"Sure, Mr. Osborne told us as much. They seem to be having financial difficulty and can't afford to keep the real silver out all of the time. So, they use the real stuff at a winners' dinner when you know that the eyes of those who could differentiate fake versus real might be at the table. Or, your ever-snooping media looking for a scandal."

"Well, I must say, I can't argue with either. It makes sense. They have missing items, but not necessarily because of theft, or at least we can't actually prove it at this time."

"Except for one," JJ cut in. "It's all about the PGA trophy. You simply can't replace something like that all that easily. I think it was actually taken. We know security was pretty lax and so stealing it would have been fairly easy. Even though it is a fake, or at least not what Mr. Osborne has been led to believe, it is still worth something. Maybe as much as ten to fifteen thousand."

"You may be onto something, JJ," Dan reinforced. "Whoever took it probably thought it was worth at least six figures only to discover that it isn't. So, where does all of this leave us?"

Maurice offered an answer. "I think you still need to call the police. Mr. Osborne has said that he believes there is the theft of the trophy. The trophy is gone. Mr. Osborne represents the owners, so it seems reasonable that the police at least begin by investigating the missing trophy. However, as I just pointed out, concluding that the trophy was stolen is pure conjecture at this point. Nonetheless, having the police focus on the trophy allows us to follow up on the other things."

JJ spoke up, "He seems to be more concerned about the missing portraits than the silver and other things."

Maurice nodded.

"That's what has been bothering me," Dan added. "He seemed far more upset about the two oils than his antique silver settings and flatware. Why? Is it possible they were actually stolen, unlike the silver being hidden and replaced by cheap knock-offs? At first I thought Mr. Osborne didn't have anything to do with the theft, but now I'm second-guessing myself."

"Point well taken," JJ concluded.

"I suggest we call it a day for now," Dan suggested. "In the morning, I'll call Commander Hines. I'll also ask that another colleague of mine, Abbey Gentry, have her Unit 33 analysts start running background checks on the principal players as soon as we get their bios."

"Ahh, Miss Gentry's special group of secret crime fighters that you have told me about in the past. Will I actually meet any of them before I leave?" Maurice asked anxiously.

"What the hell are you guys talking about?" JJ asked.

Before Dan could answer, Maurice cut in. "Please Dan, allow me to explain. Your friend describes me as an internationally renowned detective. Perhaps true, but not as true as Dan and his clandestine operation of secret analysts. These people are very smart and very experienced. They can find anyone and almost anything in the world if you give them the time."

"Well, if they're so damn good, why aren't we using them?" JJ shot back.

"In time, JJ, if we need them. Right now, they'll focus on the key players and their backgrounds."

With that, JJ departed and said he would await Dan's call as to when they were going back.

ON THE DRIVE HOME

As Dan and Maurice were driving home, Dan's phone rang. He answered it, recognizing that it was Matthew Osborne. "What's up, Matt?"

"I was just following up on what you may have uncovered today, Dan."

"I have Maurice with me, can I put you on speaker?"

"Sure." Osborne was sounding like a man torn between anxiousness and depression.

"Let me begin by asking if everything is okay? You don't sound like your usual self," Dan said as he looked over to Maurice for confirmation. Du Pont shook his head in agreement.

"I'm just worried, Dan. The board is on my back with the trophy being stolen and one of our premier tournaments is coming up this month. One board member even asked if we could somehow replace it with some sort of reproduction until after the tournament. Of course, I told her it was impossible. Can you believe it?"

"Well, Matt, I was going to call you in the morning with our initial findings. Are you sitting down?"

"I am, but I don't like the sound of where this is going."

"I think that we should get SFPD involved sooner than later. I can control them so they are absolutely discreet," Dan lied. "So, let's not worry about that. But the sooner we get this investigation underway, the greater the likelihood we can recover it. Who knows, maybe even before the tournament," he lied again.

"Let me think about that. Anything else?"

"What I'm about to tell you may be difficult for you to hear."

"Shit."

"Perhaps your board member is not that far off. Matt, JJ believes that the trophy is a fake. You may have had a valuable trophy at one time, but the one that was taken a few nights ago was probably fake. Of course, we can't prove anything until we can put our hands on it. However, what JJ knows about these things, he's pretty confident that the trophy in the photos that you provided, along with those in the trophy case, prove that it is already a knock-off."

"Fuck, what are we going to do? I can't tell my board that sometime back, the real McCoy was swapped out for a fake. I know this type of thing is always happening with masterpieces, but a fucking trophy! Shit! How do I explain this?"

"Don't despair quite yet, Matt. JJ is really connected in the silver world, especially when it comes to specialty items. He's got feelers out to his network and thus far, nothing has surfaced. That means the thieves may be having a difficult time offloading it. And, even if they try, they're likely to find out that it is only worth about twenty-five thousand and not six figures."

"So, what's to say someone offers a lousy twenty-five grand and they take it?"

"Unless they are desperate, they'll try to shop it around to get the best deal. When they do, some dealer is bound to call JJ. If they try to unload it on a private collector, well, then the collector is going to have it appraised before agreeing to buy it. Either way, whoever stole it has already found out that they haven't got what they thought they had."

"Do you think it was just someone off the street?"

"I'm not sure why you are asking me that," Dan shot back.

"Because, everyone here assumes that it is very valuable and that you can't just walk into some silversmith's shop and ask them to melt it down and buy it for the value of the silver."

It was Maurice who spoke up. "But Matt, that's the very reason we may want to consider that someone from the inside took it, or at least arranged to have it taken. They would think it was worth a fortune since that is what they have always heard. They make arrangements with a collector only to discover that they have stolen something worth only a fraction of what they thought it was worth. Listen, the average street thief doesn't wake up one morning and say to himself, 'I know, I'll slip up to the Olympic Club House and steal a valuable trophy that is under the protection of cameras and is alarmed.' Sorry, sir, but someone in your house is a thief. And the police investigation will bear this out."

As the two men in the car waited for a response, all they heard was, "I'm fucked. I'm really drowning here." Then the phone went dead.

"What do you think?" Maurice asked.

"I'm not sure. I'll call Commander Hines at his home this evening and explain things. Then I suggest, if you want, you can join me tomorrow when I go back to the club house."

"I want to go with you."

When the two of them arrived home, Dan excused himself and went into the den and called Commander Hines.

ALMOST 4 A.M.

Dan was fast asleep when his phone rang. Brenda asked who would be calling at this time of the morning. Dan looked at his phone.

The caller ID said it was Commander Hines. When Dan answered it half asleep, Hines said apologetically, "I'm sorry to wake you up, Dan, but that Osborne guy we talked about earlier tonight? Well, we believe he just offed himself."

"No, that can't be," Dan said in total disbelief. "That can't be. If I go down there, will they let me see for myself?"

"Come on, Dan, it may be a crime scene. You know better than to ask."

"Wait. You know of Maurice DuPont?"

"Anyone in law enforcement worth their salt knows of him. Why?"

"He's my house guest and was with me when we were at the club house earlier. Before I just walk away, can I pull in one favor and ask that you let the two of us take a look while the scene is still fresh? Anything he sees or conclusions he arrives at, they're yours. Matt was a good guy. Perhaps he was really anxious, but he wasn't the type to just off himself. He wasn't."

"How soon can you get there?"

"We'll be there in under an hour."

"I'll hold it open, but Dan, this time you really owe me big."

"Love ya, big guy. We're on our way."

Dan knocked on the guest room door. He heard a sleepy grunt acknowledge the knock. Dan popped his head in. "Wake up, dear brother-in-law. There's been a big twist in our Olympic Club theft. As your esteemed founder, Eugène-François Vidocq, might suggest, parroting Sherlock Holmes, 'The game is afoot!' I'm sorry, but I don't know what Vidocq would have answered!"

Commander Hines had called ahead to clear the way for Dan and Maurice to have access to the crime scene, the library. Matthew Osborne was slumped over the first table as they entered the library. Two members of the Crime Scene Investigation Unit members stood in the room, along with a plainclothes detective and two uniformed police officers positioned at the doorway. The coroner was just arriving. Osborne had a small .22 caliber derringer in his right hand, resting on top of the desk near his right temple. It appeared that the gun was discharged against his head and penetrated the skull.

Maurice looked at Dan and commented, "It's the size of a gun that could easily fit in a leg pant pocket."

Dan looked on with interest.

Maurice examined the gunshot carefully and then stepped away once the coroner was set up to do her preliminary investigation. The police detective stood nearby and said to Holmes, as Dan stood likewise a few feet away, "Looks like a suicide. Clear and simple. But there is no note."

"That's because this was no suicide," Maurice interjected.

The coroner, who was bent over examining the bullet's entry into the skull, heard Maurice. She straightened up, looked at the police detective, and asked, "Who is this gentleman and how does he come by such a conclusion so quickly?"

The detective looked perplexed, shrugged, and turned to Dan for an answer.

"Let me introduce you to Detective Maurice Du Pont of the French National Police. He is an internationally renowned homicide detective. He's currently my house guest and Commander Hines thought it might be interesting to hear what he has to offer."

"I'm glad to meet you, Detective DuPont," the coroner said as she extended her hand to shake his.

The SFPD detective acknowledged Du Pont as well and then asked, "In all due respect, you realize that you will have to testify as to your opinions if this is anything but a suicide, do you not?"

"I'm most well aware of this and it is a homicide. I can assure you."

Dan, standing back, smiled as the other two looked intensely at Maurice.

"Can I ask how you came to this opinion after only being here but a few minutes?" the coroner asked.

"Certainly. To begin with, however, this is just my opinion. We'll need to wait for you to complete your examination. And then, of course, the autopsy should tell us definitively." Maurice, trying to be ever the diplomat, smiled appreciatively. "Until then, look at the blood spattering. If this were a suicide, there would be blood spread out in all directions near the point of entry. In this case, there is a clear break in the pattern. There are splatters to the left and to the right, but nothing in the center. This suggests that there was someone standing next to the victim. When you find this individual, you'll discover blood splattering on him or her and their clothing since it is nowhere else.

"Secondly, given the small caliber of the gun, the victim's hand would not have naturally fallen the way it is lying on the desk. Rather, someone placed the victim's hand down on the desk. It is just too clean; too neat. It is as though a woman may have done this.

"Then, there is the position of the head. A small derringer was used. We know this because it is in his hand on the desk and it matches the entry point and the powder burns on the temple. Yet, with such a weapon, the head is likely to have fallen back, not forward. I suspect someone actually bent the victim forward so as to rest on the table. Perhaps the victim was drugged at the time of his death. Your analysis will confirm this or rule it out. If so, it would have been very difficult for the victim to shoot himself so accurately with such a small weapon; a larger one perhaps, but not a small derringer. Shall I go on?"

Dan smiled.

"And, of course, I'm sure your lab people are being very careful; however, please ask them to be extra careful walking around here. This is especially critical from here at the side of the table over to the fireplace where there is a hidden room on the other side. I suspect that the killer may have inadvertently let small amounts of blood smatterings fall as he or she made their way over the fireplace. It is possible that there is blood along the edge where the killer grabbed the door when stepping through."

The detective stood there, perplexed as to how Maurice was guiding the investigation. Dan asked him, "Who found the body?"

"The security chief. He said he was doing a routine patrol of the interior when he discovered the deceased around 2:15 a.m."

"Is he still around?" Dan inquired politely.

"Yes, he's in the parlor with two other people. I believe both are employees. I haven't interviewed any of them. I was going to do that just as you arrived."

"Do you think it would be alright if we asked the chief a few questions?"

"I guess so, but remember, anything you learn needs to be recorded and you'll likely be called to testify since this is now looking more like a homicide. I'll be standing right there."

With that caveat, the three men went into the parlor where Dan saw Chief Armstrong, Jennifer Hudson, and Stanley. The detective asked Stanley what his last name was. "It is Stanley. Everyone just calls me that. My first name is Robert, however."

Dan asked Chief Armstrong if he could step aside and answer a few questions. He agreed.

"Chief, I understand that you found Mr. Osborne. Correct?"

"Yes."

"Earlier when we met, you were working the day shift."

"Right. We're short-staffed so I came in early to cover my midnight rover. It's not uncommon for the security staff to work double shifts."

"I noticed that the young female security officer at the gate is still on duty as well," Maurice observed.

"Yes. When an incident such as this occurs, I want to make sure we have all the coverage we can get. I suspect that as the morning unfolds, the media trucks and news reporters will pick up. We'll need extra gate coverage."

Maurice then asked, "Earlier you told us that the night shift patrol officer only checks the external doors, and, I assume, the windows. They don't go inside. But you did this evening. Why?"

"I don't require my officers to do an internal check, but I like to walk through at least once a night to make sure all of the offices and rooms are closed and those with locks are locked. It's no big deal."

"And the library. It doesn't lock. Right?" Dan asked.

"Correct. But we like to keep the doors to rooms like the library closed. We do the same for the trophy room, dining hall, parlor, and so forth."

"Thank you, Chief. And thank you, Detective. I'll write down everything Detective Du Pont and I asked and I will forward it to you shortly." Then turning to Maurice, "Are you finished?"

"Yes. But before we leave, perhaps I could look one more time at the secret door by the fireplace in the library."

They went back to the library, leaving the detective behind to begin his questioning of the chief and the other two. Maurice went directly to the fireplace and began visually examining the area to determine if he could see a latch, or button, or anything else that would control the operation of the door. There was nothing. He examined the sides and underneath all of the tables and chairs. Again nothing. He then made his way around the rest of the room, carefully examining everything as he walked by; as before, nothing.

When he finished, he looked at Dan and said he was ready to go. Dan thanked the others for their cooperation and they headed home. On the drive back, they discussed what they had encountered.

"Is it just me, or did you notice that Chief Armstrong wasn't wearing the same type of uniform he was earlier?" Maurice asked.

"Actually, I hadn't picked up on that, but you are right."

"Yes. This uniform had no thigh pockets and he was wearing short sleeves. Is that common here with such cool evenings?"

"No, it isn't. Are you suggesting that we turn around and ask the chief if we can search his locker?"

"No, but did you get the detective's phone number? It wouldn't necessarily be out of place for him to do so and with the assistance of the crime lab people and their blue lights. Even if the locker is empty, there may still be traces of blood."

"I like the way you think, Maurice." Dan called the detective, explained the reason for the call, and smiled as the detective thanked them for the possible lead.

Chief Armstrong had seen that Matt Osborne's car was still in the lot. He went in to ostensibly check on the doors and complete an internal check of the other areas. He found Osborne sitting at the first table in the library. He was on his laptop and appeared to be looking over the budget. The chief asked how he was doing. Osborne was surprised to see him at this hour. "For God's sake, Chief, what are doing here at this hour of the night?"

"I could ask you the same thing. As for me, we are short-staffed as usual, so I'm pulling a double shift. And you?"

"I'm afraid my ass is in a sling. I just found out that our supposedly high-value trophy isn't even a fraction of what I thought it was. Somebody, some time ago, made a switch. It's the only thing that makes sense to me. When I tell the Board that the trophy was a knock-off, they'll fire me, sure as hell. How was I able to tell? It's not like I'm some sort of trophy specialist like the guy that was in here earlier!"

"So, I'm confused. Okay, the damn trophy was a pile of crap. What's that got to do with the budget?"

"You don't get it. Our revenue is way down and if we don't make a lot of money on our upcoming tournament, heads will roll. Probably not yours because we always need some security, but your staff will take some sort of hit."

"For Christ's sake, Osborne! You can't do that. We're already severely short-staffed. Look at me. I'm in here after working all day and will not go home for at least another nine or ten hours. It's just not fair!"

"Well, fuck, Chief, what exactly do you want me to do? I'm trying to figure where I can cut without severely putting this place at risk. I can't find an answer. I'm about ready to chuck the whole damn thing and walk away. Maybe even off myself!"

"I don't know either, but one thing I do know is that your great scheme with Stanley and Hudson about slowly swapping out the real silver with fake shit isn't going to make it."

"It was never intended to be a long-term solution. You can't offload a lot of real antiques at the same time without a lot of people asking questions. My hope was that some dealer might come through the front door and see our trophy and make an offer. If that happened, we could get maybe a quarter of a million for it. But now I'm told that we'd be lucky to get ten percent of that."

"Ten percent. Hell, try something closer to five percent."

"What do you mean?" Osborne stopped and looked hard at Armstrong. "Well, fuck me. You're the one who stole the damn thing!"

"Yeah. I initially wanted to scare you and the others since you don't give a crap about security. I was going to give it back but a friend of mine said he knew a silversmith and he could give me a real good idea as to its real worth. When he told me that I'd be lucky to get ten grand, I nearly crapped myself."

"You fucking fool!" Osborne yelled.

"Me a fool? You're the ass that convinced the world that the thing was worth nearly a quarter of a million!"

"What did you do with it?"

"I smashed it to bits. I drove over it and it sounded just like a box of crackers getting pulverized. I laughed my ass off. The amount of silver in that thing is close to nothing. The silversmith told me that there are high school trophies with more real silver."

Osborne sat there, stunned. He couldn't believe it. It was all so surreal. And then he started to get out of his chair. "I have no choice but to call the police. They'll still nail you for a felony. I may lose my job, but you're going to lose a lot more, especially with that little cutie at the main gate. Or was she in on the theft as well?"

Chief Armstrong could only see red. He was breathing hard and his hands were getting sweaty. That's when something snapped. He coldly looked at Osborne, now his prey. "You're going to do no such thing." He hauled off and swung at Osborne with all he had. He could hear the jaw crack as Osborne's head flung wildly back. Osborne was unconscious, or worse yet, dead. Chief Armstrong stood there staring at Osborne.

"What the fuck am I going to do now?" he said out loud and then called the main gate.

Michelle Hawley answered. "Hi, what's up, honey?"

"You alone?"

"Yes."

"Get up here right away. I need your help. I'm in the library. The front door is unlocked. Just hurry."

A few minutes later, Michelle came running in and saw Osborne sitting with his head bent backward. "Is he dead?" she asked, not believing what she was seeing.

"No. I think he's still with us. Listen, he knows everything and said he was calling the police. He said he knew you were involved as well. We have to do something."

"Donald, what are you thinking? It's not like we can carry him somewhere and even if we could, where?"

"Here's what I'm thinking. He said he was thinking about offing himself. What if he did, with our help?"

"Are you nuts?!"

"Well, you're the one with the college degree. What are you thinking?"

"Maybe we get him to one of our cars somehow and then drive down the road and push him out, over one of the cliffs. We can pour a bottle of Scotch all over him and people will think he was drunk and fell into the ravine and died."

As they began discussing her plan, Osborne started to grunt. He was becoming conscious.

"Shit, we can't have this. He'll fight us all the way!" Armstrong yelled. "Think, baby, think!"

"Do you have your derringer with you?"

"Yeah."

"I'm going to go around and hold his head up straight."

As she walked around, started, "Honey, I'm doing this for you and our baby. Hold him tight and put the gun in Osborne's hand, then raise it to his right temple. Then push the muzzle in as far as it will go." He did as she instructed him. "Now, pull the trigger." He did and Osborne's head fell back. Blood and brain matter spewed everywhere.

Michelle gently pushed him forward so he was resting on top of the keyboard. She picked up his right arm and laid it on the table next to his head. She looked up at Armstrong.

"I can't believe we just did that," Michelle said softly.

"What now?"

"We leave. You go change your clothes; there's blood all over them. Then wait about twenty minutes. That should give me time to race home, change my clothes, and I can be back at the gate when the police arrive. I'll let you know when I'm back and then call the police. Tell them that you think you just found Osborne and it looks like he killed himself. Then call Stanley and Hudson."

SIX O'CLOCK IN THE MORNING

By the time Dan and Maurice retuned home, it was nearly daybreak. Dan made a pot of coffee and went out on the deck. Maurice joined him. They chatted small talk just to get their minds settled. Not long afterwards, Brenda joined them.

"Have either of you gotten any sleep? You look wiped out."

"Honey, now I know what they mean by policing being a young person's job. I'm going to finish this cup and then go to bed. I think I'll sleep until noon. What are you doing up, we didn't wake you, did we?"

"No. I've actually been up for over an hour. I'm so frustrated. I got this new app but something is wrong. I keep putting in my pin, but it doesn't want to open. I'm about to throw this damn thing into the bay."

Maurice felt a little pity for his sister. "Can I try it?"

Just then she shouted, "Eureka! It opened. I forgot. I changed my pin earlier yesterday. It's working just fine."

Maurice smiled. His neck was a little stiff. He slowly started swinging his head back and forth and from side to side. Suddenly, he stopped and looked directly at Brenda.

"You're wonderful. You've just solved a problem I've been struggling with for hours. I've been approaching the secret doors wrong all along. They're not manually operated these days. They open with a sensor and pin on a person's phone. Technology. You got to love it; you got to hate it!"

"I'm not quite sure I'm following you, Maurice, but does this mean you two are going back?"

"I guess so," Dan said, noticeably tired.

"I've solved the issue with the secret doors!" Maurice said loudly, clearly impressed with himself. He went on, "These days, it's not manual. It's automated. My dear brother-in-law, they've upgraded their secret accesses. They're using sensors near the doors and walls and opening them and closing them with a pin off their smart phones."

"Okay. Let's say you're right. Where do we find the pin numbers?"

"Dan, we don't need to look for them. Osborne has already told us. We'll start with 1906, then 2021, then 2023. Those are the dates he was so proud of when he was discussing the portraits."

"Do we have to go back now?"

"No, Dan, but I suspect that when we do go, we're going to find a good deal of the missing silver and flatware. For now, it's not going anywhere. You get your beauty rest and perhaps we can go over early this afternoon. Do you think your police commander friend might want to join us?"

"I'll call him before we leave. We damn near drive by his office on the way to the club house."

Knowing he could not sleep now; they left for the lodge. Maurice and Dan had picked up Commander Hines and all three gave a hearty laugh when Maurice tried the first pin and the library wall slipped out. Maurice then tried the second pin and the door by the fireplace opened. They all walked in and discovered two tables set up at one end. On one was a selection of what appeared to be one hundred percent silver flat wear. Dan would get JJ to verify. On the other was a collection of antique silver tea and coffee sets along with serving dishes and bowls. One of the large bowls was engraved, "*May 6, 1860, the Founding of the San Francisco Olympic Club, King Edward VII.*"

Dan looked at Maurice and suggested, "Well, it's no trophy, but a large serving bowl engraved by King Edward VII ought to qualify as a trophy of sorts and have its own place of honor in the Main Hall."

Later that afternoon, they heard that Chief Donald Armstrong and Michelle Hawley had been arrested and charged with the murder of Matthew Osborne. Osborne's blood was found on the clothes in the Chief's locker. It didn't take long for the Chief to give up Michelle. When the police searched his car, they found the PGA trophy in the trunk, in excellent condition. Two days later, despite their long tenure, the Board voted to have Robert Stanley and Jennifer Hudson terminated for mismanagement.

As Dan suggested, when the tournament started, anyone entering the Main Hall saw the large serving bowl with King Edward VII's engraving. It was in a secured case. Above it, two new security cameras. Beneath was a monitor so everyone could see themselves as they entered. There was a sign under the monitor. It read, "Protected by security cameras, please do not touch. Alarm will sound."

At the main gate, the old security equipment was gone, replaced by an up-to-date system.

DAN HOLMES:
THE PREQUEL

MY FIRST SHOOTING

Most people never see an actual murder in their lives. I have. Sadly, several. My first was when I was seven years old. I didn't know what was going on at first, but when I saw one man angrily shoot another and then watched him fall over the rail of the ferry boat I was on, I understood that he had just killed the other man.

I'll come back to this shortly.

For now, I want to simply mention that by the time I was twenty-one, I had actually witnessed another three murders, or homicides, as my dad called them. He was a detective for the San Francisco Police and he specialized in people killing people. I know all of this sounds rather dark, and it probably is. However, over time, I've come to accept death as a fact of life, particularly death involving one person killing another.

As for my first murder, I was traveling from Oakland, California to San Francisco's Ferry Building. I was with my dad. He had traveled over to Oakland to pick me up from having spent the weekend with my aunt and uncle and two of my cousins. I had had a great time. I always loved spending my weekends there. I fit right into whatever they had planned for the few days we were together.

I particularly liked going to the baseball games. Even though I was a big San Francisco Giants fan, I rarely saw them play because they played at Candlestick Park on the south side of town, and we lived in a small house at 45th Avenue and Anza Street, quite a ways from the Giants' stadium. So, when I visited my Oakland family in the East Bay, it was always exciting to see the Oakland Athletics play.

The morning of my first "murder experience," as I refer to them, I was on the ferry boat's lower deck, standing close to the stairwell. There were two men arguing not ten feet from me. There were other people around, but no one seemed to be paying any attention. Some walked right past them; one actually stopped and yelled, "Excuse me!" because the men were blocking his path. It wasn't long before they started pushing one another and calling each other names. I remember they were doing a lot of swearing at each other, but now I can't remember exactly what they were arguing about.

After a few minutes, one of the men started to walk away. That's when the man that stayed behind yelled, "You fucking prick! You loser!"

Suddenly, the other man stopped, turned around, and pointed a gun at him. Without saying a word, he shot the man twice in the chest. He fell over the rail and into the dark water below. I was horrified and shouted out. The man with the gun heard me. Turning, he looked straight at me, lowered the gun, and said, "Get the fuck out of here. Don't tell anyone what you saw or I'll find you and shoot you too."

I ran up the stairs as fast as I could and through the passenger area until I saw my dad sitting on a bench towards the front of the boat. I ran over and stood in front of him. Later, he told me I was shaking really hard. I don't remember that. He asked me what was wrong and I blurted it out, "I just saw a man shoot another guy then that guy fell into the water. That's when the shooter said he would shoot me if I told anyone. God, Dad, what's going to happen?"

My dad pulled me close into his chest and held me. We had

another fifteen minutes before docking. Dad grabbed my hand and ran up a small flight of stairs and knocked loudly on the pilot house door. He yelled over the sound of the engines to see the captain. He showed the tall, big man who opened the door his police badge and then conveyed what I had told him. The captain turned and told one of the sailors to stop the boat. He bent over and asked me if I could recognize the man if I saw him again. I said that I probably could. He asked us to step inside the small cabin and ordered one of his men to call the Coast Guard.

"When did this happen?" he asked.

My dad told him about five minutes ago. The captain picked up a telephone that was mounted to the wall and calmly announced, "Ladies and Gentlemen, may I have your attention. This is your captain. As you have probably noticed, we have stopped and will be turning around. We have reason to believe a man has fallen overboard. I apologize for the inconvenience and ask for your patience. The Coast Guard as well as a number of other boats in the area are on their way to join in a search of the area. Once we have completed this search, we will continue to the ferry building. Thank you for your cooperation."

It took quite some time for us to actually dock. Despite the other boats that came to assist and the Coast Guard's vessels, there was no sign of the body. I later learned that this was not unusual given the strong current and tide. The body would wash up on shore somewhere around the bay in the next several days, assuming sharks and other sea predators didn't find him first.

Meanwhile, the captain directed everyone through a single disembarkation line while my father and I stood at the head of the line in hopes that when the shooter passed by, I would recognize him. While this was going on, the crew was thoroughly searching every nook and cranny of the ship. When you stop to think about it, this was very brave of them, considering the assailant was armed and they were not. As it turned out, he was discovered just as the last of the passengers were disembarking. He was unarmed and hiding in one of the lifeboats—classic. There was no gun and even though he later admitted to the shooting, the gun was never recovered. The police theorized that he threw it in the bay some time before getting caught.

"MURDER EXPERIENCE #2"

I lost my mom to breast cancer when I was four. She was the love of my dad's life, a true soulmate. They had been married almost ten years when I decided to make my entrance. Mom was a paralegal for a large firm in the financial district and they were very generous when she died, providing a full college scholarship fund for me and my sibling, John. One time, Dad told me that she always wanted one of us to grow up and become a priest. That wasn't me, but luckily my brother John expressed an interest early on and wanted to become a cloistered Trappist monk up north of Chico, California.

His early seminary days were spent at a school in Hunters Point not too far from where the Giants played baseball. He would brag that he could actually hear the announcer on the loudspeaker at Candlestick Park shout each play and filling the fans in on bits of trivia about each player, or coach, or baseball in general. "It's like listening to the game on the radio," he would tease, "all without any commercials! How great is that!" God, I hated him for that. He eventually transferred gave up on becoming a Trappist and went to a diocesan seminary in Berkeley where he was ordained and as-signed a parish in San Francisco, but not until he was drafted as a chaplain and sent to the Middle East.

Early on, however, Dad found it difficult finding someone to take care of us kids. It was problematic since his hours fluctuated all the time. He was continuously being called out at night or work-ing overtime because of his latest homicide case. Our neighbor, Mrs. Hawthorne, was one of those walking saints that seemed to be always there when Dad needed help, but given her age and medical challenges, she could only ever watch just one of us. John was the younger, so he stayed behind. For me, I went with Dad.

Things at the station house were a little more relaxed about chil-dren back then. Besides, Dad's homicide clearance rate was, as the saying goes, "out of sight." Over his career, he solved ninety-eight percent of his assigned cases. He was like a pit bull turned loose on the city whenever someone was murdered. Several started out as possible suicides, especially by hanging. That was "murder experience #2" and I was almost ten years old.

I'll spare you many of the details. Suffice it to say, Dad got the call just as we were all settling into bed. John was hurried over to Mrs. Hawthorne's where Dad knew he was going to be safe as she prayed the rosary over him. (Perhaps that is how we knew he would end up in the seminary). Dad made sure I was dressed for the weather and off we went.

The victim was found hanging in his garage so it was easy to jump to the conclusion that it was suicide. But Dad saw things that no one else did and it wasn't long before he determined it was a homicide. He came over and sat down next to me on an inverted wooden milk case. I could tell what he was going to say; I had seen that look dozens of times before.

"I need to take you home and come back. This is a murder scene. The man didn't commit suicide."

I was used to Dad telling me such things. "What makes you so sure this time?"

"There are a couple of things. First, this guy was a junkie. I found several needles in the dirt on the floor. Even though they appear to have been there for a while, you can easily see them if you are looking. Secondly, the knot around his neck is all wrong. It's too loose. When he would have started wriggling all around, the noose would have given way and he would have fallen. Not so here, he was already dead when he got strung up. All the knot had to do was hold him up. And then there are his hands. They are tied in the back. How does a guy hang himself if his hands are tied behind his back? They should be tied in front. Clearly, the killer is quite the amateur.

"Most cops come in, see a man hanging, and jump to the conclusion that it is a suicide. The indications that this was a murder just jumps out at you. I'm sorry, Junior, but what we have here is real sloppy police work. Somebody just doesn't give a damn. Don't worry, though, I'll pass it on and someone's butt will soon be in their own noose. In the meantime, I have to get you home. You call Mrs. Hawthorne and let her know you're home. If she wants to keep John until the morning, that will be okay. Just make sure he has breakfast and get him to school. Okay?"

"Come on, Dad, how many times does this make? I know the drill. You can trust me. Just call and let me know when you're coming home."

"That's easy. I'll be home in time to make us all dinner."

So, it went. Dad eventually solved the hanging, my brother learned how to say the rosary, and I spent my free time immersed in baseball until the next time dad was called out.

"MURDER EXPERIENCE #3"

My third witnessed murder occurred when I was a junior in high school.

There was quite a rivalry between my school, Richmond High and Westmount High. At that time, Friday night was sock hop night and each school would host a DJ dance. It was typically held at the gym and, since shoes were forbidden, we all kicked them off at the door and made our way to one side or another—girls typically on one side, boys on the other. Smoking was an absolute no-no, but that didn't stop the boys who saw James Dean as an idol—even though he had died about five years earlier—from ditching their shirts and rolling-up a pack of cigarettes in their t-shirt sleeve. Or, harkening back ten years, and idolizing Marlon Brando in *The Wild One*, wearing their "leathers." All of this to impress the girls, many of whom actually had eyes for members of the football team.

As my gym teacher noted at the time, "You take a school with so much testosterone raging in fifty percent of the student body, have shit Hollywood images of tough guys, and a bunch of crazed teenage girls, and it's only a matter of time before something bad, really bad, is going to happen."

And it did.

It was on one of those Friday nights that the boys from Westmount decided that they wanted to test their "luck" with the girls of Richmond High. The two schools had battled each other for years on the football field and neither could claim outright bragging rights as to who was better. The same held true in swimming, track and field, and a fairly new sport for the area, hockey.

It was shortly after nine when three cars loaded down with Westmount thugs pulled into the parking lot at Richmond. They never got through the front door before they were confronted by Richmond's version of thugs-be-us.

I was late in arriving and had just pulled into the parking lot. I could see a crowd starting to gather outside. It didn't take long before the swelling crowd of teenagers had clearly outnumbered the few chaperones who were trying to maintain some sense of order. As I exited my car, I could hear one of them yelling for someone to call the police. I saw the mother of one of my friends race back in, no doubt to do just that.

As I approached the crowd, I could see that two students were inside a large circle, each brandishing their own knife. They were facing one another and the crowd was cheering them on. I thought I was dreaming; clearly this was not happening. That's when I heard a girl's voice scream, "Stab the fucker! Stab him!" Each time, her voice became louder and louder. And then, "If you're my man, stab him!"

It was then that I saw one of the Westmount boys break from the crowd and run into the circle. He was screaming something inaudible as he plunged a knife into the back of the kid from Richmond. The Richmond student fell lifeless to the pavement.

Everyone started screaming and yelling. Pure chaos broke out as everyone started running in all directions. Many of the Richmond High students ran back into the gym. Those from Westmount raced back to their cars and took off, screeching their tires as they peeled out.

I stood there for a moment. I couldn't believe that one of my classmates lay in a pool of his own blood. As the sound of sirens approached, I bent down, rolled him over on his side, and checked to see if he was breathing. He wasn't. I stood up just as the first police unit arrived. I turned, raised my hands above my head just as my dad had instructed me some time back should I ever encounter a responding police officer with his gun drawn.

Thirty seconds hadn't passed when one of the chaperones stepped outside and yelled that the officer had the wrong person, referring to me. She stepped over and told him that the student had been stabbed by someone from Westmount High and began stammering. She was really broken up and started weeping—not crying, actually weeping and mumbling something about how could this have happened. The paramedics arrived along with several other responding police units. I was escorted to the patrol officer's car and placed in the rear seat.

I must have been in there close to an hour. Too bad there were no smart phones then. I just sat there looking around trying to see if I recognized anyone and figure out what was going on. Suddenly, there was a knock on my window. It was my dad. The uniformed officer was standing next to him and opened the door. "I guess you've had a rather interesting night," Dad said with a comforting smile.

Before I could answer, the uniformed officer said, "Sorry, Detective, but he was standing next to the body when I arrived. I couldn't take any chances."

"Officer," Dad assured him, "I would have done the same thing. Don't worry."

The officer looked at me. "I'm sorry, kid, but procedures are procedures."

I smiled back. "I guess it's okay."

My dad looked at me and simply asked, "You want to go home or get something to eat? Perhaps a little ice cream?"

That was always my dad's go-to response when bad things happened—chocolate with crushed nuts and whipped cream.

"I think I could use one of your famous cones, Dad."

"You're going to like it. I just know you will. And when we finish, I need to get you home and start working on this mess. Your mom will be worried sick until I get you home."

That's right, Dad had remarried, this time to an emergency room nurse he met one night investigating a shooting. She had a fourteen year old son, Matthew. That was when I turned twelve.

MOST DISTURBING "MURDER EXPERIENCE"

Whereas seeing a man get shot and fall overboard on a ferry boat, followed by seeing a hanging man, and then witnessing the stabbing of a classmate, are all troubling, there was another murder that I found particularly disturbing. I think it was because, in the end, it was absolutely senseless. It was one of those classic situations of being in the wrong place at the wrong time, only to witness a murder unfold right in front of you. Moreover, it unfolded so quickly, there was nothing I could do, nor anyone else had they been there.

It was after midnight and my college roommate and I were in for one of those typical all-nighters just before a big exam. We were out of Pepsi and an assortment of cheap snacks, so I decided that a quick run down two blocks to the corner convenience store was in order. Chelsie's must have made a fortune from college students in search of soda and other sugary snacks to get through these study sessions.

There were only a couple of us at the back of the store looking for something salty when we heard the sound of the door being buzzed open, something the owners did after ten o'clock each evening. I looked up and saw two men enter the store. Both were wearing leather jackets. I noticed the large logo of a street gang on the back of one of the jackets. The man who wore it was the older of the two and had a scruffy-looking beard that hung down onto his chin. He had a tattoo that covered the back of his right hand.

The younger also sported a beard but it wasn't anything like the older man's. What stood out was the gun he was pointing directly at the young clerk. Neither man spoke, but the older one gave the younger one a slight push from behind so as to say, "Go ahead." Then I heard three shots, each in rapid order. Smoke from the gun momentarily filled the air.

From my vantage point, I watched the store clerk fall back onto a counter filled with cigarettes and an assortment of other behind-the-counter items. He slowly slid down to the floor and out of sight, leaving a trail of blood running down the counter behind him.

The younger one then did something that I couldn't understand at all. He turned and shot out the surveillance camera. He fired two shots and then both men calmly walked out as though nothing had happened.

After they left, I raced to the front, but it was obvious that he was dead. I dialed 911.

As it turned out, the clerk wasn't even supposed to be on duty. His uncle owned the store and had asked his nephew to take the evening shift because the regular clerk had called off sick a few hours earlier. Using the tape from the camera before it was shot out, the police were able to quickly identify the older man as a member of one of the local motorcycle gangs. This was a so-called "initiation shooting" designed to test a new member's commitment to the gang.

Sadly, the tragedy did not end that night. Two weeks later, just before ten o'clock at night, two men entered the store, both wearing leather jackets. They stopped at the front counter and the eighty-two-year-old owner quickly pulled a large revolver out from under the counter and fired at both of them. Neither man was armed nor did anything that might otherwise have warranted such an action. But the store owner was scared and actually feared for his life.

The media was quick to report the homicides but there was no follow-up as to the disposition of the owner and impact on his family losing two members in a matter of days—one dead, the other arrested and in jail. My dad called me several weeks later and said that his Berkeley police colleagues had informed him that the owner pled out to a charge of manslaughter and was placed on probation. The family was fined and they were putting Chelsie's on the market.

It always seemed strange that the young shooter shot out the camera after the incident and not before. When I asked my father, he was not surprised. He explained, "These types of shootings are not uncommon. To get up the courage, the shooter ingests a large number of drugs, usually some type of stimulant. They're not thinking straight and oftentimes gets confused. They know they have to shoot out any surveillance camera they see and honestly believe they did so before the killing. They'll swear by it only to see themselves later on the tape doing just the opposite."

That one haunts me to this day.

VIETNAM AND THE MIDDLE EAST

After high school graduation, I enrolled at Cal Berkeley, majoring in political science, and joined their Reserve Officers' Training Corp, or ROTC program. There were a lot of anti-Vietnam protests starting to spread across universities. Some schools experienced protests that got out of hand and it didn't take university administrators long to invite the police on campus. Some protests were so violent that the National Guard was called in to restore order and enforce curfews. Perhaps the most notorious, but far from the most violent protest, occurred at Kent State University when one of the National Guard soldiers shot and killed a protestor.

My step-brother, Matthew, was not as fortunate as me. While I avoided the draft due to my being in ROTC, he was drafted right after graduation. How strange when you think that on Saturday, you are sitting with your classmates wearing a graduation cap and gown, and on Monday, you're being loaded onto a bus and by nightfall, you are wearing a completely different outfit, a set of military fatigues. Mathew was shipped off to Vietnam within the week and returned a few weeks later in a coffin.

My days in the ROTC were emotionally mixed. On the one hand, I felt it was my duty to serve. On the other hand, I wasn't convinced by a long shot that my country was engaging in far-off wars for the right reasons. It still leaves me wondering these days why I made the military a twenty-five-year-plus career, spanning tours in the Middle

East. In fighting the Taliban, I saw the most bloodshed, especially among the innocents—mothers and their children.

At one point, my brother John actually served by my side. He was a Catholic priest by then and was serving as a missionary in a small village outside the control of the Taliban. Since they were advancing, I was ordered to assist the local religious volunteers in helping to evacuate the village to a safer place. When my unit arrived, much to my surprise, the first person I encountered was John. We only had time for a quick hug and a promise to see one another shortly. He was leading a group of women and children out of the village when the Taliban broke through our defenses and rushed into the village, opening fire on everyone.

My unit returned fire and engaged them directly in hand-to-hand combat. The invading force only numbered about two dozen and my unit was able to repel them, killing nearly all of them. They say killing in the time of war is not murder. Yet before we could take control and push them back, I witnessed a lot of their murders. Their killing was so indiscriminate and their victims so innocent, the scene still frequently haunts me.

John must have been under the direct hand of God that day. His small caravan of three convoy trucks drove out the back of the village just as the Taliban was rushing over the hill bordering the front and down into the village. He, and everyone else in the trucks, escaped without injury.

It took me nearly three days to catch up with him. Our reunion was great but far too short. John was heading stateside in a matter of days so I didn't see much of him until I returned home a year later. In that time, my unit saw a great deal more action, which meant a great deal more killing. There is no doubt in my mind that that was when I became so jaded towards living and dying.

As I've said many times before, I don't feel morbid about it, I just understand and accept it.

ELLEN FISCHER

I finished my last tour with an interesting addition to my unit. We were joined by five Israeli commandos. Among them was a highly skilled Mossad-trained sniper, Ellen Fischer. Her skill was remarkable; I've never seen anyone shoot like her. It didn't matter what the conditions were or what the target was, stationary or moving, she could literally hit her target in one shot, dead center of where she was aiming.

She had a young spotter with her, Peter. His sole job was to look out for anything that was unusual or any advancing enemy. As a team, they left me and the members of my unit in awe. We drew upon her services a number of times. In situations that we thought were lost, she showed remarkable poise and focus. She would calmly take out selected targets, scattering the remaining insurgents.

At one point, she introduced me to her closest friend, Abbey Gentry. She, too, was an excellent addition to my small team. She proved herself and, years later, I would hire her as one of my Corporate Security managers, taking charge of a number of units. Eventually, I appointed her in charge of the clandestine intelligence group I developed within 2nd National Bank.

One time, there was an attempted assassination of Abbey, one of her managers, and myself. Even though Abbey and I survived, her manager was killed. On the day of the attempted assassination, Ellen was there. As the perps were fleeing, she shot both of them on a crowded San Francisco street, killing each of them with a shot to the back of their heads. Later, she used her sniper skills to take out the leader of the street gang that planned and executed the attempt. Along with her spotter, in a matter of seconds, she shot the leader, his wife, a bodyguard and his driver. For her, it was sweet revenge since they tried to kill her best friend. She successfully escaped to Tel Aviv with the help of her Mossad handlers.

2ND NATIONAL BANK

I finished my military career in my early forties and then met my wife Brenda. I started out with the title Vice President, Director of Security. When I was hired, 2nd National was one of the largest international commercial and business banks in the world; that is what the banking world called such financial institutions. Today we are simply referred to as a global financial institution. Originally my primary duties were like those of most security managers, overseeing the bank's guards, security systems (e.g., cameras and alarm devices), and investigating retail robberies to determine our level of liability. Responsibilities extended to International Banking, Wire Transfer Frauds, Intellectual Property Protection, and IT security would eventually come.

About two years into my job, I received a call from my boss. She wanted to see me in the president's office right away. When I arrived, she was there, along with the Executive Vice President for International Banking. The EVP began while the other two listened. "We have a delicate situation unfolding in Mexico. Our branch manager's nanny has been kidnapped. She's family to her employers and they are beside themselves. They are prepared to pay the ransom, a quarter of a million dollars, but we have told them to hold off until we talked to you."

"That was smart. To pay that large of a ransom will only encourage others. Let me get right on it. I have resources that I think can quickly bring this to a positive conclusion. I'll need some basic information like names, when she was last seen, any photographs, and the address of the branch manager's home."

They were quick to provide all of it. I thanked them, saying I would be back to update accordingly. And, this was not going to cost the bank a quarter of a million dollars. It would be small enough to discourage them from targeting us in the future but large enough to ensure they would not kill the nanny. President Sands simply nodded his head and told me to do what needed to be done.

I don't necessarily need to go into detail here; however, within forty-eight hours, the nanny was safely home. Instead of trusting it to the police, I took matters into my own hands, using my resources. Although no one was killed, the kidnappers were made to understand the folly of their ways. Let's just leave it at that. That lesson taught the executive management team a long overdue lesson about the inherent risks associated with being a "big American bank" in nearly twenty countries globally.

A few days after things settled down, I received a phone call from President Sands. He wanted to meet me in the executive dining room. He was alone when I arrived and, in a friendly way, grilled me about my resources. I explained that they were largely former operatives and branch managers among various intelligence agencies, including not only the CIA and some of our Military Intelligence organizations, but also from among various like agencies in foreign countries.

"How reliable and timely are they? Are they as good as they were with our recent Mexico situation?" he pressed.

"It depends. These organizations, some private, some not, have a large clientele base. They always mean well, but in some cases they cannot help due to a lack of in-country resources or the monies necessary to fund certain operations," I answered.

"Say we had our own intelligence group. Could we even develop such a group? And, if so, how big would it have to be and what would be the cost?" he continued.

"Wow, you ask a great number of very good questions. First, we could most certainly develop such a group. Ours, however, would be far more technology-oriented. It's a developing area and it means more information, quicker and cheaper because we wouldn't have to contract many operatives. That translates directly into lower personnel-related costs, lower liabilities. We would rely on skilled analysts that could access systems globally given the emerging power of the internet."

"Here's what I want," President Sands said, leaning in closer. "We tell no one, not even your boss since she's leaving for another opportunity."

I was taken aback since this was the first time I was hearing this.

"I'm transferring Corporate Security to report directly to me. I know that'll piss off some people, especially our General Auditor since he has long wanted security to report to him, but fuck him. You'll have a new title, Senior Vice President, and you need to get going on developing this intelligence group. Okay? Oh, and of course there will be appropriate compensation, but HR is not to know about your new group. I'll figure out a way to bury the cost, don't worry about that."

"Can I ask why? It sounds like we're headed for a number of mergers or acquisitions domestically and internationally."

"I like the way you think, Holmes. Yes, it's all about expansion. That means new markets and some, quite frankly, that can't be trusted—well, not now anyway. The Board and I want to know what we're getting into before any announcements are made and before we put our signatures on dotted lines."

"But doesn't that require approvals beyond our Board of Directors? What will Fed Reserve have to say, not to mention our Treasury Secretary and even our Secretary of State?"

"Don't you worry about all of that. Just get me my team, the equipment they'll need, a good manager to keep them in line and a place that is nearby but no one suspects what they are doing."

"Consider it done."

Two weeks later, I had secured a place a couple of blocks away at 33 Beale Street. The clandestine group would be housed in the same building as our IT department but no one other than the group would have access. In short, they would be hiding in plain sight.

Eventually, as I said earlier, I transferred Abbey to head the unit. She grew the department to eight highly skilled analysts and another eight program developers. Relying on what today has become known as hacking, they essentially have access anywhere in the world and within most organizations, military, foreign intelligence and even your local DMV.

Their name?

Unit 33.

www.ingramcontent.com/pod-product-compliance
Lightning Source LLC
Chambersburg PA
CBHW030401020726
47493CB00003B/902